Book Boyfriendish

LISA WELLS

Contents

This book is dedicated to my wonderful momma. Some would say she spoiled me rotten—you know how those pesky older siblings
can be.
I'd say she spoiled me perfect.
I love you mom.
Thanks for teaching me how to enjoy life a little
on the ornery side.

Book Boyfriend*ish*

LISA WELLS

Chapter 1

"They'll see you now," said the *Naked Runway* receptionist as she returned the receiver to the cradle, her sleek bob and perfectly arched brows giving her a polished edge. "Just knock on the door and then enter."

Sophie E. Clark, who was on the verge of getting the last laugh, blew out a breath. "Thank you." She stood and made her way across the hall to the conference room. With every step, sweet belly nerves tickled her stomach. "You can do this." One more hurdle and all of those who had told her she'd never make a living as a professional daydreamer could kiss her ample derriere. The thought brought a smug smile to her lips.

Here she was, the girl voted most likely to never get her head out of a book, standing in the sleek, fashion-forward halls of *Naked Run-*

way, about to meet with the editors-in-chief, one for digital and one for print.

She tugged at the hem of her custom "Book Boyfriend Connoisseurs" tee—a vivid splash of personality against her chic black ensemble—and knocked on the door.

"Come in," she heard.

Squaring her shoulders, she pushed open the door and stepped inside with confidence buoyed by her passion. There were two women sitting at the conference table, both highly recognizable by anyone who'd bothered to do their homework.

While Sophie had expected to meet the digital editor-in-chief who had called her in for the interview, she had not expected to see the magazine's owner present as well.

Unsure of the protocol on who to introduce herself to first, Sophie decided the owner trumped the other. She extended her hand to the older woman in the room. "Sophie E. Clark, at your service," she declared, her insides fluttering with excitement.

"Ms. Birdie Fairway," the owner said as she stood, holding out a hand. "But please, call me Ms. Birdie."

"It is such an honor to meet you," Sophie gushed. "I had no idea you'd be a part of this interview." She reached out and shook the woman's hand. "Your charity work in the city is simply phenomenal, especially your legendary bachelor auctions. For which I have a fabulous idea for you to consider."

"Why, thank you, dear," Ms. Birdie said, then waved at the other woman in the room. "This is Isabella P. Chance, *Naked Runway*'s Digital Editor-in-Chief."

Sophie turned her attention to the woman who held her dreams in her hand. "I loved your designs back when you competed on *Fashion Runway*, and I never miss an episode of your podcast. Your coverage of the feud between the Rake of Manhattan and Dr. Stone kept me in stitches. It is an honor to be in your presence. I'm Sophie E. Clark." Too late she remembered she'd already introduced herself.

"I love you already." Isabella stood and shook Sophie's hand.

"You do?" Sophie said, just as a bored-looking brunette entered the room on a cloud of perfume. "Why is that, exactly?"

"Because someone wise obviously taught you to include your middle initial when you introduce yourself," Isabella said. "It increases people's perceptions of your intellectual capacity, performance, and status."

"Actually, *Junie B. Jones* was my favorite book when I was little, and I liked how she used her middle initial, so I adopted the habit as well," Sophie admitted.

The newcomer to the interview looked Sophie over, shrugged, and said, "You must be Sophie. I'm Frankie Peterson." She raised a rude eyebrow at Isabella. "I do not need a middle initial to be validated as important."

"Nice to meet you, Ms. Peterson," Sophie said, bobbing as if she'd just met a queen. "I've heard frightfully wonderful stories about you."

"Heavy on the fright, I'm assuming," Isabella said without a hint of humor in her voice.

Sophie was disconcerted by the dynamics playing out between the two. "Not at all—"

"If we're quite finished with the pleasantries," Frankie said, "could we get down to business? I have back-to-back meetings all day." She took a seat, leaving Sophie the only one standing. "I've not had a chance to read over your pitch, but Isabella assures me it's fabulous. Of course, her opinion seldom sways mine. So please, give me the condensed version of your idea for our column."

Sophie squared her shoulders, her heart beating heavily with excitement as she looked each executive in the eye. "Thank you for having me," she began. "As I said in the proposal I sent you, Manhattan isn't just a backdrop for the most heart-fluttering romantic comedy movies and books. It's also where fantasy meets reality on every corner, in every coffee shop, and in the unexpected encounters that feel like they've stepped straight out—"

"For the love of time, get to the point," Frankie interrupted.

Sophie gulped. "*Find Your Book Boyfriend* will be a monthly column dedicated to bringing the allure of rom-com boyfriends into the lives of our readers. This column will engage our audience in a quest to find real-life, Manhattan men who mirror our favorite fictional heroes." Her smile widened as she envisioned the column coming to life. "Each edition will dive into the world of a different rom-com hero trope—be it the charming bookshop owner with a secret or the ambitious lawyer with a heart of gold. Within each column, I'll tie in a popular rom-com novel that celebrates that hero trope. Then I'll explore the city's nooks and crannies, seeking out men who embody these qualities, and report back to our readers on my finds. Thus the title *Find Your Book Boyfriend*."

Sophie paused. Frankie had said to make it short. But there was so much more to say. "We'll invite *Naked Runway* readers to join the adventure through interactive challenges, themed events, and even nominations for their own real-life rom-com heroes. The column I'm proposing will connect, inspire, and maybe, just maybe, lead to real-world romances."

Sophie took a breath before giving her closing line. "*Find Your Book Boyfriend* will not only set trends but also celebrate the joy of romance in the real world, proving that the search for love—inspired by the characters from our beloved rom-coms—can be as thrilling as the novels themselves."

She sat back, her pitch complete, hope building as she awaited the response from the three women.

Isabella squealed. "It was a fabulous idea when I read your letter of inquiry, and it's even better in person. I can envision it now. We can interview your book boyfriend finds on our podcast."

"I'm just not sure how we're going to tie it into fashion. Sure, we went off-brand with our *RAKEish* column, but having a prince behind that column sold magazines. What is so special about you that will bring new subscribers to the table?" Frankie asked.

"I'm the president of the Manhattan chapter of the Book Boyfriend Connoisseurs," Sophie offered.

Frankie rolled her eyes. "And that matters why?"

"Because they are a national club of romance readers with an impressive number of members," Ms. Birdie said.

"And you're the president of the Manhattan chapter?" Isabella asked Sophie.

Sophie grinned. "I am, and it's a hoot. We get together once a week and rate the boyfriends from our latest read."

"How many are in the Manhattan Book Boyfriend Connoisseurs?" Frankie asked, a glint of interest in her eyes.

"We have around ten thousand members. Over a thousand active ones, who show up for our meetings which requires us to have a multitude of meeting locations throughout Manhattan."

"Hmm. It's not a terrible idea," Frankie said. "Ms. Birdie, what do you think?"

Ms. Birdie studied Sophie with kind eyes. "Your proposal had me at *book boyfriend*, but I do have a concern, which is why, after reading your inquiry, I decided to attend this interview today."

"And what is that?" Sophie asked.

"Your safety. You propose to travel all around Manhattan, interviewing men as prospective living book boyfriends, and, well... That could be dangerous. Rom-com sounds benign, but some of their heroes have unsavory reputations...in the beginning. For instance, Lucian Rollins, the hero in the third book from Lucy Score's *Knockemout* series."

Sophie's jaw dropped. Ms. Birdie read romances.

"I've read that book—fell in book-boyfriend lust with Lucian—and you have an excellent point," Isabella said. "I hadn't thought about Sophie's pitch from that angle. It's one thing to drool over a man like Lucian while reading a book, but interviewing a living, breathing duplicate of Lucian might not be safe."

Sophie closed her mouth as her spirits plummeted. She'd thought for certain this was it. She'd get the gig and could finally stop worrying that everyone was right—that her daydreams were a waste of time.

"Ms. Birdie, are you vetoing her proposal?" Frankie asked in a neutral tone.

For three very long seconds, Ms. Birdie didn't reply.

"Not at all," the queen bee finally said. "But, as the owner of *Naked Runway* and the one who could be ultimately slapped with a lawsuit, should Sophie's journey go awry, I feel the need to demand she hire a bodyguard."

"A bodyguard?" Sophie couldn't afford to hire a bodyguard, and if they deducted one from her paycheck, that would undo all her have-the-cake-and-eat-it-too plans. Plans that would allow her to live out her dreams and still manage to cover the cost of the rent hike on her grandfather's apartment. A hike he couldn't afford, thanks to Sophie's last good-for-nothing rotten son-of-a-bitch boyfriend.

"Yes, dear," Ms. Birdie replied.

"Surely, that's not necessary," Sophie replied, scrambling for a way to ensure it wasn't. "I mean, I know a little jiu-jitsu, carry mace, and have a very healthy set of lungs in case a scream is required."

"I can't risk being sued because I deemed those adequate ways for a star columnist to protect herself," Ms. Birdie said.

"I promise not to sue in case of a mishap," Sophie said. *Star columnist* had a nice ring to it.

"Darling, don't look so glum. It will be fine. We can start by hiring someone for a month. If, at the end of the month, the expert feels you're not in need of protection, then I'll reconsider my stance."

"A month," Sophie repeated. Maybe she could pick up some extra shifts at her current, non-daydreaming gig. "Do I get a say in who it is?"

"Do you know a bodyguard?" Isabella asked.

Sophie blushed. "Not an actual one...but I know a few bouncers who—"

"Nothing against bouncers, but I think we need someone with better credentials," Isabella said. "And I have just the person in mind. He's a former Navy SEAL who I'm pretty sure would be up for some light duty while he recovers from an injury. He's part owner of a security firm."

"He doesn't sound that impressive at what he does if he's been injured." Frankie's tone could have taught classes on how to kill with inflection.

Isabella didn't die. Instead, she turned her back on Frankie and spoke to Ms. Birdie and Sophie. "Anyway, because of his injury, he hasn't been cleared for the type of security situations they specialize in, but I think his doctor would give the go-ahead for being your bodyguard."

"Excellent idea," Ms. Birdie said, clapping her hands. "Which one of them was injured?"

"Stone," Isabella said.

"How serendipitous," Ms. Birdie said enigmatically, but didn't expand.

"Ms. Peterson has a point," Sophie said, darting a glance at Frankie. Her instincts told her she needed to get on the woman's good side for her project to work. "If he's injured, will he be all that helpful?"

"His injury is hardly an injury at all," Isabella said. "Or at least that's how I heard it described. For a few weeks, he's supposed to wear a thick bandage on his middle finger, which impedes the speed with which his shooting finger can react."

"What good is a bodyguard who can't shoot?" Frankie asked. "Why don't I—"

"Somehow, I don't think he'll have a need to shoot anyone while protecting Sophie," Isabella said. "I envision him hanging around more as a scare tactic than anything else."

"If he's there to scare people," Sophie said louder than she intended, "I won't get any men to grant me an interview, let alone be willing to consent to be declared a book boyfriend twin." A scary bodyguard was the last thing she wanted to have to deal with right now. "I really think we should pick someone less frightening. In fact, I have a colleague—"

"Nonsense," Ms. Birdie said. "Stone's a professional. I use him and his brothers for security at my social events. He's perfectly capable of blending into the background."

Sophie hated the idea. A guy like that would not understand the assignment. He'd be all condescending and irritated at her for...everything, probably even the lack of world peace.

Much like her last boyfriend, who'd started out quirky and ended up deceptive.

"If we're going to go down this rabbit hole, and I'm not convinced we should," Frankie said, "the solution to Sophie's worry is an easy fix. She and her bodyguard can adopt a fake relationship as a cover. That way, he won't scare anyone off. They do things like this all the time in romantic comedies."

"You read rom-coms?" Isabella asked, looking truly startled.

"Bite me," Frankie snapped.

"What a lovely idea," Ms. Birdie said, succinctly ending the exchange between the two editors. "Don't you agree, Isabella?"

Sophie was too busy watching to see how Isabella would handle being told to bite the other editor to give much thought to the suggestion that she was to be a part of an honest-to-goodness fake dating trope.

"I do agree," Isabella cast a wistful look toward Frankie. "Remember the time we watched *Pretty Woman* instead of studying for our college exams our senior year?"

Sophie's gaze whipped to Frankie. Her mouth had pinched, and her nostrils were flared.

Now sounding vulnerable, Isabella continued, "It was right after we found out—"

"No one is interested in our time as college roommates," Frankie shot back.

Sophie jerked her attention back to Isabella. She looked slightly sad.

The silence that ensued was finally broken by Ms. Birdie. "Frankie, once again you've come up with a brilliant idea."

Frankie nodded.

The older woman gave Sophie an expectant smile. "Are you on board?"

Sophie had to flip back through the conversation to recall what they'd even been talking about. *Oh yeah. That.* "For a fake boyfriend?"

"Please say yes. It will be a rom-com come to life," Isabella purred. "Not that the two of you will fall in love, just embrace the trope."

"At the risk of you shutting down the whole pitch," Sophie said, hesitantly, "I have to say I'm not sure my budget will cover the cost of hiring a bodyguard." She absolutely knew it wouldn't but if desperate times called for desperate measures, she'd sell her toenail clippings to freaks on the internet.

"Darling, *Naked Runway* will cover all your costs. Just keep your receipts," Ms. Birdie said.

"Even cardboard cutouts of book boyfriends?" Sophie asked. "And matching themed T-shirts. And—"

"Anything that helps you with your project is approved," Ms. Birdie replied, her eyes twinkling. "Tell me more about these shirts."

"It's one of my side hustles to pay the bills. I design and sell quirky, book-related merchandise on Etsy. It's my way of putting to use my associate degree in merchandising," Sophie said. Someday, she'd go back and get her bachelor's degree, but that would have to wait until Poppie was more stable. "My T-shirts are my bestsellers."

"How absolutely lovely," Ms. Birdie said. "I do love a person with initiative."

"How many side hustles do you have?" Frankie asked. "It was my understanding you'd be working for us full-time if we hire you."

"Just a few. My Etsy shop, and dog walking for the elderly. And I run a monetized YouTube channel where I read Junie B. Jones stories to children at bedtime. And, once in a while, I'll cover a shift at the local bar so my friend can stay home if her child is sick."

"Good God," Frankie snapped. "Are you even capable of staying on task? It sounds to me like your career life is a hot mess."

"Leave her alone," Ms. Birdie admonished. "I currently own over fifty businesses, and I manage just fine to be a professional. Sophie, the job is yours with the understanding that *Naked*

Runway takes priority. If any of your side hustles get in the way, you'll have to put them on hold."

"Deal." Sophie squealed. "I can't believe this is all happening. Thank you so much."

"You're welcome," Ms. Birdie said. "Isabella, be a doll and find Sophie a fully equipped office she can work out of. Those cardboard cutouts she mentioned will need someplace to hang out. I don't imagine your apartment is big enough to hold twelve extra people...real or not real."

"Fabulous idea," Isabella said with a smile. "There's an empty office down the hall from mine. Sophie, did you have any other concerns, or are you on board with our bodyguard slash fake boyfriend plan?"

"Of course, I'm in," Sophie replied. And she was. Sure, that part of the plan wasn't something she wanted, but they'd given her so much more than she'd expected. Who was she to say no to their one condition? "What could possibly go wrong?"

"Probably nothing," Ms. Birdie said.

Isabella chuckled.

"What's so funny, dear?" Ms. Birdie asked her.

"I was just recalling some of the funny plot twists that have caused things to go wonky in the romantic comedies that this whole endeavor is being based around."

"Oh my," Ms. Birdie said.

"Not to worry," Sophie jumped in before *Naked Runway*'s owner could change her mind. "I mean, really, how bad could a fake relationship plot twist be?" Unlike the real relationship plot twist she'd recently survived.

One time. One freaking time, Sophie had gone off-brand in her preferred boyfriend type of choice and had quickly regretted the decision.

Never again.

Chapter 2

Stone stared in exasperation at the woman who had adopted him and his brothers when they were in elementary school. "Have you lost your mind?"

"I have not," Clarabelle Peabody replied sharply. "It's a perfect solution to your current problem. You've never been good at being idle. This will keep you from idling on every one of our last nerves."

"Babysitting some airhead columnist in search of the perfect living, breathing book boyfriend"—the most asinine thing he'd ever heard, and he'd heard a lot of asinine things in the past couple of years—"is not my idea of a perfect solution to my inability to do my damn job." He glared at the bandage on his middle finger.

"Language," Clarabelle said, rearranging her skirt around her legs.

"Sorry." He dropped into the chair across from her.

"Darling, I recently spoke to a psychologist who moved into the... neighborhood, and she said your current predicament could quite likely be psychological and not physical. She suggested you take a mental vacation."

On the surface, the comment seemed innocent enough, but Clarabelle did not live in a normal neighborhood. Her friends were anything but normal everyday people. Hell. Most of them no longer breathed.

"How will watching this fluff piece be a mental vacation?"

"One, she's easy on the eyes. Cute as a button, I'm told. Two, the assignment is a cakewalk. The odds of her being harassed, once word gets out that she has a six-foot-four, broody boyfriend who is built like a fortress and has a serious jealousy issue, are nil."

"If that's the case, why isn't this god of all men filling in as her bodyguard?"

Clarabelle sighed. "Don't be dense. You're that guy."

He laughed only to cut it short when she didn't laugh in return. "Mom, I'm six-two. Not broody. I don't have a jealous bone in my body. And I've never even met this woman. How can I be her boyfriend?"

"You absolutely are broody. And everyone exaggerates their dimensions. And once you find the right woman, you most certainly will be the jealous sort. Think of her as your practice forever person. Get all the kinks out with her so you don't screw it up when the real thing comes along that you want to impress."

Stone refrained from reminding her of his plan to never get married. His reasons were solid. Amongst them a blood oath with his brothers to remain bachelors until retirement. Love distracted men, and in their line of work, distractions became deadly. "Let me get this straight. The gig is an undercover one, and I'm to pretend I'm this woman's boyfriend?"

"Didn't I mention that?" Clarabelle gave him a serene smile. A smile that hid so many secrets. "I could have sworn I did so."

"You did not."

Clarabelle had always been scattered, but ever since coming back into their lives a few years ago, that *scattered* had become magnified to the point of concerning.

"It must have slipped my mind, what with all the worrying I've been doing over you. It was bound to happen," Clarabelle said, dropping the worried mother card with the finesse of a Vegas blackjack dealer.

"There's no reason for you to worry about me." As much as he'd like to call her on her tactic, he couldn't. Not too long ago, he'd thought he'd never see her again. Having her back in his life, bizarre as it was, meant the world to him. "Mom, I'll be fine."

She tutted. "Physically, I'm sure you will. But a lot has happened in your life over the last several years."

"As it has in yours."

"It's really no wonder that things have gone bonkers for you," she said as if he'd not spoken. "I suspect your brothers will face the same hurdle any day now. Well...not the injured finger, but the glitchy part."

"As long as I'm glitching, I have no business working as a bodyguard," he said, grabbing on to the built-in excuse to say no.

"Oh, fiddle, faddle," Clarabelle said, waving a dismissive hand. "It's not like your client will be in any real danger. You'll just need to scare the weirdos away without using your weapon of choice." She whispered the last part as if afraid the walls of their office had ears.

"And I need to do that without her finding out the family secret." And it was one damn startling secret. Or it had been to the woman he'd just started seeing right before Clarabelle had reappeared and turned his and his brother's lives upside down.

Stone, believing he'd found his perfect match, had given serious consideration to changing careers for her. Completely besotted, he'd gone so far as to hint to her of the family secret by admitting he believed in things otherworldly. He'd been certain he'd found a woman who would indulge this side of him.

He'd been wrong. Lesson painfully learned.

"True." Clarabelle repositioned herself so her eyes were level with his and studied him. "Is that what's bothering you? Not being able to tell a woman your secret until after she says *I love you?*"

After Stone's failed relationship experiment, he and his brothers had decided that in the future—if one of them were to ever again become a love-besotted fool willing to change careers for a woman—they would, at the very least, wait until after love was declared by both parties before they mentioned the family secret and leaving the business. "Considering I have no plans to fall in love and get married, no, that's not it."

Clarabelle waggled her finger. "If I've told you all once, I've told you a zillion times, that just because one woman couldn't handle your true-blue, honest-to-goodness identity, doesn't mean none of them can. I went to battle for you to have the right to get married while maintaining your position, and I would have never done that had I thought there weren't women out there that would understand."

"That's not the only reason we made the pact to never marry. If you recall, the agreement was in place before you showed back up in our lives and did the thing you did."

"I gave you a skill set that has helped the three of you tremendously in your new venture as security specialists. And all but eliminates any real danger you face, which makes your pre-me-back-in-your-life pact unnecessary."

"That you did, and we are grateful." As a result of their new weapon of choice, they were able to eliminate most danger before it could get off the ground. But not all. His recent injury proof positive. "But the fact remains I'm currently out of commission. Not suitable for this new gig you've booked me."

"I'll be the judge of your suitability, and I judge you just fine for the job." Clarabelle had insisted on filling in for their current receptionist, who was out on parental leave. "It's not like you're going to be protecting the president or something. You'll be providing security for a real sweetheart, Sophie E. Clark. She's a new columnist at *Naked Runway*. She took over for the Prince of Manhattan."

The mention of Scott Landshire made Stone smile. "I'm still recovering from his wedding celebration."

"Anyhoo, I've scheduled for you to meet with Frankie Peterson who will be running lead on this assignment. And at that meeting, you'll be introduced to Sophie. This will provide you with an opportunity to better understand what it is you've agreed to do...via my acquiescence."

Chapter 3

One week later, Stone stood in line at Espresso Runway, waiting to give his order. The place, tucked away in the ground lobby of the building that housed *Naked Runway's* offices, was bustling with early morning traffic.

The woman in front of him stepped forward to place her order. "Could I have a Fairytale Latte, please? Make it with oat milk, a shot of vanilla, and a swirl of caramel. Oh, and could you sprinkle some cinnamon on top? And if it's not too much trouble, a dash of edible glitter? It's like a sip of magic to start the day."

Stone grimaced. What in the hell kind of order was that?

"I'm sorry, we don't sell a Fairytale Latte," the barista said. "Nor do we have edible glitter."

"Oh," the redhead said. "Then, let's make it a..." She paused dramatically, glancing at the menu. "A Grande Couture Cappuccino, please?

With almond milk, a shot of rose syrup, and a sprinkle of pink sugar crystals on top."

"Will that be all?" the barista asked, not glancing up.

"Hmmm," the redhead said. "Could you add some of those chocolate curls? They look like little scroll embellishments—so fun."

The high-maintenance woman stepped aside, and he moved forward. "I'll have a coffee—black, no sugar, no fuss."

As he waited, he scanned the café, cataloging exits and noting faces, until his gaze inevitably fell on the redhead. She now stood to the side facing him, a contagious smile on her lips. The smile, despite it being a Monday morning, made sense once he read the front of her pale pink T-shirt. *Professional Daydreamer.*

He glanced away and snorted derisively. The shirt was probably designed to be a joke, but Miss Fairytale Latte seemed the type to be declaring it literally. How could he sign up for that gig? His way of earning a living couldn't be more different. The notion of someone making a living as a daydreamer seemed ludicrous, but then again, who was he to judge? Some would say his secret weapon of choice in his job was far more outlandish.

The barista called out, "Order for Stone," and thrust a cup toward him. "An order for—"

Stone took the cup, got a whiff of something super sweet, and read the name written on it. He cleared his throat and held out the cup to the redhead who'd just accepted the other order. "I'm assuming, Fairytale is you." He twisted the cup so she could read the name written on it.

"Oh, that would be mine, thank you," she said, her voice light and airy as if mix-ups were a normal occurrence in her life. "And that would make you..." She glanced at the name on the cup she held and frowned ever so slightly. "Stone Cold."

"I've been called worse." Her fingers brushed against his as she took the cup, sending an unexpected jolt through them. Stone retracted his hand slightly, masking his reaction with a neutral expression.

"It appears we are mirror opposites," she mused.

Under normal circumstances, he avoided small talk. But he was early and had a few minutes to spare. "Life would be dull if we were all living fairytales."

"True, but everyone could use a bit of enchantment now and then," she said, emphasizing the word *enchantment* as she gave him an assessing look. "Don't you think?"

"Perhaps," he conceded cautiously, "but in my experience, reality tends to be complicated enough."

Her lips pursed, drawing attention to their heart shape because, of course, they were shaped like Cupid's bow. "Who says reality can't have a bit of whimsy, too?" she said before making her way to an open table. "Care to join me?"

Everything about her was a stark contrast to his own existence, which was entangled in shadows and secrecy. He shook his head. "I have an appointment."

Her response was to immediately start chatting up another man. Stone gave her one last look and, for a nanosecond, could have sworn he saw a spark come out of her hair. No doubt it had been nothing more than how the light landed on it, but still, what with her shirt and her coffee shop name, he couldn't help but admit to himself:

That woman just might actually embrace our family secret.

Not that he'd test his theory. His heart no longer took such painful gambles. He was a bachelor for life.

Chapter 4

L eaving the coffee shop, careful not to spill her drink on her *Professional Daydreamer* T-shirt, Sophie navigated the hallway leading to the conference room at *Naked Runway*, barely thinking about Stone Cold and his vibes of anti-book boyfriend material.

Each step took her by fabulously styled individuals wearing designs she couldn't afford. As such, she'd decided it was the perfect day to debut her latest creation. A bright pink tee she'd embellished over the weekend with her career of choice all in celebration of her new gig. She'd decided to pair it with a black tulle skirt sporting a field of dancing wildflowers along its hem.

Over the past week, every time she reminded herself she'd landed the gig for a year-long column at Manhattan's premier fashion magazine, giddiness had filled her with cheeky smiles and bubbly laughter. According to a follow-up gab session with Isabella, they'd had over one hundred applications.

Isabella had also informed Sophie that Frankie had insisted she needed a month-by-month breakdown of Sophie's planned columns so she could properly plan the non-digital magazine's layout, thus today's gathering.

Arriving at the meeting room, Sophie discovered it empty. Had she gotten the dates mixed up? Or the time? Or had Ms. Birdie changed her mind and sent Sophie a pink slip?

Stop spiraling, Sophie.

The admonishing voice in her head was that of five-year-old Sophie's therapist, a grandmotherly woman who'd worked with Sophie in the months after her parents had died in a boating accident. The three-word command triggered a memory-muscle response. Sophie closed her eyes, inhaled deeply, and exhaled slowly.

It wasn't until she heard someone clearing their throat that Sophie realized she wasn't alone. She opened her eyes.

"You okay?" Isabella asked, viewing her quizzically.

Sophie grinned. "I'm better than fine. I'm fabulous. Just grounding myself for today's presentation."

Isabella nodded and then tilted her head and eyed Sophie's whimsical ensemble.

Taking care not to fidget, Sophie waited.

"I love your look. It's fresh and enchanting and gives me an idea of how to brand you to our readers."

"Thanks," Sophie beamed, tucking her curls behind her ears. "I can't wait to hear your plan." She'd never considered the idea of *Naked Runway* branding her. Now that she was, she rather liked it. They'd branded the Prince of Manhattan as a rake. What would they come up with for her? Hopefully not as a flake.

The sound of voices prevented her from inquiring more.

Ms. Birdie, Frankie, and the man from the coffee shop walked into the conference room. Stone Cold. A man who had both intrigued and startled her earlier. His shaved head and broad shoulders were completely at odds with the suit he wore. One shouted menacing, the other important. Why was he—oh.

"Hello Stone," Isabella said. "I'd like to introduce you to Sophie E. Clark." She glanced at Sophie. "Sophie, meet Stone Blackthorn, your bodyguard."

"He's going to be my fake boyfriend." Incredulity painted her words as she stared at his scowl.

"You're my new client?" Stone asked.

"Is there a problem?" Frankie inquired. "We can call this whole thing off. It's not too late."

"Nonsense," Ms. Birdie said. "No one is calling anything off. Sophie, dear, why do you look so concerned?"

Sophie waved open palms; fingers splayed. "Look at this guy. No one will agree to an interview with him in the picture, fake boyfriend or not. He'll scare them off."

Stone tugged at the collar of his suit jacket. "I suggest you—"

"Why don't we all take a seat?" Isabella said. "Sophie, you can start your presentation. Perhaps that will help us all better understand your concern and give Stone a solid understanding of his upcoming mission. Stone, I was so sorry to hear about your accident but was very happy you could do this job. How is Ryder?"

Stone's expression went carefully blank. "He's doing fine."

"Wonderful. He's a great guy and deserves happiness."

"Yes. He does." Stone turned his attention to Sophie. "I'm ready when you are."

Sophie wanted to ponder that weird exchange but now wasn't the time. She had bigger problems to consider. The biggest was how her daydreams could survive in the shadow of Stone's towering presence. His impenetrable gray storm aura would cast ugly thunder clouds over her sparkly, iridescent one.

She stepped to the front of the conference table where a computer was set up and slid her flash drive into the slot.

The ladies took a seat, and Stone leaned against the wall while Sophie pulled up her PowerPoint. The title page appeared. "Stone, my column will be titled: *Find Your Book Boyfriend.*"

She really liked the graphics for this screen. It had vectors of men, holding the book in which they were the hero. Or at least they were her vision of what each of the heroes looked like from the descriptions given by the authors of their book stories.

"Each month, one of these images will be featured in my column and next to them will be the real-life single man who matches them."

Stone snorted.

"I missed that, Stone," Sophie said sweetly. "Did you have a comment?"

"Other than the whole thing sounds ridiculous," he responded, "I don't."

"I'm certain it does sound rather odd to a man like you. My column is geared toward those with the heart of a romantic. The keywords are *heart* and *romantic*. On the surface, you appear to neither have a heart nor know the first thing about romancing a woman." Under normal circumstances, Sophie would never be so rude, but if he was on the fence about accepting the position as her bodyguard, her mission was to dissuade him.

He raised a brow. "You're very astute."

Sophie took a deep breath, focusing on the screen. This was her moment, her dream. She couldn't allow Stone's intimidating appearance to distract her. With a determined click of the remote, Sophie dove into her proposal, hoping her passion would be enough to eclipse any doubts from the women in the room—and maybe, just maybe, soften the foreboding edge that Stone brought into the mix.

"Book Boyfriend Connoisseurs conducted a survey of all its members to discover their top one hundred book boyfriends," Sophie said. "The survey was broken down into categories. My column, for this year, will focus on the top twelve winners in the contemporary romantic comedy category."

"Why romantic comedy?" Frankie asked.

"Because it will set the tone for the column," Sophie replied. "One of happiness and ease."

"I'm not totally sold on that, it's a bit boring, but move along, time is wasting," Frankie ordered.

"The top twelve books in the rom-com category were: one, *Aggie the Horrible versus Max the Pompous Ass* by—"

Stone grunted.

Sophie paused and glanced at him. "Comment?"

"Sorry. The title just surprised me."

She gave him a benign smile and continued. "Two, *Anyone But The Billionaire* by Sara L. Hudson. Three, *Funny Story* by Emily Henry. Four, *Falling for My Enemy* by Claire Kingsley. Five, *Things We Left Behind* by Lucy Score. Six, *The Magnolia Chronicles* by Kate Canterbary. Seven, *Love Hacked* by Penny Reid. Eight, *Made in Manhattan* by Lauren Layne. Nine, *The Bride's Runaway Billionaire* by Pippa Grant. Ten, *Most Eligible Billionaire* by Annika Martin. Eleven, *Single Dad on Top* by J. J. Knight. And twelve, *Tangled* by Emma Chase." She showed each book cover as she read the name of the book and its author.

"I read half those books on vacation last summer," Isabella said. "I can see why they were chosen."

"Of course you've read them. It's not like being the editor-in-chief of the digital side of things is too demanding. I, on the other hand, have no time to vacation, let alone read," Frankie said.

Isabella scratched her nose with her middle finger but said nothing.

"Since Stone wasn't here to hear your original pitch," Ms. Birdie said, "explain a little about your proposal."

Sophie clicked to the next screen. An image of the cover for *Aggie the Horrible versus Max the Pompous Ass* popped up. "In this book, the business tycoon hero has a meddling grandmother who has manipulated his need for a temporary assistant to push her latest matchmaking efforts upon him. As a result, he's quite a total bosshole to the heroine, all in the hopes she will quit."

Maybe Sophie should be a bosshole to Stone to get him to quit, should he decide to take the gig.

"Bosshole?" Stone asked.

"Nice word for asshole in charge," Sophie explained. Who was she kidding? Life was too short to fake assholeness.

Stone rubbed the back of his neck, bringing her attention to his bandaged finger, but said nothing.

"My thought is to have Isabella do a podcast asking all of Manhattan to anonymously nominate their favorite bossholes with hero possibilities—given the right person—to be spotlighted in my column."

"Hero possibilities?" Stone asked, frowning.

"Most men—abusers and narcissists absolutely excluded—can be salvaged if they're willing and able to be educated on what it takes to be a living book boyfriend, a.k.a. a swoony hero."

"Lucky them," he said sarcastically.

She ignored his tone. "I'll interview the nominees, weed out the stinkers"—she glanced at Stone—"and declare one a book-boyfriend match. Midway through the column's run, Ms. Birdie has agreed that all the book boyfriends who have been discovered by that point will be required to participate in her annual bachelor auction. My Book Boyfriend Twins will go to the highest bidders."

"Auction?" Stone asked.

"A charity auction," Sophie said. "The money this year will go to Childhood Cancer Research."

"I was so thrilled when I learned of your idea," Ms. Birdie said. "I predict it will be our best fundraiser ever. A date night with your book boyfriend will sell out faster than any other auction we've ever hosted."

"If this is the entirety of your plan," Stone said. "I see no reason to be your bodyguard. You won't need one, and I won't take money that's not earned."

"Sophie, tell us a little about each type of man you will be scouring the five boroughs to find," Ms. Birdie urged. "I do believe that will help Stone get a better grasp on just why it is you need protecting."

Sophie nodded. "In the book *Tangled*, the boyfriend trope is a New York City playboy, so I'll be on the hunt for one of those. The novel *Funny Story* requires me to find a living, breathing, lovable cinnamon roll."

"A what roll?" Stone asked, his brow creasing.

"Cinnamon roll. Those are the nice guy heroes. They're not broody, or snarly, or anything that is off-putting. Instead, they have a gooey heart and are just waiting for the right person to appreciate their niceness."

"Good God," he shuddered. "I pity the poor fucking man who gets described as a cinnamon roll. Could you be any more cruel to their ego?"

Sophie frowned. "I beg your pardon?"

For a moment, Stone looked confused by her outrage. Then he grimaced. "Pardon my language. I hope I've not offended your sensibilities."

Sophie was plenty offended, but not by his language. "I'll have you know *my* perfect match will be a cinnamon roll. While yes, I love reading about all the other types of heroes, when push comes to shove, give me a big teddy bear, and I'll be superbly happy."

He gave her a look of incredulity, glanced at her T-shirt, and then nodded as if his brain had suddenly been illuminated with blinding understanding. "Of course that's what you would want in a man."

She slapped her hands to her hips. "What does that mean?"

"It means...nothing. Forget I said anything. Please continue."

Sophie clicked to the next screen with more force than necessary. Stone was getting on every one of her lifetime preserve of last nerves. By the time this meeting was over, she'd have no last nerves left for future frustrating situations. Which would leave her as one of those people who immediately overreacted with emotion instead of biting her tongue with patience. Like Frankie.

She took a breath. *Don't spiral.*

"*Anyone But The Billionaire* will have me scrutinizing all the single billionaires in search of one who likes to have fun. *Falling for My Enemy* will require me to find that super-smart geek who will make the right woman a perfect boyfriend. *Single Dad on Top* will have me searching out single dads. *Made in Manhattan* will send me to the seedier side of town looking for a guy from the wrong side of the tracks in need of a makeover. *The Magnolia Chronicles* requires me to find a bachelor who has been recently dumped and is on the rebound. And *Most Eligible Billionaire* requires me to take a look at the eligible billionaire list and find just the right grumpy one. Oh, and *The Bride's Runaway Billionaire—*"

Stone made a noise, and there went another of Sophie's stock of last nerves. She waited for him to explain the context of the noise.

"What?" she finally snapped.

"I asked nothing," he said looking at her like *who pissed in your Cheerios?*

You did, you big idiot. "You scoffed at my mention of searching out a grumpy bachelor. Why?"

"I'm picking up on this whole theme of billionaires. It appears that for a guy to be book boyfriend material he must be at billionaire status."

"Book Boyfriend Connoisseurs read for the fantasy and the escape. Thus, we like our men, for the most part, filthy rich. So, sue us. Don't tell me the women you fantasize about aren't stacked and curvy and willing."

He gave her a wolfish grin. "I'll concede your point."

She straightened. "*Things We Left Behind* highlights a hero with a shady past. And *Love Hacked* has a hero with a secret. A really big secret."

"That one will be fun," Ms. Birdie said, a twinkle in her eyes. "Sophie will ask for nominees of guys who have secrets that they believe make them non-boyfriend material but are willing to share it with the person who buys him at auction. Isn't that right, dear?"

Sophie nodded. "It might be a little tricky to find a guy who meets the dimensions of that type of book boyfriend, but that's not going to sway me from hunting."

"If you don't mind, let's back up one," Stone said. "What do you mean a hero with a shady past?"

"Just that. The hero hasn't always followed the law. And his current dealings may still be landing on the line." As had Sophie's last boyfriend who she'd thought was past that part of his life. Turned out...not so much.

"And just exactly where do you plan to look for such a man?"

"Wherever the listeners of Isabella's podcast point us," she replied, syrupy sweet. If he was going to deprive her of all her last nerves, she was going to send him home with a toothache from all her sugar.

"First of all, it's not Isabella's podcast," Frankie mused. "It's *Naked Runway's*. Second of all, Stone, we've hired you to protect Sophie, not question her assignment."

"I haven't signed a contract yet," Stone drawled. "I'm here to see if the gig is one I want to pursue."

Frankie rolled her eyes. "In my opinion, Sophie should start with the sketchy hero. It's the most exciting and will kick off our new column with a bang."

Stone winced. "I'm certain you didn't mean that as a pun, but from where I'm standing, it's not funny."

Sophie laughed. "Look at you having a sense of humor. You might be salvageable as a fake boyfriend after all." She did shooting fingers at him. "Pew. Pew."

"Again, I've not signed a contract," Stone said. "Tell me more about this fake boyfriend thing you keep harping about."

"Rude," Sophie said. "I most definitely was not harping."

Ms. Birdie stood. "Sophie, darling, you've done a wonderful job in your presentation. I agree with Frankie, you should start with the sketchy hero." She pivoted to look at Stone. "Shall we discuss what it will take to get you to sign the contract? Clarabelle said you have done a lot of undercover work in the past couple of years, and doing so as a boyfriend would present no problems for a man of your talent. Was she wrong?"

"Of course I can. It's just—do I want to?" Stone gave Sophie a less-than-sweet look. "I can't imagine your real boyfriend would be happy with this plan."

"I'm between, at the moment," Sophie said. And by *moment*, she meant it had been six months.

"Still, I thought my purpose was to deter men from trying to take advantage of you. Why is it your wish I do so as your boyfriend and not simply as your bodyguard?"

"I think I can answer that," Ms. Birdie said when Sophie didn't immediately reply. "You see, as her boyfriend, you'll not only deter gentlemen from getting handsy, but you'll also deter them from hitting on her."

"As in asking her out on a date?" Stone asked. "Would that be so bad?"

"Actually, it would. You see, we can't have Sophie getting too chummy with any of her choices because they will need to remain eligible for the bachelor auction. It would be a shame if one of them was off the market when the event rolled around."

"She's a professional...or at least I assume she is if you hired her," Stone replied. "I would think, as such, she can behave in a professional manner around the men she interviews and just say no to date opportunities."

"Stone, darling, I get the feeling you're here under duress," Ms. Birdie said. "That is probably my fault, since I called in a favor with Clarabelle to have you help us out. If that's the case, please just say so, and we will search out another to protect our Sophie. Clarabelle can repay the favor another day."

"That won't be necessary," he said. "And please forgive my surliness. It appears that being out of commission has soured my normal cheerful position."

It was Sophie's turn to snort. "Please. Like anyone in this room believes you're anything but what you've shown so far." It was too bad he wasn't a billionaire; he could be her grumpy billionaire candidate. Not that she got the feeling he was salvageable.

He raised a brow her way. "Is that your way of saying you'd prefer *Naked Runway* find another bodyguard?"

For more seconds than Sophie could track, they stared antagonistically at one another. "Let the record show, it's my belief you will be the worst fake boyfriend in the history of fake boyfriends, but if you're up for the challenge of going undercover as a guy I'd actually date, then sure, I'm all in. You?"

"Let's do this," he snapped.

Sophie swallowed hard. What in the devil had she been thinking, provoking him to say yes?

Isabella stood. "Frankie, how about we have the Glam Team give Stone a makeover to kick this off."

"Oh, hell no," Stone said, then grimaced. "I mean, no, thank you."

"Isabella might have said it like it's an option, but let me assure you it's not," Frankie said. "You will be repping *Naked Runway*. So of course you will be prettied up for the position."

"It is standard operating procedure," said Isabella. "Sophie, you mentioned a Cinnamon Roll hero was your type?"

Sophie tilted her head and eyeballed Stone. In what world could this bald hulk of a man be turned into any semblance of that kind of book hero? "I did." She wrinkled her nose.

"If this boyfriend thing is nonnegotiable, I'd prefer to go undercover as the shady past hero," Stone said.

"Sophie, are you okay with that?" Ms. Birdie asked.

"Truthfully, I'm not." Sophie gave a fairly convincing sigh of regret. "It will be awkward enough pretending he's my boyfriend, but I could never pull off pretending an attraction to that sort of man. It's just not in my DNA." She did a Vanna White gesture with her hands around the words on her T-shirt for emphasis.

"Then the Glam Team will have its work cut out for them, turning Stone into a sweetheart," Frankie mused.

"This, I can't wait to see," Sophie said, smiling serenely at Stone.

"I just bet you can't." He gave her a hard stare. "But just remember, once I'm transformed, I expect you to sell it to the public that you can't keep your hands off me."

She grimaced. "I'm not an actress; I can't just fake lust. You're going to have to do your part as well."

"Excellent point, both of you," Ms. Birdie said. "I suggest—and it's only a suggestion—why don't the two of you take a week to get to know one another? If, at the end of that week, it's determined you cannot pull off the fake boyfriend plan, then we will pivot...perhaps hire a female bodyguard to protect Sophie. She could go undercover as Sophie's girlfriend"

"Or we could just dump the whole idea," Frankie said. "It does seem to have a lot of potential pitfalls. I'd hate to invest a lot of money in a new project only to have it flop. It was bad enough that the prince bailed on us after only one year. Not to mention, I need her first column ASAP."

Sophie gulped. "Please don't cancel my column. I'm quite certain Stone and I can muster up some chemistry. Ms. Birdie's idea to have us spend time together before duties commence is brilliant." She glanced at Stone, willing him not to rain on her happiness. "Plus, I'm sure I can find a book boyfriend ASAP to kick off my feature column."

Stone cleared his throat. "Did you say one of the book boyfriend tropes you were in search of was a New York City playboy?"

Sophie nodded.

"I can hook you up with one of those," he said, a wicked grin lifting his lips.

"Stone, if you're thinking of who I'm thinking, you're diabolically brilliant," Ms. Birdie said.

"Ryder," Stone replied.

Frankie gave an evil laugh. "You're suggesting we feature Isabella's last-lover-before-marriage, your brother, for our first column?"

Stone nodded.

"I love it," Frankie said, glancing at Isabella with raised eyebrows as if daring her to veto the idea.

"He was never my lover," Isabella snapped. "And I don't think you can call him a playboy."

"Agree to disagree," Stone said quietly. "Last week he had three dates in one day."

"Oh." Isabella looked a little sad at the revelation.

Sophie jumped in before another disagreement could escalate between the two editors. She'd find out more about the soap opera playing out in front of her later. Right now, she wanted to seal the deal. "Excellent. I have a guy for my first column, and it sounds like Stone's on board to spend a week getting to know me."

"Is she right?" Frankie asked him.

He nodded curtly. "Just as long as our daydreamer here can assure me she will keep all feelings to herself," Stone added. "I'm not looking for a real-life professional daydreamer girlfriend."

"As if my heart would ever get excited about the likes of you." Her heart might be filled with daydreams of butterflies and joy, but it wasn't stupid. It knew when to protect itself, and if ever there was a reason to protect, it would be against Stone.

As if reading her thoughts, he gave her an assessing look that made her just a little bit scared. Damn, he had the whole enforcer persona down to an art. Not good. Not good at all for her plans to sweet talk men into agreeing to the part of real-life book boyfriend hero and go to the highest bidder at auction. Then again, imperfect plans were better than none.

Weren't they?

Or had her lovely pitch just become what grandfather liked to call FUBAR?

Fucked up beyond all recognition!

Chapter 5

S tone hesitated outside Sophie's apartment. A pastel pink plaque hung on the door. On it, written in a swirling white cursive, were the words: *Beware: Unattended Book Boyfriends May Be Claimed.*

He grunted. It was because of her damn hard-on for book boyfriends that he'd just endured a makeover by *Naked Runway's* Glam Team which had ended with a wig being glued to his scalp before he'd had a chance to say *hell no.*

Never in his life had he loathed something as much as he'd loathed that experience. This coming from a man who had grown up in the foster system for a big chunk of his young childhood.

Right now, he had one goal and one goal only. Convince Sophie that making him look like a cinnamon roll hero hadn't worked. It was a look he could not pull off.

If she didn't burst out laughing and whole-heartedly agree the moment she opened the door, then she was totally warped by her ideals versus reality.

The snug pastel sweater that had been foisted upon him by a dude named Ziggy, along with the comment that it would "soften Stone's rugged masculinity," would no doubt show up in Stone's next nightmare. And don't even get him started on what he thought of Alberto's underhanded tactics.

Prepared to be laughed at, he raised his fist and rapped his knuckles against the door.

As if she'd been standing on the other side, waiting for him to knock, Sophie immediately answered. Only she didn't laugh. With a perfectly blank expression, she looked him over like he was a new piece at an art gallery.

"Well?" Why in the hell didn't she look shocked? "Are you ready to admit you were wrong? I cannot pull off this whole pastry boyfriend thing."

"It's called a cinnamon roll hero, and I'll admit nothing of the sort." She slowly cocked her head to the left. "Pink is a nice color on you."

He narrowed his eyes. Suspicion built inside him. Why didn't she look even a little startled?

"Were you looking at me through the peep-hole? Did you get all your laughing out of your system before you answered the door?"

"Of course not. I was reading when you knocked." She held up a book, *VOGUEish*, as if for proof.

"Then I take it you're in shock," he said. "And the laughter will come any minute now."

"I'm not feeling any laughter building."

He shuddered. "Trust me when I tell you, you can't be any more appalled than I was when they finally let me see myself."

She rolled her blue eyes. "Stop carrying on like an ungrateful slug. I'd give anything to be done over by the Glam Team. I mean, look at what they've accomplished with you. You're a total dreamboat in a cardigan and wig."

He yanked at the piece on his head. The damn thing still didn't budge. "Good God, you actually approve of this idiocy?" Why was he surprised? She wore a damn T-shirt with the words *My Book Boyfriend Is Better Than Yours* emblazoned across the front. Her grip on reality was blurred by her endless quest for fictional perfection. He'd need a unicorn and his magic wand just to compete.

"Full approval," she said, before quickly glancing away.

"May I come in?" he asked gruffly, irritation fueling his already sour mood.

"Oh. Of course. Sorry." She took a step back and absently gestured for him to come inside, all while continuing to tilt her head from side to side, studying him like a hero who'd just jumped off the pages of a not-yet-released, highly coveted new romance novel.

He moved into the cramped space and took stock. A person's home was a testament to how they thought. Hers was cozy to the point of being cluttered, with books and notes scattered about. Sophie E. Clark had a very busy mind, as opposed to his brain, which processed with a cool, analytical approach. His thoughts rarely wandered. He'd be willing to bet Sophie's seldom stayed in one place.

"Thank you for agreeing to morph into my idea of the perfect guy."

He had to unclench his jaw before he could answer. "I look ridiculous. Like someone who'd be more at home at a knitting circle than doing bodyguard detail. And don't even get me started on the damn hairpiece."

She eyeballed it. "I have to admit, I'm sort of surprised you didn't ditch it the minute you left the Glam Team."

"I would have, but it's glued in place and won't fucking budge."

Sophie bit her lip, her gaze flitting away for a moment as if considering her next words carefully. "It's... perfection," she said dreamily. "Exactly like... a guy I would date."

He rubbed the back of his neck. "You can't possibly find this hot."

"It's not nice to mock a girl's taste in men," she chided softly.

"My apologies." It was time to attack the plan from a place of common sense. "But Sophie, I've been hired to intimidate men into leaving you alone. That will not happen with my looking like this."

She scrunched her nose. "Agree to disagree."

"On what grounds? Look at me. I'm wearing pastel socks with hearts."

"Stone, the men I interview will leave me alone out of respect for the fact I'm in a relationship," she said. "And the less you look like a bodyguard, the less likely anyone will suspect you're a fake."

It was time to counter with a compromise. "Can we at least change your type to the grumpy billionaire? That one is way more doable than this."

She fluttered her long, thick lashes, casting delicate shadows on her cheeks. "But that's not my type."

"I thought every woman liked their men flush. Didn't you rattle off, like, a bazillion billionaire tropes on your list?"

"I'm not into yachts and private jets. I'm into books and whimsy. A filthy rich grump is not going to appreciate my quirks, nor I his wallet."

As Sophie's words hung in the air, Stone felt an unexpected twinge in his chest, a reaction that startled him. Her candid confession about her tastes—not the flashy, shallow kind, but something deeper, something real—struck a chord. He had been trained to be observant, to read people like open books, yet here he was, confronted with a complexity he hadn't anticipated.

For a moment, temptation urged him to let his guard down, to tell her that he, too, had little care for superficial things. But that wasn't his role here—he was the bodyguard, not a man to share his personal reflections.

He turned his gaze away and focused on a spot on her bookshelf that was crowded with well-worn novels and trinkets. Clarabelle had asked him not to screw this up. To follow through and complete the mission because she'd assured Ms. Birdie that he could complete any assignment...not just the ones where bullets were flying.

Tightening his jaw, he turned back toward Sophie. "Noted." The only thing that made this all bearable was that Ryder had been coerced by Clarabelle into being Sophie's first subject for her *Find Your Book Boyfriend* column. Ryder had fought a good battle but faced with Clarabelle's strong will, he'd finally caved—not without words for Stone, who'd made it known it had been his idea.

Sophie's smile came quickly, catching him off guard. What had he said to earn that dimple-inducing grin?

"Then you'll do it?" she asked. "You won't tank my dream?"

The earnest question kept him from scowling. This was a job. He was undercover. There was no reason for him to continue to rain on her parade by trying to change the rules of engagement.

He touched his hair and promised revenge someday against Alberto, who'd plopped it on there and glued it in place before Stone had known what was going on. "I won't tank it, but I would remind you of Ms. Birdie's mention of possibly hiring a female protector. Someone who could easily be passed off as your best friend. My feelings won't be hurt if you decide to go that route."

Sophie moved closer, her small apartment making even this small distance seem intimate. "Upon hearing that option, Frankie mentioned dumping the whole plan." She spoke quietly, almost to herself.

He'd first heard about Frankie from the Prince of Shiretopia while working security detail at his wedding reception. According to Scott, the woman was a loose cannon. Not to be trusted to act rationally in any given situation. "I believe Frankie likes to hate on any ideas that are not her own. I wouldn't worry too much about her."

"You may be right," Sophie said. "But you may also be absolutely wrong, and I'm not willing to take that chance."

"You'd prefer to take a chance on my pulling off a cinnamon roll boyfriend ruse? A ruse that may fail despite our best efforts?"

"It won't fail. The Glam Team has given you the look. Now, all that's left is my teaching you the body language and actions that are consistent with the hero type."

Stone looked around the tiny apartment, at the stacks of romantic novels lining the shelves, bookmarks sticking out of several. A small, reluctant smile tugged at the corner of his mouth. When was the last time—other than with Clarabelle—that he had been bested in an argument? By someone who believed book heroes could come to life?

"All right," he conceded, "let's see how this goes. But if I start getting invited to book clubs and brunches, I'm going to shoot someone."

Sophie's laughter, genuine and relieved, filled the room, easing the tension. "Fair enough."

"And, once I manage to get this wig off my scalp, it's not going back on. I'll let my hair grow out. It grows fast."

"In that case, let's get started."

"Get started?"

"I need for you to see other cinnamon roll guys in action."

He raised an eyebrow. It wasn't a bad idea. "And where does one go in Manhattan to see them in the wild? The zoo? The flagship Apple Store? The line at a sample warehouse?" The last he only knew about because Clarabelle had dragged him to one yesterday after they'd had lunch together.

"You'll see." Sophie picked up her purse, flipped off the lights, and scooched around him to open the door.

Just as she did, the door across the hall creaked open, revealing an elderly man leaning heavily on his walker, the faint scent of Bengay wafting from him as he peered out. "Sophie, you going out again?" He shot Stone a glance. "And with a different guy tonight?"

Stone glanced at Sophie and waited for her reply. She'd said she was between boyfriends. He'd taken it to mean she'd not been on a date in a while. Obviously, he'd assumed wrong.

"Poppie, I won't be out long. I promise. When I get back, I'll fix us both dinner and tell you all about my back-to-back nights out with different gentlemen." She linked her arm through Stone's, her grip firm and reassuring, pulling him slightly as she spoke.

The hallway lights flickered.

Stone stiffened.

"I bet our damn landlord didn't pay the electric bill," Poppie muttered. "He's going to try and—"

"Poppie, you and I can grouse about the landlord later. Right now, I'd like for you to meet Stone."

Stone made a mental note to check into their landlord.

"Stone," Poppie repeated. "Like a damn rock."

Sophie sighed. "Yes, but don't let his name fool you—he's a big teddy bear. Isn't that right?" She glanced up at Stone and gave him a cheeky grin.

"Only with you, darling. Only with you. If anyone else asks, I'm a grizzly." He stepped forward, the old wooden floors groaning under his weight, and offered his hand to the frail-looking man, whose eyes were sharp despite the wrinkles. "It's a pleasure to meet you, Mr. Poppie."

"Just Poppie. No *mister*." Poppie took his hand, his grip surprisingly firm for such a fragile frame, a hint of old strength lingering in his veins, and squeezed lightly.

Stone, despite his fear of breaking a bone, squeezed back. His instincts told him it was a test of his character. "You've got a lovely granddaughter."

Poppie pointed a gnarled finger at him. "If you hurt her, I'll do to you what I did to the last, and you can bet your wig he's not coming back around anytime soon."

Stone groaned and touched his hair. Was it crooked? Of course it wasn't. If it could move, it would have been in the bottom of the East River by now. "How'd you know?" he asked Poppie. "I was assured it would be my secret and my secret alone unless I took a woman into my shower and let them watch me remove it with shampoo, warm water, and a witch's brew."

Poppie chuckled. "I'd know a wig anywhere. Used to help my wife put hers on before cancer took her. You don't got cancer, do you?"

"Healthy as a horse. Just trying to impress Sophie. She told me on our first date she prefers her men with hair. Said her last guy had nice hair."

"You ain't got much competition with that one. Biggest weasel in Manhattan. And a crybaby at that. Should have heard him caterwauling as he hightailed it down them there stairs over there just 'cause I was shooting rock at him with my slingshot."

What exactly had Sophie's last date done to deserve that? Another person he'd have to run a background check on. "I promise to be nothing but a gentleman with your granddaughter."

"Good. Because you just might be a keeper. Other than those damn clothes you're wearing. You look like a preschool boy dressed by his nanny to go to the park."

Stone, not knowing how to respond, turned his attention back to Sophie. "Perhaps your granddaughter will take me shopping and help me buy clothes more suitable for my build."

"She'll do you one better than that. She'll whip you up a few of her famous T-shirts. Girl sells them like hotcakes. They've been paying the bills ever since I went and let myself get weaseled out of all my money."

Stone filed that information away along with the other tidbits Poppie was dropping all over the place. It was as if he wanted Stone to know everything just in case his granddaughter hadn't planned on sharing the information on her own.

"Did you need anything before we go?" Sophie asked Poppie, her cheeks tinged with pink, but her lips twitching as if she found it hard to get upset with the man.

He pulled a letter out of his shirt pocket. "Got another one of those damn notices again that I have to come back in for a follow-up session. I swear, any day now, men in white jackets are going to show up at my door and take me somewhere you can't find me."

Sophie untangled herself from Stone and went to the elderly man. "I've told you, that's not ever going to happen. You'll see. In another week, those notices will stop and all will be back to normal. We're a team, you, and I."

The guy wiped his eyes. "Listen to me, carrying on while you're trying to go on a proper date." He turned his walker and aimed it back inside his apartment. "You forget I said anything and go have yourself a good time," he said, already shuffling away. "I'll see you tomorrow. Think I'll fix myself a sandwich and go to bed early."

Before Sophie or Stone could say goodnight, he'd shut the door.

"Should we stay here?" Stone asked. "I mean, I can go, and you can stay."

"It's okay. If I drop my plans now, he'll worry about interfering with my love life. I'll check on him when I return."

They left the building in silence and headed down the street. Stone's mind flooded with new insights about Sophie, each one igniting his protective instincts in ways he hadn't anticipated. Yet, he forced himself to clamp down on the rising tide of questions. Fake relationship aside, theirs was a strictly professional association, and he needed to maintain those boundaries.

What had transpired in the foyer of Sophie's apartment building—those intimate revelations of her life by Poppie—had nothing to do with his contractual duties.

Besides, despite her fondness for fairy tales, Sophie exuded a resilience that suggested she sought understanding, not rescue. And for Stone, offering understanding might unintentionally invite an intimacy that could unravel both the secrets he guarded and the walls he meticulously maintained around his heart.

"Thanks for going along with being my boyfriend," Sophie said, drawing his attention to her.

"It doesn't feel right lying to him," Stone said. "I wish you would have asked me my thoughts before passing me off as your date to your grandfather."

"My last boyfriend was a catastrophe. Poppie's fretted about me ever since. He thinks I let my guard down because I was worried about him, and that's why I made such an unwise choice in men."

"And is he right?"

"Maybe. I don't know. Anyway, telling him you are my boyfriend gave him peace of mind. He looked at you and saw what I saw."

"And that is?"

"A decent human being with really bad fashion taste."

"Wait." He slowed his steps. "I thought you loved everything about my new clothes."

She giggled. "I do...just not on you." More laughter broke free from her lips. The deep belly kind that had her bending over, clutching her sides.

He jerked to a stop. This was the reaction he'd expected the moment she'd opened the door. He'd been duped. "How did you keep from cracking up when you first saw me?"

She straightened and wiped the tears running down her cheeks. "Ziggy sent me a picture."

Everything made much more sense now. "I see. I'll have to have a word with the man." But even as he said it, he was fighting back a smile.

Sophie's eyes widened. "Oh, you can't tell him I told you, because he made me swear to keep it a secret. Frankie will fire him if she finds out."

Stone's desire to smile vanished. Sophie had just revealed a man's secret—one she'd promised to keep—and with no apparent real regret in her eyes at having done so.

He filed away the damning knowledge, stuffed his disappointment out of the equation, and offered her the crook of his elbow. In the scheme of things, her inability to keep a secret wasn't an issue, thus no need for him to pass judgment. He was a bachelor for life. "Shall we continue?"

Chapter 6

Sophie steered Stone down the bustling streets of Alphabet City, part of Manhattan's East Village, navigating through the eclectic mix of cafés, murals, and busy sidewalks. Stone had been broody ever since she'd laughed at him. Even after she'd apologized. She'd not taken him to be the sort to have his feelings hurt so easily.

"It's not that you don't look handsome," she said, trying one more time to ease the situation, "it's just I know the real you beneath the fake-hair, pastel-sweater façade, and it's like that saying about you can't stuff a sausage back into its casing. You know the one I'm talking about?"

He grunted.

"I've already seen you in your whole macho persona and, well... The Glam Team tried to stuff all that hotness into the casing of a sweet guy, and it just didn't work."

"You think I'm hot?"

"You're not *not* hot," she countered. "I mean for those who like the strong, silent sort," she said, steering them around a corner.

"I thought you said the place you were taking me was close. Did you change your mind? Are we headed someplace no one knows you, so you won't be embarrassed to be seen with me?"

"Oh, get over yourself." They were headed to her not-so-secret boyfriend hunting ground, a cozy little café tucked away on East 9th Street, near Tompkins Square Park. It was notorious among the single ladies of the Book Boyfriend Connoisseurs Club for both its literal cinnamon rolls and the sweet-natured men who frequented it. "I'm sure you've had worse undercover gigs."

"That's what I keep telling myself," Stone said. "But none have popped to mind."

The air was crisp, swirling around them as they walked, the sounds of the city creating a rhythmic backdrop. Sophie had chosen her outfit with care, donning a pair of well-fitted jeans and her favorite gray T-shirt that usually garnered smiles and knowing nods from fellow book lovers, a playful wink to her literary escapades.

As they approached the café, Sophie paused, her gaze sweeping over the scene through the glass. "This place," she began, her voice tinged with excitement, "is like a live catalog of cinnamon roll guys."

Stone's expression remained unreadable. His steely brown eyes scanned the cozy interior as if assessing a strategic position rather than a potential romantic hotspot. He followed her through the door, the bell above it jingling softly as they entered the inviting space filled with tinkling laughter, the clatter of cups, and the robust aroma of coffee and baked goods.

As they weaved their way through the crowd to a small table near the window, Sophie wondered if the laid-back atmosphere would crack Stone's tough exterior. One that hadn't been the least bit hidden with a pink cardigan. The makeover had tried to turn a thriller novel into a sweet romance, and it had failed. Stone's gruff demeanor remained unchanged. She'd have to make the best of it and try to soften Stone bit by bit.

As Sophie settled in, pulling off her scarf, a man at the next table glanced over, his eyes bouncing from her face to the text emblazoned across her chest. He chuckled, a warm, hearty sound. "Hope I don't have to worry about my book boyfriend being claimed," he joked, his grin friendly and open.

Sophie laughed, which made Stone scowl. Her fake boyfriend sure was fond of collecting future frown lines on his forehead. Ignoring Stone, she turned to the nice guy. "Only if you leave him unattended," she quipped, her lips twitching with amusement.

Her attention briefly flickered back to Stone, and she was not the least bit surprised to find his scowl had morphed into something fierce and unyielding. Intimidating others sure seemed to be his favorite pastime. To remind him to chill, she reached across the table and touched his hand just as a cloud covered up the sun, casting the entire café in shadows.

"Well, I'll make sure to keep a close eye on him, then," the stranger said, pulling her gaze toward him. "What's your favorite book boyfriend type?" he asked, leaning slightly forward, genuinely interested in her response.

Sophie waved an open hand, palm up, toward Stone. "You're looking at it. The guy with a heart of gold. How about you?"

The stranger gave her a sheepish grin. "I'm into the sexy bad boys. The kind who barks orders in and out of the bedroom." He tittered and then plopped a hand over his mouth and winked.

"Aren't you just a naughty little book reader?" she said. "You'd get along swimmingly with my best friend. Donna is totally into the same type of man."

"You'll have to bring her here someday so we can meet. I'm here most Tuesday nights."

"I'll do that." Sophie removed her hand from Stone; the sun came back out, and the café brightened instantly. "Are you a member of the Book Boyfriend Connoisseurs Club? If so, you should definitely join us at the end of this month for our discussion of Ana Huang's *Twisted Love*. If ever there was a sexy bad boy, it would be Alex Vokov. Have you read it?" If any book was going to tempt Sophie to try one more bad boy before throwing in the towel on the lot of them, it would be *Twisted Love*.

"Read it? Honey, I devoured it in one sitting. That guy had me all hot and bothered before he ever spoke a word. The car ride in the rain… O-M-G!"

Sophie nodded as she handed him a card. "Here's the information for the club. I hope to see you there." With that, she turned her attention back to Stone.

He said nothing, a pulse throbbing in his temple.

Guess someone's not a fan of making new friends. "Too many smiles for your taste?"

"Something like that," he admitted, the hand she'd earlier touched now fisted on the table.

"Lesson number one on being a cinnamon roll boyfriend," she whispered. "No scowls, snarls, or sulking."

"I never sulk."

"Lesson two, you need to read *Funny Story* by Emily Henry. It will help you understand the role you're playing."

"You want me to read a romance?"

"You do read...right?"

"Of course, I read. I listen to audio thrillers on stakeouts."

"Have you ever read a romance?"

"Absolutely not!"

She sighed. You'd think she'd asked him if he'd ever committed a cold-blooded murder. "Then you are in for a real treat. Every guy should read romances. They are a road map to what women want from a lover, both in and out of the bedroom."

He raised a brow. "And your idea of spice in the bedroom is a cinnamon hero?"

"Newsflash," she said, flattening her hands on the tabletop. "Just because a woman wants a cinnamon roll hero outside of the bedroom doesn't mean that's what she's looking for once the lights are turned off."

"She's not?" he said, leaning in, his eyes narrowing with interest, drawing her attention to a tiny scar next to his left one.

"Not in the least." She resisted the urge to jump to the topic of the scar. It was no doubt the result of a daring rescue of a damsel in distress. One who could have saved herself, but he had to barge in all alpha-hero-like.

"Then what is she looking for?" he asked.

"I could tell you but trust me when I say you'll have much more fun reading and discovering the hard way." She gave him a cheeky grin. "Pun intended."

He blinked. Scowled. Chuckled. "Can we get out of here? All the happy vibes are giving me a headache."

"We haven't even ordered yet," she said, her eyes momentarily settling on a couple nestled in a quiet corner, their heads together over a shared book. A soft sigh escaped her lips, a silent yearning for something genuine that might exist beyond the pages.

"We could grab a coffee somewhere else," he countered.

She folded her hands and laid them on the table. "Fine. There's a delightfully quirky bookstore not far from here that serves the best Storybook Espresso. Are you game for that?"

"Anything but this." He stood and came around behind her chair and pulled it out.

Walking out, Sophie glanced back at the café before turning and tucking her hands into the crook of his elbow.

Thunder rumbled.

He glanced down at her hands, then looked into her eyes, a flicker of something unreadable crossing his face. She shrugged. "This is us practicing pretending to be a couple."

"We need practice?" he asked.

More thunder.

He glanced up at the sky and scowled as if the thunder were a personal affront.

"Practice makes perfect." She smiled up at him, feeling quite content with how things were progressing.

He gave a noncommittal grunt but didn't pull away. "Has anyone ever told you, you smile a lot?"

"Has anyone ever told you, you grunt and scowl a lot?" she countered.

"Which way to the bookstore?" was his response.

She tugged him to the left. "Let's go break your romance cherry and get you a rom-com."

LISA WELLS

Chapter 7

As Stone and Sophie maneuvered—arm in arm—through the busy Manhattan streets, thunder rumbled all around them. Not that Sophie seemed to notice—she was busy chattering excitedly beside him about their next stop: a bookstore she claimed was a haven for every literary soul in the city.

Her enthusiasm was palpable, infectious even, but Stone kept his expression measured, his mind preoccupied with the task ahead. *Keep their relationship strictly professional despite playing the part of her boyfriend.*

"Did you hear me?" Sophie asked when they came to a stop at a crossing light.

"Um. No. Sorry. What was that?" he asked.

Sophie glanced up at him, her brows furrowing slightly. "Poppie will grill me the moment he sees me tomorrow. And he will interrogate you the moment I leave you two alone," she said, a mischievous twinkle in her eye. "Which means we have to start to really get to know each other."

Stone tensed. He understood the necessity of their ruse, but it had been a long time since he'd really gotten to know a woman. Why go to the trouble when you're a two-dates-and-move-on guy? "All right, you come up with three questions," he conceded. "We'll both answer them."

Sophie's face lit up with the challenge, her mind obviously racing through possibilities.

The light turned, and he guided them across.

"How about we start with your *I'd never*—something you swear you'll never do."

"That's a rather odd question. What prompted it?"

"It's one of the things we talk about at book club. What is each book character's *I'd never* statement, and do they end up doing it before their book life comes to an end? It's a common plot device authors use."

"I see. My *I'd never* is easy. I'll never get married. And before you ask, it's because in my line of work, the ability to focus is the difference between life and death. Love makes a man lose focus." The last thing he'd ever tell Sophie was that the decision had originated in heartbreak and congealed in caution.

"Oh, my God. That's such a sad *I'd never*," she exclaimed, stopping abruptly so she could put her hands on her hips and stare at him. "It could never be used in a romance because how could an author ever get around it? Unless, of course, the guy decides to change his career, but even then...he'd probably end up resenting her. Wow. Just wow. That's a super sad *I'd never*."

"It's fine," he said, continuing to walk. "As you've probably already figured out, I'm not much of a people person, anyway. And just because I'm not in search of love doesn't mean I don't have women in my life. Your turn. What is your *I'd never*?"

"Easy. I'll never settle for less than the fairytale."

"What does that mean?" He scanned the crowd for danger as they walked and talked.

"My mom and dad died when I was five...boating accident. My mom did my nursery with a fairytale theme. On the wall above my bed, she wrote the words: *Never settle for less than the fairytale, my darling Sophie.*"

"As in the fairytale Prince Charming?" he asked. "Is that why you're obsessed with book boyfriends?"

"Poppie said it meant never give up on my dreams, no matter what they are or how silly others might find them."

"And what exactly is your dream?"

She gave him a mischievous grin. "To be a professional daydreamer...of course."

"Of course. And what does a professional daydreamer do?"

"They find the magic in the world and share it with others. Which is one of the reasons I create and wear fanciful T-shirts."

"I see. I'm glad to know there are those in this world who strive to embrace that career." Little did she know just how much he could relate to that vocation. Life was funny sometimes in how it brought two people together. Not that he believed in serendipity, but still...

"Are you ready for the second question?" she asked.

"I am," Stone said.

"What is one of your personal demons?"

At this rate, Sophie was going to know him better than he knew himself. "Is this another book club question?"

"Of course."

Deciding there was no harm in responding honestly, he said, "The last gig I was on, things went haywire because our...intel was faulty, and a child almost died. I blame myself for all of it. I should have done a more thorough check of the situation and didn't."

"Is that how you injured your finger?" she asked. "The one that's bandaged?"

"It is."

"How long will you have to wear the bandage?"

"Not certain. Tell me about one of your personal demons."

"Remember the guy Poppie talked about? My last boyfriend?"

"I do," he said, an unexpected feeling of something close to jealousy hitting him in the gut.

"I met him when I put my daydreamer job hunt on hold and took a regular job to help pay some bills. Turns out, he was nothing but a con."

Stone found it hard to imagine Sophie in a regular job. "What kind of con?"

"I asked him to stay at my place and keep an eye on Poppie for me while I was away at a readers' retreat. Poppie thought he was staying there to retrieve a package for me when it came. Anyway, while I was gone, he tricked Poppie into giving him all the information he needed to steal his identity and drain his retirement funds. Among other things."

"Did you report him to the police?"

She gave him a bright smile. "That's a story for another day. We're here."

The shop's quaint, inviting façade mocked the churn of Stone's thoughts. Just because Sophie presented as a woman capable of handling his secret did not mean a damn thing. He'd been fooled once. Never again.

"Are you ready for me to have my romantic way with you?" Sophie asked.

"Can't wait to see what you bring to the table."

"Just know, once I take your romance virginity, you'll never be the same again."

Stone raised a hand to tousle her riot of curls, only to lower it again. She wasn't really flirting with him. She was practicing, pretending he was her boyfriend. He needed to keep that in mind. "Talk is cheap."

She playfully nudged his shoulder.

Thunder boomed.

"Yes, but reading is priceless," she said. "Let's go pop your cherry."

As Stone looked up at the cloudless sky, his gut told him the mere act of having met Sophie E. Clark had forever changed his life. He just wasn't exactly sure yet how it would play out.

LISA WELLS

Chapter 8

A week later, after getting a crash course on romance novel tropes, Stone knocked on Sophie's front door, prepared to embrace tonight's homework. The woman loved giving exercises for him to finish.

"Come in, sweetie," she shouted.

Rolling his eyes at her insistence that they stay in character even when no one else was around, he let himself in and found her in the kitchen plating spaghetti, the steam wafting up in warm tendrils.

Tonight, her T-shirt proclaimed: *Book Boyfriends Do It Better.*

"It's a good thing I'm not vying to be your real boyfriend," he said, as he took in the scene and shuddered.

At one time, this would have been his dream: settling down and starting a family. A cozy home filled with laughter and love, children's drawings on the fridge, and the scent of home-cooked meals wafting through the air. Lazy Sunday mornings spent in bed with Sophie. Wait. Fuck. Not Sophie. He and the redhead were oil and water.

"Why exactly is it a good thing you're not secretly hoping to become my real boyfriend?" Sophie paused to give him her full attention.

For one, he'd have to compete with all the book boyfriends who currently held her heart. Not that he'd ever say anything along that line. No Navy SEAL worth their salt would ever back down from a challenge.

Instead, he held up his copy of *Funny Story*. The hero in the book, Miles, was so un-James-Bond-like that Stone had found himself wincing at several of his actions and words. "I've read your damn book, and I don't possess one thing in common with the hero." Not that there was anything wrong with Miles—in the end, he'd been quite likable. He just wasn't wired the same as Stone.

"Wow." Sophie looked at him like he'd just declared he hated puppies and kittens and sex.

He bristled. "Wow, what?"

Her look of dismay slowly faded away and became one of feigned nonchalance. "It's nothing."

"That sounded like a something." This was how most of their conversations had gone over the past week.

"I just assumed you were...at the very least...probably good in bed...like Miles. Not that that's the reason he's my newest most favorite book boyfriend."

Stone didn't react. Not on the outside, anyway. Instead, he considered which part of what she'd just said he most wanted to address. The one that questioned his ability as a lover, or to inquire how in the hell Miles had taken the honor of most favorite book boyfriend? "Darling, the things I could do to you in bed would make Miles' sexual knowledge fade to black."

That was a new phrase Sophie had taught him while they'd been getting to know each other. In some romances, the sex is out in the open, and the reader gets to enjoy the journey. Other romances have a closed-door policy where the bedroom door is shut on the sex, a.k.a., fade to black. And then there were clean romances where sex simply didn't happen.

Now, he watched in amusement while Sophie boldly eyeballed him up and down and then back up.

"Do you have any references that can verify your grandiose statement?" she finally asked. "I mean, it's quite obvious when Emily Henry created Miles, she made him all that and a good book when it came to pleasuring a female."

"How, for the love of common sense, do you consider that obvious?"

Sophie rolled her eyes. "The guy owned several pairs of not sexy shoes."

"Your theory is based on his collection of Crocs?"

"Spectacular sexual prowess was a must for the author to give Miles in order to salvage him from that wardrobe detail. Not that I'm bad-mouthing men who wear them. In fact, the detail endeared Miles to a multitude of women worldwide, because they shouted good guy who doesn't take himself too seriously. Which makes Emily Henry a genius at creating book boyfriends."

"Good guy but not sexy guy?"

"Correct."

Stone pondered the revelation. Romance readers possessed layers of complexity that rivaled some of his former SEAL assignments. "I thought his personality saved him from his less than spectacular introduction to the reader."

In all honesty, he'd spent a considerable amount of time thinking about Miles and what it was about him that flipped Sophie's skirts. Stone had decided it was Miles' willingness to be vulnerable. An attribute that might work on the written page but was an ingredient for heartache in reality.

"All heroes worth a damn," Sophie said, "have a most excellent personality that comes out to play with the right woman. Now, back to the question at hand, do you possess proof of your claim to possess off-the-charts sexual aptitude?"

Having forgotten the origin of their conversation, sex, he chuckled. "Damn straight I do." Seldom did a person surprise him, but Sophie's brazenness continued to catch him off guard. Starting with her declaration of her intent to break his romance cherry.

"I'm listening," she cooed, fluttering her lashes.

"You don't need proof, because I am not your type." While that last bit was for her sake, he took it to heart as well. A confirmed bachelor would be a fool not to load up with all the ammunition at his disposal to keep *what ifs* at bay.

"Which works out nicely," she mused, "considering I know your *I'd never*, and that doesn't mesh at all with my *I can't wait*. Of course, we've not mentioned toying with the idea of a torrid fling. But I'm guessing that's a thought better left unthought. So, forget I even spoke it." She waved her hand in the air as if she could erase words already spoken.

A *torrid fling*? He rubbed a hand over his jaw. Her I-take-that-back technique had failed. No shocker there. If he'd learned nothing else this past week, it was that Sophie E. Clark was going to be the death of his serenity. A word he'd never once used in his thirty-five years before meeting her, but now found himself pulling it out several times a day.

She glanced at him as if expecting him to comment. He said nothing—another thing he found himself doing a lot around her. Not because he chose to hold his tongue, but because she mostly left him speechless.

"Have a seat." She pointed to one of the two chairs around her minute kitchen table. "Dinner's served."

He shoved away thoughts of casual sex with Sophie, took a seat, and felt a tiny bit disappointed at the thought of her saying I *Do* to a normal relationship with some Miles-like man in the future.

Which was ridiculous. His relationship with Sophie was professional, and he never mixed business with pleasure.

Sophie handed him a bottle of wine. "Do you mind pouring while I take the brownies out of the oven?"

He glanced at the label. *Romance in a Bottle: Uncork the Passion.* He raised an eyebrow, smirking as he looked back at Sophie. "Seriously?"

"Hey, don't knock it. I design these wine labels and sell them on my Etsy store. They're perfect for date nights and book club meetings."

"For someone who likes to appear as if you play life casual, you've got a real knack for business," he said, popping the cork and filling the drinks. When he glanced up, he caught sight of a hint of pride in her eyes.

Quickly glancing away, she took a seat and picked up her goblet. "Shall we toast to being each other's opposites-of-what-I'm-looking-for-in-a-romantic-relationship person?" She held her glass out toward him, waiting for him to clink his to hers.

He hesitated, his brain needing time to catch up to what she'd rattled off. "What makes you think you're the opposite of what I'd look for in a woman...if I were looking?"

"Easy. I've read enough romances to figure it out. I'm the sunshine to your unfixable grump. You want a woman who doesn't need romance but is instead content with little conversation and who allows you your broody opinions about the world without trying to fix you or change your mind."

He raised an eyebrow, prepared to challenge, but then lowered it. The fact that he'd engaged in more conversation with her over the last two weeks than he'd done with anyone else over the last year didn't count. They'd conversed so they could best pull off the fake-boyfriend ruse. Not because he'd suddenly become chatty. He did indeed date women who required little con-versation. "You're not wrong. But in my de-fense, my job is best suited to cynics who spend more time contemplating than discussing book boyfriends. A romantic in my position would give someone the benefit of the doubt and end up dead...along with the person they were supposed to protect." With that declaration, he clinked glasses with her and took a sip.

"That is an unarguable excuse to keep love at bay."

The fact that she agreed gave him heartburn.

She sat down her wine and swirled spaghetti on her fork, using a spoon as a prop. Then she glanced at him and gave him a smile. "Besides finding nothing in common with Miles, what did you think of your first romantic comedy book?"

"It wasn't what I expected." He took a bite of spaghetti so she wouldn't ask him to expand.

She retrieved a folded sheet of paper from the pocket of her jeans. "As the reigning president of the Book Boyfriend Connoisseurs Club, I've prepared a few questions to see if you fully grasped why Miles is the epitome of a dreamy cinnamon roll hero."

"In other words, you want to make sure I actually read the book." He picked up his garlic bread and took a bite. If ever there was a sure sign a woman didn't have romantic feelings toward you, it would be her serving you garlic bread.

"First question: What do you think makes Miles not just a love interest but a character with depth that resonates with readers like me?" Sophie twirled her fork in the spaghetti, then lifted it to her mouth.

"Hmm." Stone took a sip of wine, his gaze steady on her, smugness filling him because he had an answer he didn't have to pull out of his ass. "At first, I was ready to write him off as nothing but a crybaby. I mean, where I come from, no man would wallow in self-pity while watching a damn chick flick." Or if they did, it would be their secret and theirs alone.

"But?" she asked when he stopped talking.

"But somehow the author—"

"Emily Henry," Sophie said.

He nodded. "She turned Miles around. Saved him from himself." A mental video of Sophie saving Stone from himself flashed before his eyes. He set his glass down, the clink resonating in the quiet kitchen, and shook his head to clear the fantastical musings.

"In what way?" Sophie prodded.

"For one, Miles stopped smoking weed inside."

"And?" Sophie asked.

Stone tore off a piece of garlic toast, the aroma mingling with the rich scent of the spaghetti. "A douche, caught up in the whole I've-been-hurt scenario, wouldn't have been so considerate."

Sophie giggled. "True. What else."

"He's likable, and I can see why some women would find that attractive." He popped the bread in his mouth.

She raised her brows, her fork pausing mid-twirl. "You say that like you're not likable?"

"Being likable is the kiss of death in my line of work. I can be scary, intimidating, a dick, frosty, any of those, but I can't be likable."

"That's too bad. Women like kind." She leaned back, the flicker of candlelight casting shadows over her face as she chewed her food.

"So do criminals," he countered. "Kind is equivalent to an easy mark."

She twisted her lips as if wanting to dive deeper into what he'd said but instead asked another question. "Miles faces several personal conflicts that force him to grow. How did those elements contribute to his appeal as a book boyfriend to the heroine?"

"Isn't that a question you should answer? I don't know how women think."

"You know how Daphne, the heroine, thought because you read the book."

"Yeah, but—"

"There's no but."

"I guess, it made him more..."

"More what?"

"Can't we just eat in peace?"

"Not if you want anyone to believe you're my authentic boyfriend."

"Somehow, I don't think anyone will quiz me about the hero in a book." He finished his wine, refilled his glass, and topped off hers.

"Of course, they'll quiz you," she said, toying with her goblet. "Any guy of mine will be well read and more than happy to discuss book boyfriends."

"Are you for real?" A wave of irritation washed over him. The kind that happens when a guy realizes he's not going to get the girl...even though he doesn't want the girl. It was a male pride thing. "You expect the guys you date to sit around and talk about book boyfriends? That's like me saying any woman of mine will be expected to sit around and talk about—"

"About what?"

He swallowed, shocked that he'd almost let slip the one thing he couldn't reveal. The family secret. It was the real reason behind his being out of commission for the time being, the way his injury had caused his magic to glitch. "Nothing. It doesn't matter. This isn't about me, it's about you and keeping you safe."

"On that note, I have something for you," Sophie said. "Wait here." She popped up and hurried out of the room.

While she was gone, Stone pondered how Sophie would respond if she learned of the side gig Clarabelle had set him and his brothers up with when she had come back into their lives. A side gig that made Sophie's look insignificant by comparison.

Actually, it wasn't a side gig. It was an equal gig. For every normal case they took, they had to take one abnormal case. Otherwise, as Clarabelle would say, what was the sense in going to all the trouble to get them certified in the field?

His gut told him Sophie would be thrilled.

But when it came to romance, his gut couldn't be trusted.

Sophie whipped back into the room carrying a gray T-shirt and wearing a smirk.

He stiffened. Damn, he knew that smirk. Had experienced it several times since meeting her. Whatever came next, he wouldn't like it.

"Here." She thrust the shirt at him. "This is for you to wear on your first official outing as my boyfriend while I interview potential candidates for my second column."

He took the shirt by the shoulders, slowly turned it around so he could read the words and groaned. *Real Life Book Boyfriend in Training.*

"Was that a groan of pure love?" she asked, rubbing her palms together like a foster child who had just been asked if they'd like to be adopted. "I mean, of course it was. What's not to love about it? It's absolutely perfect. I sell it in my Etsy store. It's a huge hit with wedding parties, book clubs, and girl's night out events."

He shook off the shock. "I am not wearing this."

Her confident smile wobbled. "Why? What's wrong with it? I thought you'd be thrilled to wear it compared to the sweater vests that *Naked Runway* wants you to wear. I heard Ziggy found a black and white striped Beetlejuice cardigan in your size at a vintage shop that he plans to pair with pink trousers designed by

Isabella. And Frankie actually approved it without argument, which is supremely rare...according to Ziggy, who seems to know a lot of things."

An image of Beetlejuice popped into Stone's head. The rambunctious spirit had been extravagantly strange. Stone ran his hand over his jaw and weighed his options. The T-shirt was better. Barely, but better. "If I wear this"—he held up the garment like it contained a man-eating bacterium—"can I ditch the Dockers and loafers and wear my jeans and combat boots, and you'll back me with the Glam Team?"

Sophie wrinkled her nose. "Do your combat boots have blood on them?"

"Not that you can see."

"Then I don't see why not. I mean, you've already ditched the hair," Sophie said.

"Thank you. I owe you."

"Great. I know what I want."

"What?"

"I want nothing but smiles out of you on Monday even after you've had a chance to read what my T-shirt says." She took a seat and picked up her wine.

"I'm not great with surprises," he said gruffly. "Why don't you show it to me tonight?"

"Eww," she squealed, but not in disgust. She wore a huge smile. Instead of immediately explaining the exclamation, she paused and took a leisurely sip of her wine.

He raised a brow. "Eww?"

"That's your fatal flaw," she said with a shrug as if he should have figured that one out on his own.

"I'm going to need more context," he said.

"It's the thing you'll need to overcome to become book-boyfriend-material worthy."

"Say what?" He picked up his goblet and took a drink.

"You'll need to learn how to be okay with not having full control in any given situation," Sophia explained, eyeballing him like a pet project.

"Being in control is not a flaw." He spoke the words slowly, clearly as if talking to a child.

"Isn't it?" she said, tilting her head.

He fisted his good hand. "Stone-cold control is a superpower that was branded into every fiber of my being by the fucking United States Navy. It's because of that superpower that I was so successful as a SEAL. And am successful in my current line of work."

"What can I say?" Sophia said. "One woman's heartthrob characteristic in a guy is another's meh."

"Meh?" She found his best asset a meh? He took a large gulp of wine and emptied the rest of the bottle in his glass.

"It's not personal," she said, picking up her fork. "I'm sure your superpower does come in very handy for what you do for a living. It's just not my cup of tea in a guy I wish to pass off as my boyfriend. So, for the sake of us both being happy in our forced time together, you'll pretend to be working on your control issues, while I pretend you are my boyfriend. Deal?"

"And what will you be working on? Or is it just me that gets assigned a fatal flaw?"

She finished chewing and then smiled sweetly. "Just you. I'll be so busy executing my superpower that there won't be time for me to work on myself."

"But if there were time, what would you need to fix?"

"Honestly?"

"Every time."

"I have a slight blurting problem."

"Expand?" This sounded very much like another solid reason why he could never give Sophie his heart. In a case where he tried love again, the woman would have to be able to keep a secret.

"I say things better left unsaid."

No matter how much she might possibly love his secret, he couldn't share it with a blurter. "Such as?" he asked, sounding like a man hoping he'd misunderstood.

"The usual. Jeopardy questions, Wheel of Fortune Puzzle answers. World-domination secrets."

It wasn't until he saw her lips twitch, that he realized she was messing with him, and his lungs filled with air again. "What exactly is your special power and who gave it to you?"

"Finding living book boyfriends for others...and it's a power I got from my mother."

Barely, just fucking barely, he kept from spouting off, *That's who gave me my super power as well.* "If that's your specialty, what's your kryptonite? What will stop you in your tracks? After all, as your boyfriend, I should know that."

"A grand gesture. They get me every time."

"Just how many have you experienced?"

"Zero."

"Then how do you know grand gestures are your kryptonite?"

"Because I read romance novels. They all have one, and I always fall for the guy who lays it all on the line with one."

"You like guys who grovel?" Stone resisted an urge to be an ass and say real men didn't do grand gestures. Because, honestly, there were probably a few who did. None that he knew of, but then again, he mostly hung out with ex-military types who would rather take a bullet than grovel.

"I like a guy who is willing to do whatever it takes to win the heart of the heroine. That might mean groveling. It might mean over-coming a fear. It might mean being the first to say I *love you*."

"I'll add that to my protection du-ties—shield you from random grand gesture attacks."

Sophie raised an eyebrow, amusement flickering across her features. "You see that you do. I wouldn't want to have to com-plain to Ms. Birdie that you only did your job half-ass."

Stone's lips twitched as he nodded. He now knew her *I'd never*. And her kryptonite. Two things he didn't know about any other woman he'd ever dated.

He was prevented from saying as much when both their phones dinged at the same time. Ignoring his, he watched as Sophie flipped hers over and read the screen.

She frowned. "I have a message to give Ms. Birdie a call."

He pulled out his phone and read his mes-sage. It was from Clarabelle.

Your glitches have been brought to the attention of the council. Your assignment with Sophie is temporarily on hold. Possibly forever.

He glanced up at his dinner companion. Would this be their last encounter? The thought gave him heartburn.

"Is yours from Ms. Birdie as well?" Sophie asked.

He shook his head. "It's from my mom. A family matter needs my attention. I'm sorry to eat and run, but—"

"No apologies required," Sophie said, waving him off. "Family trumps fake girlfriends...or even real ones as far as I'm concerned."

"On that we agree." He stood and hurried to the door. With one hand on the knob, he turned for what might be his last glimpse of Sophie. Damn if the thought didn't leave a lump in his throat. "Send me a text and let me know if Ms. Birdie is changing things up."

Chapter 9

The following morning was unusually quiet in Stone's condo as he sat broodily looking out at the city.

He'd not been surprised at being pulled from duty. Ever since meeting Sophie, his glitching magic had magnified.

What had started as nothing more than minor sputters and random sparkles had grown into weather glitches and power outages when he and Sophie touched. The council, who tracked these things, had decided action was needed. No fieldwork of any kind for him until the matter was resolved.

Stone had never abandoned an assignment, and for the first time to be his protection of Sophie made him irritable. Somehow in the two short weeks of working with her, his opinion of her had shifted.

He no longer thought of her as an annoying fluff assignment. Her laughter, her relentless optimism, the way she looked at the world as if it were a book filled with endless adventures—they had completely disarmed him.

His phone lit up. He grabbed it and grinned when he saw who'd sent him a text.

Sophie: *Good morning. Ms. Birdie lined up three perfect candidates for my first columns. Looks like I won't need a bodyguard for now. How are things with your family?*

Stone hesitated, his fingers hovering over the keyboard. He hated texting. If one wasn't careful it ended up being nothing but an on-going chat that wasted precious time.

Then again, he had asked her to keep him abreast of what Ms. Birdie had wanted to speak about just in case it had nothing to do with him being pulled from bodyguard duty.

Stone: *News here too. Off duty for a bit. Trigger Finger Fumble.*

He made the term up. To reveal the true name given to his injury, Wand Rub, would be to reveal his secret.

Sophie: *Trigger Finger Fumble? That sounds too adorable for your grumpy ass. If I were you, I'd tell everyone you have tactical twitch. Of course, once you resume bodyguard duty, we'll for sure refer to it as something cutesy to stay with your cover.*

Stone chuckled softly, the sound surprising him. He typed a response.

Stone: *Like what?*

He could live with tactical twitch. In fact, that's exactly what he would start using.

Sophie: *Snuggle Sprain. Nuzzle Niggle. Caress Crick.*

His eyes paused over the last two words. The phrase's reference both unmistakable and startling. Then again, she was the same woman who'd pronounced her intent to break his romance cherry. So why be startled over implied finger fucking?

The thought of caressing her sex caused him to harden—an involuntary reaction. He was used to maintaining control, his emotions and physical responses disciplined from years of training. Yet here he was, affected by a simple text, a hint of innuendo from Sophie stirring something within him that he hadn't anticipated.

It was unsettling, how she could make him think of things beyond the professional boundaries they were supposed to maintain.

A new message came through.

Sophie: *You still there? Or have you perished from your injury? Trigger Finger Fumble isn't fatal, is it?*

Stone: *It's survivable.*

Sophie: *Good to know. Now that we're not professionally involved—at least for the next couple of months or so—what are your thoughts on our remaining reading buddies?*

Technically, she was right; they were no longer professionally involved. But also technically, he was on deck—injury permitting—to be her bodyguard once she started interviewing some of the more unsavory sorts.

They were in morally gray waters. He didn't do gray. He did black or white. Right or wrong. Good or bad.

Stone: *I have none.*

Sophie: *I was hoping you'd say that. Our next book will be: The Magnolia Chronicles by Kate Canterbary. What do you say we reconvene this chat thread in say—a week?*

Stone: *Did I say yes?*

Sophie: *You didn't say no. Drats. I lost track of the time. Got to go. Duty calls. Talk in a week. Yours in all things romance books, Sophie*

Stone hesitated, his finger hovering. Normally, he'd not allow himself to be manipulated. But he wasn't opposed to her plan. And agreeing to be her book buddy was not the same as agreeing to that damn torrid fling she'd mentioned. It was a safe reason to experience more of Sophie E. Clark. What did the E. even stand for? He felt like he should know.

Stone: *Okay, Stone Cold*

CHAPTER

One week later, Sophie pulled her copy of The Magnolia Chronicles off her bookshelf and settled on the couch with her phone.

Sophie: *Testing. Testing. Stone Cold are you there? Over and out.*

Sophie waited to see if Stone responded. She found herself oddly nervous, realizing she cared a little too much about his reply. Caring too much about a guy with a *never getting married* stance would be to risk forfeiting her fairytale ending.

Stone: *I thought you'd never ask.*

Sophie: *I'll be honest, I'm a lot relieved right now that you replied.*

They'd not set a time to reconvene, only that they would in one week. She'd meant to text him a time but had been side-tracked with the interviewing of her first book boyfriend candidate, his brother, which had been a blast. Her first column for *Naked Runway* was now off her plate.

Stone: *Relieved?*

Sophie: *I thought you might have decided to ghost me. I can be a little pushy when I really want something, and I sort of ambushed you into being my reading buddy.*

She hesitated before sending, wondering if she was too honest. Stone had a way of making her feel exposed, in a way that was both exhilarating and terrifying.

Stone: *Speaking of that. Why exactly did you want me to be your partner in reading crime? Don't you have a whole club of romance readers at your fingertips?*

Sophie: *Absolutely. In fact, my best friend, Donna and I met last night to discuss book boyfriends who excelled at dirty talk.*

Stone: *Explain.*

Sophie: *Dirty talking book boyfriends is a whole other side-trope of book boyfriends.*

Stone: *And you like them?*

Sophie: *I've never had a dirty-talking lover, so they intrigue me. I'd probably fall off my stilettoes if a guy ever ordered me to get down on my knees.*

She blushed just typing that, imagining Stone being that guy. Her heart sped up, and she had to remind herself falling for him would be the worst idea.

Stone: *Maybe if you broadened your horizons and ventured away from your cinnamon roll heroes, you'd get your dirty-talking cherry burst.*

Sophie: *As with all decisions in life, there are pros and cons one must weigh. What did you think of the meet cute in The Magnolia Chronicles?*

Stone: *You mean their Sunday dinner?*

Sophie: *I do.*

Stone: *It reminded me of something that would happen at one of our family Sunday dinners. I can clearly imagine Clarabelle doing that to any one of us boys. Even though we've all taken a blood oath to never marry, she's determined to see each of us revoke that oath.*

There it was again. The reminder that Stone wasn't the forever kind. She wished she could ignore how much it hurt to hear it.

Sophie: *A blood oath sounds extreme. Then again, declaring never to marry is also extreme. Maybe it does require a monumental action to seal the deal.*

Stone: *Why did you want us to read The Magnolia Chronicles?*

Sophie: *Because its hero falls under the recently single hero trope, and my next column covers that one.*

Stone: *Readers like heroes with broken hearts?*

Sophie: *Adore them.*

She bit her lip, resisting the urge to tell Stone he'd become her new favorite kind of hero. The broody grump.

Stone: *How did your interview with Ryder go? He clammed up when I asked him.*

Sophie: *He told me all your secrets.*

Stone: *I doubt that very much.*

The certainty in his reply made her pause. What secrets could he be hiding? Was it something about his past, or perhaps a vulnerability he kept well-guarded? There were so many chapters to him she hadn't yet read. She pushed away her speculations and focused on teasing him instead.

Sophie: *He told me you're afraid of the dark, still break out in pimples when you eat greasy food, and you can't pick up a woman in a bar to save your ass.*

Stone: *LMAO. Tell me about the interview.*

Sophie: *You'll have to wait and read about it in my first column just like everyone else. How's your Trigger Finger Fumble?*

Stone: *We're now calling it Tactical Twitch, and the healing process is slow. What's your tee say today?*

Sophie: *We believe in the power of the book boyfriend.*

She sent him a screen shot of her T-shirt.

Sophie: It's one of the slogans of the Book Boyfriend Connoisseurs Club.

Stone: Our company slogan is: Guardians of the Innocent.

Sophie: Want me to make you a tee with that on it?

Stone: We try not to let the bad guys know who we are.

Sophie: Gotcha. Care if I try out on you a few of the interview questions I'm considering adding to my book boyfriend questionnaire?

Stone: Are you asking to have your way with me?

Sophie: OMG. You made a joke. There's hope for you yet.

No reply. Her heart skipped a beat, wondering if she'd said too much.

Sophie: I'm going to take your lack of a reply as a yes to my request. Here's my first question: If your love life had a hashtag, what would it be?

Stone: #Dirtytalker.

Sophie: Ha. Ha. Be still my heart. What's in your nightstand drawer?

Damn, she probably shouldn't have mentioned her heart.

Stone: My passport. A picture of my brothers and I on our gotcha day with Clarabelle. And an item I'm not willing to name at this moment.

Sophie: *Let me guess. Condoms, handcuffs, blindfolds...am I warm?*

She sent it before she could overthink. Imagining him squirming on the other side of the screen made her grin.

Stone: *Duty calls. What book are we reading for next week?*

Did duty call, or had her light-hearted flirting shut him down? At least he'd asked about next week's book. That was a good sign.

Sophie: *Anyone But The Billionaire by Sara L. Hudson*

Stone: *Got it. Is there a secret handshake or anything we do to officially close our book buddy meeting?*

Sophie: *Since we're not meeting in person, it will have to be secret words instead of a handshake. How about—Keep the bookmarks handy.*

Stone: *Or—and hear me out on this one—Dog Ears for the Win.*

Sophie: *Please tell me you don't bend the pages to keep your place in a book.*

The mere thought made her shudder.

Stone: *Ok. I won't tell you that.*

Sophie: *Deep Sigh. You truly are not book boyfriend material.*

Silence.

She grimaced. The comment had been meant to reassure him she wouldn't fall for him. Time to end this chat before she blurt-typed something stupid.

Sophie: *Keep the bookmarks handy, Sophie the Page-Turner Princess*

Thirty seconds later he replied.

Why had it taken him so long?

Stone: *Keep the bookmarks handy, Stone the Reader.*

Chapter 10

S tone finished *Anyone But The Billionaire* thirty minutes before it was time to text with Sophie. His week had been busy. His brothers had been involved in a particularly volatile rescue of a child who'd been stolen from the home of a diplomat and sold into child sex trafficking. Since his magic was still glitching, Stone hadn't been able to be on the scene, but he'd stayed behind and helped from a distance. He fucking hated staying behind. He'd also had to cancel last week's book buddy chat with Sophie.

Thinking of Sophie brought a mix of emotions. He missed their banter, her quick wit, and the way she made him forget, even for a little while, about the chaos of his life. He'd even stopped by *Naked Runway* under the pretense of needing to speak with Ms. Birdie, hoping he'd run into Sophie. But he hadn't, and it had left a strange emptiness in him.

The last he'd heard from Clarabelle, the council had put her in charge of researching how to best treat his condition. She'd promised to be in touch as soon as possible.

He picked up his phone and fired off the first text, eager to reconnect.

Stone: *Best opening line of all the books I've ever read.*

He waited for Sophie to reply. Five minutes later, he fired off another text.

Stone: *Has a guy ever picked you up in a park with an animal prop?*

More silence. His impatience grew, mingled with a hint of worry. Why wasn't she replying?

Stone: *Are heroes with commitment issues a trope? Do women secretly love guys who fight commitment like it's a bout of diarrhea on a nine-hour flight?*

Still nothing. He cursed under his breath. Maybe he'd been too crass. He didn't want her to think he was just some jerk.

Stone: *That was insensitive. Sorry. You there? You ignoring me? Did you forget to read the book, and you're too embarrassed to admit it?*

Silence. He checked the time, wondering if something had happened to her. Should he be concerned?

Stone: *Keep the bookmarks handy, Stone the one who read this week's book.*

Two hours later, his phone buzzed. Relief washed over him as he saw Sophie's name.

Sophie: *Sorry I missed our meeting. Life happened. I also loved the book's opening line. No, I've never been picked up by a guy who had a pet prop. I don't know about all women, but for myself, I can say I definitely do not secretly long for a man with commitment issues. Life is too short to beg someone to love you.*

Her words hit harder than they should. He knew she was joking, but it stung. Did she think he had commitment issues?

Was he just another cliché guy afraid of love? The thought gnawed at him. His reasons for staying single had always felt valid, but now...he wasn't so sure.

Sophie: *Which is why you're marked safe from ever having Sophia E. Clark fall in love with you.*

He frowned, a pang of something unsettling twisting in his chest. The idea of Sophie never falling for him...why did it bother him so much?

Was he just fooling himself about his reasons for avoiding commitment?

Sophie: *Next week's book is Single Dad by JJ Knight. I promise not to miss the meeting. Keep the bookmarks handy, Sophie, your missing chapter mate.*

He stared at her last message, feeling a strange mix of longing and confusion.

He missed her more than he wanted to admit, and the thought of losing their connection gnawed at him.

But how could he reconcile his past experience with the growing feelings he had for her? Not to mention, his job was fucking dangerous. What kind of mixed-up asshole would he be to encourage a woman to love him knowing he could be setting her up for heartache?

On that thought, he pocketed his phone without replying.

Chapter 11

S ophie waited for Stone to reply. She'd looked forward to tonight's book buddy chat more than she cared to admit. The anticipation had been like a sweet ache, a small thrill that made her heart race as she hurried through the week.

When he didn't respond, she had to fight back a desire to cry. Not good. She quickly texted Donna. If anyone could talk her down from a spiral, it was her friend.

Sophie: *Help. I'm falling for a commitment-phobe.*

Donna: *Meet me at the pub. I'm leaving now.*

Sophie grabbed her sweater and purse off the couch and rushed to the pub. It was located halfway between her place and Donna's.

When she walked through the doors, Donna was already there tucked away in their favorite booth, located in a dimly lit corner. She waved Sophie over.

Sophie took a seat and Donna thrust a glass of wine at her.

"Tell me all about him and don't leave out any detail," Donna said. "Starting with who he is. I wasn't aware you were dating."

Sophie's heart pinched at the thought of Stone. She had really wanted to talk to him. "My bodyguard."

"The guy you described as an irreparable grump?"

Sophie nodded. "Turns out, he's got a hidden sense of humor."

"Oh no. That's your kryptonite."

Sophie smiled but it was bittersweet. It really was her kryptonite. That hidden humor, the way he made her laugh even when she didn't want to...it was dangerous territory. She'd lied when she'd told Stone her weakness was grand gestures. While they were charming when executed with sincerity, they weren't the thing that made her swoon.

Donna took a sip of her wine, considering her friend with a thoughtful frown. After a moment, she leaned forward. "What's his commitment-phobe number?"

"Ten. He and his brothers took a blood oath to never marry."

"Ouch. Does he know you've fallen for him? Did you blurt it out by accident?"

"No. Thank God. Right now, our only form of communication is text."

"Wait. What? I thought he was guarding you while you went about town interviewing strange men." Donna had been away on a writers' retreat in Sophie's place.

"That's on hold, for now. But we've been meeting once a week online and talking books."

"I see. While I've been gone, you've been cheating on me?" Donna grinned.

Sophie knew she was teasing, but she wasn't wrong. "I have. I'm so sorry. It's just, I was afraid we'd never see each other or talk to each other again, and I jumped at the only thing I could think of to keep him in my life."

The admission hung in the air. Sophie felt the weight of her words—the truth she hadn't wanted to admit to herself. She was afraid of losing him, afraid of what that would mean for her heart.

"I forgive you," Donna said. "What is the reason behind their blood pact?"

"I don't know. He didn't tell me."

"Then I suggest you invite him to dinner and ask him to elaborate."

"But what if that scares him off?"

The fear was real, gnawing at her. What if pushing for more meant losing everything they had? Friendship was better than nothing.

Donna reached across the table, placing her hand over Sophie's. "Then he wasn't the right person to dine with in the first place."

Sophie nodded, absorbing the wisdom of Donna's words. She knew Donna was right, but it didn't make the idea of losing Stone any easier to bear. "I guess it's time to find out if we're reading from the same book or if he's just skimming through the pages."

"Exactly," Donna smiled, squeezing Sophie's hand. "And whatever the outcome, I'm here. Just like I was after your ex showed his asshat true colors."

"Fuck him," Sophie said. Stone was nothing like her ex. *Nothing.* Her ex had been a master at deceit, hiding behind a charming façade. Stone, on the other hand, was brutally honest—even about his flaws. That honesty was what drew her to him, even if it scared her.

"May ten thousand fat ticks crawl up his asshole and attach," Donna said.

They toasted to the sentiment.

Sophie pulled out her phone. "I'll text him and ask if he wants to meet in person next week for our book chat."

Donna nodded her encouragement.

Sophie took a deep breath, steeling herself for whatever response might come. The idea of seeing Stone in person made her heart race, but the fear of his rejection loomed large.

Sophie: *Let me make it up to you for not being on time tonight and buy you dinner next week. We can discuss Single Dad in person.*

She hit send and put her phone away. She glanced at Donna. "Now what?"

"Now we can plan what you'll say to the grump whose bones you want to jump."

Sophie threw back her head and laughed. This was why she adored Donna. "I won't lie, I have definitely thought about getting him naked."

"Of course, you have. Otherwise, there'd be no fear you were falling for him."

Donna's words struck a chord. The fear of falling for Stone was real, and it terrified her. But the thought of never knowing what could be was even worse.

"Speaking of getting laid," Sophie said to Donna, "I haven't forgotten you owe me the rest of the story about the guy whose bones you jumped right before leaving for the retreat."

Donna's smile crashed. "Not much to tell. He turned out to be not that effective as a lover."

Sophie's phone dinged. She yanked it out of her purse and quickly read the message.

Stone: *Something has come up, and I will be out of pocket until further notice. Keep the book-marks handy, Stone, a guy you once read books with.*

Her heart sank, the words souring her stomach. All the hopes and excitement that had been building deflated in an instant. Sophie twisted her lips trying to stem the desire to cry. How could he be so casual about it? Did their connection mean nothing to him?

"New plan," she said to Donna, her voice trembling slightly. She turned her phone around so her friend could read the text. "Turns out, we're not reading the same book."

The disappointment was overwhelming, but beneath it, there was a flicker of anger. How dare he make her like him so much and then just dump her? She deserved better.

Chapter 12

Stone was an ass, and he knew it. He'd jumped ship on Sophie the moment it hit him he wouldn't mind falling for the professional daydreamer. Which made *him* a fucking daydreamer. The realization that he could actually fall for her had terrified him. It went against everything he had sworn to himself, everything he thought was best for all concerned.

He'd had no choice but to cut things off before he lost his way and broke them both.

Now, almost two months since their last interaction—two months in which he'd read every book on her damn list of romantic comedies for her columns—it was time to professionally reunite. Emphasis on *professional*. Never in a hundred lifetimes could he let Sophie know he'd been damn close to giving her his heart.

The thought of seeing her again both excited and scared the hell out of him. How could he keep his distance when all he wanted to do was pull her into his arms and kiss her?

In a perfect world, he'd never had to see Sophie again. Fuck. There wouldn't be anything perfect about a world in which he'd never see Sophie again. But at least it would be a safe world, free from the risk of heartbreak.

But he didn't live in a perfect world or a safe world. Without telling him, Clarabelle had contacted Ms. Birdie to let her know he was once again available to help.

Ms. Birdie had quickly arranged for him to return to Sophie duty.

If Stone had been strong, he would have told Ms. Birdie to find another bodyguard for her columnist. But the idea of some other guy protecting Sophie had turned his gut sour. No one would be as invested in her well-being as him. Hell, he'd give up his life ten thousand million times to keep her safe.

All commitment-phobias aside, giving her his heart and asking for hers in return wasn't in the best interest of *her* heart or her safety.

"What's got you scowling?" Clarabelle asked Stone, glancing over her shoulder at him from her position in the kitchen.

He snapped out of his thoughts, realizing his emotions were probably written all over his face. He and his siblings were sitting around the kitchen table at Ryder's place, while Clarabelle stood at the stove stirring something that smelled delicious.

"I'm just hoping the spell you cast over me to keep my magic from glitching holds. I'm back on fluff duty starting tomorrow."

"I was assured it would do the trick," Clarabelle said. "Unless—"

A knock at the door interrupted her sentence.

"Did you invite someone else?" Clarabelle asked Ryder. "Should I set another place?"

The question reminded Stone of the meet cute scene in *Anyone But The Billionaire*. A memory that made him smile. He'd thoroughly enjoyed that book, not just because of the story, but because it was something he and Sophie had shared.

"No way. Family time is sacred time," Ryder said exiting the room to answer the door. When he returned, he wasn't smiling. "We've got a case. Another complicated one."

"I'll put Sophie on hold and join you," Stone said, instinctively ready to jump back into action.

"Nonsense," Clarabelle snapped. "You've given Ms. Birdie your word you'd finish what you started."

"But—"

"*Honor* and *but* don't go together." Clarabelle removed her apron. "You're either a man with honor, or you're a butt. You can't be both. Does Sophie deserve your best or your ass?"

Stone straightened, feeling a pang of guilt. He should have had dinner with Sophie and tried to explain why continuing their book chats wasn't in either of their best interests. That would have been giving her his best. "She deserves all the best parts of me."

When he realized everyone was staring at him like he had two heads, he realized he'd worded his answer a little too honestly.

"It's not like that," Stone protested, though his heart told a different story.

"If you say so, dear," Clarabelle said, patting him on the cheek.

Chapter 13

Sophie adjusted her camera strap as she stepped onto the subway, scanning for open seats, Stone trailing behind her. They'd not texted since the night he'd abruptly dumped her.

Well, to be fair to him, his dumping had obviously been a result of her triggering his she's-falling-for-me radar with her request they meet for dinner. He'd bailed to save them both from the embarrassment of her giving a guy—who'd been nothing but blunt about his commitment issues—her heart. Perhaps, someday, she'd buy him a drink for doing that.

Since then, Sophie's second and third columns had been published. The second had featured the single-dad book boyfriend trope. The thirty-something she'd decided to interview was the father of a precocious six-year-old boy. He'd turned out to be the perfect book-boyfriend twin to the hero in J. J. Knight's book *Single Dad.*

The third column had been a nod to Sara L Hudson's hero in her novel *Anyone But The Billionaire.* Sophie's choice to feature for this boyfriend trope had been a billionaire who was the spitting image of how the author had described the hero, Chase, in the book. And his rise to billionaire status had been a hoot to write about.

Part of Sophie still wanted to get herself a hairless cat.

Now, with so much time having passed, the mood between her and Stone since he'd met her at the subway station could only be described as awkward. All the momentum they'd built up with their week of getting to know one another and their texting down the drain.

Still, it was a lovely day and Sophie was determined not to let anything spoil their first official outing as an interview couple. Yes, the fake boyfriend thing was still a go. As such, she'd been chatting Stone up. Or at least trying to, so they could pull off the illusion they were a thing during the interview. Not that he was helping.

In the fifteen minutes they'd waited for the train, he'd kept all his responses to one syllable or grunts.

Now, spotting two seats together, she made her way to them.

Stone surprised her by sitting, his broad shoulders taking up more than his fair share of space. She couldn't help but wonder what he'd been up to in the last couple of months other than rehabbing his injured finger, which no longer had a bandage.

Of course, she'd asked, and he'd replied, "Work."

When she had asked how his tactical twitch was doing, he'd uttered, "Fine."

Thus, when he'd asked, "Where are we going?" she'd replied, "You'll see."

It was as if he blamed her for something.

On the bright side, he'd worn the T-shirt she'd made for him and given to him the night of their spaghetti meal...and this without her reminding him. An act that thrilled her. He could have so easily pretended he had forgotten that part of their pact. She glanced down at his combat boots. Yep, there were stains.

He was a striking figure in his *Real-Life Book Boyfriend in Training* T-shirt. He wore it like a second skin. The guy's muscles bulged in a very un-cinnamon-roll-like fashion. Something she wasn't hating at all.

He caught her scrutinizing glance and scowled. "I look ridiculous."

"On the contrary. You wear my creation well. And if I recall, per our last in-person conversation, you're supposed to be all smiles today." She could sell the hell out of that T-shirt on Etsy if he'd model it for her.

"I do not recall that conversation, but here you go." Stone gave her a half-assed grin.

"If that's your idea of a smile, we're going to have to practice them over lunch." She refused to be baited into a bad mood. Today, they were on a quest to find a book-boyfriend twin from the wrong side of the tracks.

He gave her another smile. "Better?"

"Only by a margin. How about we swap the smile out for your making more of an effort at conversation?"

He sighed. "What would you like to talk about?"

"I'm glad to see you kept your promise to let your hair grow out and to see that it seems to have done so evenly. No permanent damage from the glue of the wig." His hair was dark and curly, leaving her fingers twitching to touch.

"Alberto and I will have words the next time I run into him," Stone said in a low voice that sent a shudder through Sophie, reminding her he made a living embracing conflict.

"Don't you dare bully that sweet guy. I'm certain he only did what he was told to do. Besides, you have more important things to worry about."

"I'm capable of worrying about more than one thing at a time. Speaking of which, now that we're working together, what's on your agenda for me to worry about?"

She'd had him meet her at the subway but hadn't told him where they were headed. Mainly because she'd known he'd get all bristly when he found out. She decided to stall some more. "Seeing you here—looking extra macho despite my shirt—it has become painfully obvious I won't be able to pass you off as a boyfriend that I'd actually pick in real life."

For some reason, that caused his brows to furrow. "And?"

"And we're going to have to revamp our plan."

Stone grunted but didn't expand.

"I'm not fluent in grunts," she said.

"You've finally said something that makes sense. Do you have a backup plan? If not, may I offer the obvious one?"

"There is no need for backup plans when you operate under the philosophy that all of your endeavors will succeed." Gah, she'd missed his testy banter.

He rubbed his forehead. "Then let me offer a strategy. Ditch the whole idea of presenting me as a boyfriend?"

Oh. Two and half months apart had not fixed that broken record. "That is quite an obvious backup plan, except that my contract with *Naked Runway* states I will have you with me at all interviews and will present you as my boyfriend to the public." Sophie tugged at the hem of her own T-shirt, drawing his attention there. It read *Book Boyfriend Finder* in playful, bold letters.

He didn't roll his eyes, but his nostrils flared, and that was pretty much the same thing on him. "And it also said you would take me with you to every interview, yet you left me out of your first three."

"Because you were otherwise occupied. Besides, Ms. Birdie personally knew all three men. Thus, your scary presence wasn't needed." Realizing his eyes were still on her chest, she snapped her finger in front of his face to get his eyes to move upward. Once they did, she continued, "Anyway, we need a new boyfriend type for you."

He stood, towering over her. "How about we don't define my type and leave everyone guessing?"

She opened her mouth to argue but decided it wasn't the worst idea. "Fine. I won't pigeonhole you, but I will introduce you as my boyfriend. I can only hope our wearing matching mission gear does a lot to soften your image in the eyes of my boyfriend candidates. If not, I predict no one will talk to me."

"Speaking of which, where exactly are we headed? I don't normally take the subway."

"To a repair shop in Little Italy."

His eyes narrowed. "Our interview is with a guy who works in the Bronx?"

Was he a Bronx snob? That was very short-sighted of him. "The person who nominated Antonio says he embodies the tough exterior but has hidden depths worth drilling down for. I can't wait to see if he lives up to the hype."

"And what type of book boyfriend hero is Antonio supposed to represent?"

"The wrong-side-of-the-tracks fixer-up-per." The train screeched to a halt. "This is our exit." She stood and turned to face the doors. As soon as they opened, she swept out with the rest of the passengers and made her way to street level. There, she slipped on her sunglasses and opened her phone to check for directions. "This way."

Stone slid on his own pair of dark sunglass-es. "What's the name of the place?"

"The Wrenchfather Repair." She tucked her hand into his arm just as the siren of a car they were walking by went off, causing her to jump.

Stone didn't jump. Instead, he frowned. "Fixed, my ass," he muttered under his breath.

Deciding not to ask about a comment he'd obviously not meant for her to hear, she said, "After the interview, we can grab lunch at one of the restaurants. I'm sure we have a lot to catch up on. For instance, I'm still not dating anyone. How about you?"

"No one."

As they entered the garage, the smell of oil and metal filled the air. Sophie raised her camera, ready to capture their first potential book boyfriend in his natural habitat.

"No cameras allowed," said someone off in the distance.

Sophie took the shot of the exterior and quickly lowered her camera, glancing around to see where the voice had come from. It appeared to have come from nowhere. "Did you see who spoke?" she asked Stone.

"No. But I see a lot of surveillance equipment. I'm guessing someone inside is watching." Stone dropped an arm across her shoulders and pulled her in close, just as a cloud blacked out the sun. Another muffled curse from Stone.

"You okay? I feel like every little thing is agitating you. A car alarm goes off, you mutter. Sun goes behind a cloud, you curse?"

"Never better," he whispered, as they ventured deeper into the world of wrenches and car parts.

"Remember, with every interview, we're bringing my dreams to life, so please don't fuck it up," she said sweetly.

He chuckled. "Got it."

Sophie and Stone approached the only mechanic on location. He leaned confidently against a classic car, his broad shoulders draped in a grease-stained work shirt. His hair was slicked back, revealing a hard, unsmiling face with sharp eyes that seemed to miss nothing. A thick gold chain hung around his neck, glinting under the sparse lighting as he crossed his tattooed arms with an air of casual menace.

Going strictly on appearances, he was a perfect fixer-upper. *Please let him show signs of hidden lovability under all that hardness.* "Hi, I'm Sophie."

The guy slowly wiped his hands on a clean rag. The action, combined with a scratchy radio playing in the background, cast an edgy backdrop to her hopes.

Finally, he bestowed upon her an easy smile that vanished all her worries. "I'm Antonio. What brings you to my shop?" Like icing on the cake, he had a dreamy Italian accent to go along with the whole wrong-side-of-the-tracks bad-boy persona.

She practically bounced from stiletto to stiletto with happiness as they shook hands. "We're scouting for a special feature," Sophie explained, trying to keep it vague but interesting. "I'm looking for real-life heroes to interview." She raised her camera and snapped a photo of him before he could stop her.

Antonio laughed, a booming sound that filled the garage. "Darling, taking photos around here is asking to have your camera broken. Among other things."

With his arm still around her shoulders, Stone shifted slightly, his body subtly angling toward her in a silent promise of protection.

"Sorry," she said, wiggling out from under Stone's arm. "I'm just so excited I forgot. This, by the way, is my boyfriend." She gestured toward Stone. "His name is Stonie. Well, actually it's Stone, but his middle initial is E., so I call him Stonie. He loves it. Did I mention my middle initial is also E?"

Antonio studied her as if trying to decide if she was a true ding-a-ling or if she had ill intentions. When his gaze landed on her shirt, and then Stone's, his whole demeanor changed. "Quit the bullshit. I know why you're here."

Sophie gulped and inched closer to Stone, her hand touching his bicep. "You do?" Lightning struck outside with a loud thwack.

"I've been told I was nominated for some chick's book boyfriend nonsense. You're that chick. And you"—he eyeballed Stone—"are the muscle."

"I told you, he's my boyfriend," Sophie said, very, very glad Stone was here. Having him so close felt reassuring.

"Doll-face, I know muscle when I see muscle," Antonio said.

As if the moment had been choreographed, a burly dude appeared, taking a wide-legged stance and showing the weapon tucked in his waistband.

"Just because you hire bullies to protect you doesn't mean everyone does the same," Sophie admonished. "You should be ashamed of yourself for calling me a liar."

"Well, here's what I think about that," Antonio said. "If he's your boyfriend, go ahead and kiss him."

Sophie's stomach churned at the thought of kissing Stone in front of these strangers. Her cheeks burned with indignation. "I most certainly—"

"Darling," Stone said, "I know you like to argue, but I think this will go quicker if you kiss me and then sweet talk this man out of that interview you dragged me down here to do."

Sophie turned toward Stone. Had she heard correctly? "You know I don't like PDA."

"It's a kiss, not a fuck," Antonio said. "Now, either kiss him or get the hell off my property."

Stone raised an eyebrow at her, the I-told-you-so smirk barely hidden from Antonio. It was obvious Stone knew which choice she'd take.

He was wrong.

Sophie E. Clark was a professional daydreamer. She'd do what it took to get the interview.

Not giving herself time to overthink the why of her decision, she stepped into Stone's space and raised her chin. He stood straight, staring down at her like a still-framed photograph.

She reached up, her fingers trembling, and looped her hands around the nape of his neck. "You're going to have to help me here," she murmured. Even on tiptoes, she couldn't reach his lips if he didn't bend.

A half-amused smile curled his lips. "I thought you'd never ask."

He bent down and their lips touched. A surprising warmth spread through her, followed by a clap of thunder outside.

Mission accomplished, she waited for Stone to step back. He didn't.

Instead, he adjusted his head so that their noses weren't quite so next to each other. His hands, which had been shoved in his jean pockets were suddenly gripping her hips, pulling her into him.

The chaste kiss took on a new verve. Gentle no longer applied. Rough could and did, though.

His breath had a hint of coffee and cinnamon. When his hands moved and fisted the material of her shirt, she opened her mouth to say *we better stop now*, only he chose that moment to slip his tongue in between her lips.

Common sense flew out the window and was replaced with thrills and skipping heartbeats. Sophie, who had never experienced such headiness during a kiss, was not surprised when her tongue decided not to sit this one out. Nor did her nipples as they tightened against his chest. When he pushed into her, and she felt his erection, she moaned into his mouth.

Outside it began to rain. Hard. The sound pelting the tin roof like hail.

Unfortunately, or fortunately, that's when Stone seemed to get a grasp on his common sense and stilled.

As they parted, a breathless moment hung between them as their gazes locked.

There was a flicker of something in Stone's eyes—was it surprise? Approval? Frustration?

"I stand corrected," Antonio said. "What questions do you have?"

Sophie's breath was shallow as she glanced at Antonio, her mind so befuddled she had no idea what he was asking. "Umm."

Stone cleared his throat, stepping back into his role with much more ease than she was capable. "Sophie, darling, where's that list of questions you've been preparing?"

Sophie pulled an index card out of her skirt pocket. "Tell me about your hero moments."

"Most of my hero shit can't be repeated to a reporter," Antonio said.

His muscle, a guy with a gold tooth and a scar on one cheek, patted the gun on his hip and chuckled. "You could tell her about how, back in the day, you could hotwire a car in under thirty seconds."

"Shut the fuck up," Antonio said, his easy smile never leaving his face.

Sophie swallowed hard. "Actually, all I needed to do today was meet you. If you're included in the feature, I'll let you know." She grabbed Stone's hand and turned ready to escape.

"Not another step," Antonio said softly.

Sophie turned back. Stone, once again, placed his body between her and Antonio.

"Was there a problem?" Stone asked in a voice that could freeze fire.

Sophie peered around his shoulders to see Antonio. "Did you need something?"

"I'm going to need to watch you delete those photos you took while on my property."

"Oh. Of course." Sophie stepped out from behind Stone, turned her camera around so Antonio could see the photos, and deleted them.

Antonio held out his hand. "I'll need the SD card, as well."

"But—"

"We have rules." He pointed to a sign that said *no photography*. "You knew them, and you broke them."

"But I didn't see the sign until after I took the photo."

"Which is why I'm asking for your SD card instead of breaking your fancy camera," Antonia said. "Isn't that right, Buzz?" he said to his security.

Sophie had never been threatened, and she didn't like it. Not one little bit. "Stone?"

"It's okay, darling," he said, surprising her with the calmness in his voice. "Give him the card. I'll buy you another."

What the hell? Wasn't he supposed to be her security? Sophie fumbled with her camera and did as she was told.

"Satisfied?" Stone asked.

Antonio nodded.

"Great. Now, before Sophie and I leave, let's get one thing straight. She is my girl. Mine. I protect what's mine. If you ever say another threatening thing to her, I will tear you apart limb by painful limb."

With that, he took her hand and strolled them out of the garage. Thank God, the rain had stopped almost as soon as it had begun.

"I really hope this hasn't hurt my chances of being chosen," Antonio shouted after her.

Sophie didn't say anything until they'd rounded the corner and were out of camera sight of the garage. "Why did you let him have my SD card?"

"I assessed the situation and decided the most secure way to keep you safe was to acquiesce. There were two of them and one of me, and I had you to worry about."

"Is that why you kissed me?"

"If I recall right, you kissed me, I simply helped you make it appear more believable."

"Oh." She wasn't sure what she'd hoped he'd say about the kiss, but it wasn't that. "Why did you feel the need to threaten him? We're not really a couple."

"Sure, we are. Just not the traditional kind. And, as it turns out, a dear friend who recently pointed out to me that I'm the possessive sort was right."

They walked for a while, both lost in their own thoughts. When they came to a stoplight, she said, "Go ahead and say what you're thinking."

Stone said nothing.

"It's okay. I know you're dying to."

"What is it exactly you think I'm dying to say?" he asked, stepping into the street to cross.

"I told you so," Sophie said, hurrying to keep up with him. "You want to say, 'I told you they wouldn't buy me as a boyfriend.'"

"I could, but that wouldn't be very nice. And honestly, you are equally justified in throwing an I-told-you-so back at me."

"I am?"

"Seeing the way Antonio reacted when he realized I was your protection gave me a better understanding of your reason for wanting to pass me off as a boyfriend. His hackles went up and there was no way you were going to chat him up."

"Do you think that's why he was such a dick?"

"I do believe so. Anyway, I promise to work harder to blend in for tomorrow's assignment. Unless you plan on coming back here?"

"Never," Sophie said emphatically. "Antonio is not now nor ever will be boyfriend material...real or book."

"His fatal flaw can't be overcome?" Stone asked.

"It most certainly cannot."

Stone's, on the other hand—the jury was out on that one.

Chapter 14

Stone walked down the corridor to Ms. Birdie's office, his steps measured and his demeanor composed, yet his mind was anything but calm. Yesterday's kiss lingered in his thoughts, replaying with an intensity that caught him off guard.

What in the hell had caused him to throw his she's-mine-keep-the-fuck-away card down at Antonio's feet? It was a sure bet move to invoke another alpha to want something he couldn't have.

Now, Stone couldn't help but worry his lack of control around Sophie had something to do with his still glitching. Unfortunately, until Clarabelle returned from her visit to Mayhem, Missouri, there wasn't anyone he could turn to for support.

It had been a relief when he'd learned Sophie hadn't needed his services today. According to the text she'd sent him, she'd not yet decided on a new across-the-tracks candidate to interview. He'd caught a break there. The warmth of Sophie's lips and the slight tremble he had detected in her touch had haunted his dreams last night and had chased his thoughts all morning. He needed the day to reset.

He couldn't help but wonder if she, like him, had spent the last twenty-four hours convincing herself it had been just a kiss to prove a point to an asshole. That the two of them were best suited as the occasional book buddy. Nothing more.

He reached the sleek glass door marked *Executive*, took a deep breath, and smoothed down his jacket—a futile attempt to settle his thoughts as much as his appearance. With a slight nod to Ms. Birdie's assistant, he pushed the door open.

Ms. Birdie sat poised behind her desk, her sharp eyes looking up from a stack of papers as he entered. "Stone, it's so nice to see you again," she began, her voice cutting through his reverie with its usual brisk efficiency. "I appreciate your dropping everything to see me this morning."

"Not a problem. Sophie ended up not needing me today, so my schedule was free."

Ms. Birdie sighed. "I'm afraid I'm the reason she didn't need you today. I've tasked her with putting together a more detailed outline of her plans for the remaining columns."

"If I know her, she will be thrilled with the excuse to dig deeper into her book boyfriend files." Stone just hoped it didn't require him to read additional romances. The ones he'd read had already thrown him off his bachelor-for-life plan. As it was, he was hanging on to its ledge by his fingertips. One more happily ever after could spell the death of his common-sense approach to his future.

"Oh, you're not wrong," Ms. Birdie said. "I dropped by her office and saw her process, and it involved a corkboard with colorful threads crisscrossing all over the place. Reminded me of one of those crime scene boards you see on television cop shows."

"That sounds on brand for Sophie."

"Anyway, I hate to tell you this..." Ms. Birdie continued shuffling the papers into a neat pile. "But we've received a rather unsettling threat against our star columnist."

Stone stiffened. Thoughts of Sophie being hurt sent a cold fury down his spine. "When? Who?" If it was Antonio, Stone would make good on his threat. No one would hurt Sophie on his watch.

"It came sometime in the last twenty-four hours. Dropped off downstairs in our mailbox. Nothing was caught on the cameras, so the who is not known."

"I don't understand." Stone paced to the window and glanced out before turning and leaning against the wall. "You said you've asked for a more elaborate plan. Why not cancel the whole assignment? Surely, her safety is more important than the column."

"I gave her the option, and she wouldn't even consider the possibility. In her words, that's why she's got you." Ms. Birdie waved at the chairs in front of her desk. "Sit. You're making me nervous."

Stone nodded, forcing his professional mask firmly into place, and did as he was told. "I'd like to see the correspondence." The room felt too warm suddenly—or maybe it was just him.

Ms. Birdie handed him a file folder. "That's a copy of the note. The original went with the police."

He opened the folder and read. *Watch your back, Sophie E. Clark.*

"Have you met any of her prospects that gave you reason to worry for her safety?" Ms. Birdie asked.

"There's one individual, a guy she interviewed yesterday. He was interesting, to say the least.

Worked as a mechanic but gave off mob vibes. The business might have been a front. Anyway, he didn't take kindly to Sophie snapping a couple of photos. He demanded her SD card."

Ms. Birdie's brow furrowed. "I'm not surprised. That's why I insisted she have security during certain interviews. This world is full of unique individuals who would love to do harm to someone so sweet. I suggest we tighten security around Sophie, effective immediately. I want you on this 24/7 until we sort this out."

"Understood," Stone replied, even though the command felt like a double-edged sword. More time around Sophie meant wrestling with this unexpected, unprofessional attraction, yet it also meant keeping her safe, which, he had to admit, had become more personal than usual.

"Excellent. I spoke to Clarabelle, and she assured me your injury has healed and your schedule is cleared. But I wanted to run it by you in person since I can't say how long around-the-clock protection will be required. I mean, in a perfect world, we'll catch the culprit before the day is over."

When had Ms. Birdie reached Clarabelle? She'd not been returning his calls. "I'll protect her no matter how long it takes. Once I commit to a job, I'm all in."

"That's not what I heard from the Glam Team. Alberto said he'd heard you'd completely ditched their makeover attempts."

When in the hell had Alberto seen him to snitch on him? "That was a mistake on my part. Considering this threat, from now on, I'll be the perfect cinnamon roll boyfriend. Other than the wig."

"Excellent. Now, if you don't mind, would you break the news to Sophie? I'm afraid I'm due at a board meeting and won't be able to stop by and talk to her on my way out."

"I'll head that way as soon as you and I are done," Stone said. "It will give us a chance to work out the logistics of our being in forced proximity for the time being." The idea of such continual nearness disturbed him on a couple of levels. One, it would be harder to hide his secret from her if they were continually together. Two...well, that kiss had been anything but benign. It had left him wanting much, much more.

"And for now, we're not sharing this turn of events with Frankie," Ms. Birdie added.

He picked up on a thread of weariness in Ms. Birdie's tone. "Any special reason why?"

"Let's just say she's under a lot of pressure from a personal matter, and Isabella and I believe it's best to keep as much of the stress from the job as possible off her radar for the near future."

"I'm sorry to hear that," Stone said. "I hope everything will be okay."

"As do we, dear. As do we." Ms. Birdie stood. "Now, I hate to rush you off, but my schedule leaves little room for chitchat."

As he left Ms. Birdie's office and walked toward Sophie's, Stone took stock of his feelings. Something he'd never done until Clarabelle had come back into his life and given him the skills for his other career. A career that often required encouraging others to ponder their feelings.

While Stone still pretty much sucked at that part of the job, he was improving. Which brought him back to his current emotions. *What do I feel right now?*

Part of him dreaded the close proximity he and Sophie would be sharing for the near future, while another part—a part that kept presenting itself as valid—was thrilled.

But mostly, he was pissed that someone had threatened Sophie E. Clark.

Chapter 15

Sophie stood in her compact office, poring over the large planning board that dominated one wall. She was reworking the strategy for the remaining nine columns. It wasn't that she believed the plan required an overhaul, but this morning, Ms. Birdie had sent her an urgent message asking her to present another outline of her plan, this time with a tighter focus—one that allowed for all the interviews to be completed in one month.

Sophie couldn't help but think the one-month thing had something to do with Stone. Had he formally requested to be done babysitting her? On the bright side, if she completed all the interviews within the month, the candidates could all participate in the bachelor auction that was coming up soon.

On the other bright side, being done in a month meant kicking her grumpy shadow out of her life once and for all. Only, there was a slight problem. And it absolutely wasn't that she couldn't stop thinking of the kiss. Because she could...if she wanted to. She just hadn't wanted to, yet.

The problem was Sophie wasn't good with details. She was more of a big-picture person.

She liked the freedom to dream of new possibilities over being committed to just one path. Not possible if she had to pick her men in the next couple of days and line up interviews ASAP.

Sophie pushed her worries away. Things would work out the way they were meant to—they always did. Right now, all she needed to worry about was preparing a detailed list of the full names of those who had nominated a guy for her consideration and giving it to Ms. Birdie.

The magazine's owner had given Sophie an edict that if the person nominating another did so under the pseudonym anonymous, Sophie was to toss the nomination.

This sucked big time because there were some excellent nominations that fell in that unfortunate category.

Especially for the sketchy background nominations where ninety-nine percent of the nominations fell under the category anonymous. This also presented Sophie with another problem. Frankie had insisted that Mr. Sketchy—whoever he turned out to be since Antonio was a hard no—be featured in next month's edition of *Naked Runway*.

Currently, Sophie was mapping out qualified leads on color-coded index cards, each hue representing a different type of book boyfriend. Strands of colorful yarn connected the cards, creating a vibrant spiderweb that would eventually help her chart her and Stone's day-to-day journeys across Manhattan over the next month.

A sudden knock at the door spun her around, half-expecting to find a delivery person burdened with the life-size cardboard cutouts of her book heroes. Each figure was a crafted replica of how the members of the Book Boyfriend Connoisseurs Club imagined the protagonists from the featured books would look. She was particularly excited to lay her eyes on the life-size Miles from Emily Henry's *Funny Story*. That character had been living in her daydreams ever since chatting about him with Stone.

Instead of a delivery person, Stone stood there...just as rugged and unyielding as always.

"Hi." Her gaze darted across his face, searching for any signs of regret from their kiss. Was that why he was here? Had he come to quit? Remind her for the gazillionth time that he was a bachelor for life? That would explain the intense stare. "You're not dressed for the job," she blurted.

He cocked his head. "You gave me the day off."

"Oh, right. Sorry." What was it about him that made her say stupid things? "Then why are you here? Did you miss me?" Like that. That was a stupid thing. Of course he hadn't missed her. Gah.

"Like a toothache," he deadpanned.

"Very funny. I'm not that bad."

"You're right. You're not," Stone said, looking almost contrite. "Ms. Birdie sent—" He paused mid-sentence as Sophie stepped aside.

She followed his gaze and realized she'd given him his first clear view of her elaborate boyfriend board. "Do you like it?" she asked, sounding like a proud momma.

"Ms. Birdie mentioned your board, but words didn't do it justice." He edged closer, his shoulder grazing hers in the cramped space, and he scanned the detailed connections on the board. They heard the loud sound of a car backfiring somewhere, down on the streets below.

"I know it looks chaotic, but it helps me organize my thoughts," Sophie explained, watching his reaction closely.

Instead of replying directly, Stone plucked a tiny sticky note from the board and read the scribbled words aloud. "Don't fall in love with him." He turned to her, one eyebrow arching. "Who's him?"

"One of the Cinnamon Roll candidates," Sophie admitted, her cheeks warm with embarrassment. "The nomination described him as almost too perfect to be real."

"And if he turns out to be everything promised, you don't want to fall in love with him?" Stone asked, a hint of teasing underlying his serious tone.

She shrugged. "At least not until after the auction. Ms. Birdie was clear—all these guys must agree to remain on the market to be featured and to participate in the auction next month."

"Why not just buy him at auction if you fall for him?" Stone suggested, his voice laced with a blend of humor and practicality.

"Because all my disposable income is currently helping to keep Poppie in his apartment." And bribing the superintendent not to toss him out because he'd forgotten to pay last month's rent on time.

"That's a good granddaughter of you. He's lucky."

"I'm the lucky one. He took me in when I had nowhere else to go."

"Then you're both very lucky to have each other."

"Highly agree. He's the one who taught me to live my best life," she said, then paused. Was she revealing too much? She didn't want Stone to think she was hinting for help or pity or that she was a flake. "Did you drop by for a reason?"

Stone's expression went extra-grumpy.

"What? What is it?" she exclaimed. "Just spit it out. If you've come to tell me you've given your one-month notice, I've already figured that much out."

"There's a credible threat against you. We need to discuss your security," he said, his voice not quite as steady as normal.

"Like on a scale of one to ten, with one being it won't happen and ten being it's happening, where does credible fall on the scale?" she asked.

"Eight," Stone replied immediately. "Until the threat is eliminated, I've been instructed to ensure you have constant protection."

"The threat is actually against me?" Sophie asked, her mind reeling.

He nodded.

Panic fluttered in her chest. Stone had once mentioned—in a variation of his standard *I'm never falling in love* spiel—that threats against him could lead to threats against those he loved. Would the same hold for threats against her? Was Poppie in danger? Of course they would, and Poppie would be.

Damn it. Poppie had survived the danger she'd inadvertently brought to his doorstep with her last boyfriend, and now she'd brought danger to Poppie again. Things were—

Stone must have seen she was spiraling because he quickly offered, "I have a secure two-bedroom condo. I propose you move in temporarily, and I can keep a closer watch on you there."

"I can't just leave Poppie, especially not now," Sophie said. There had to be a better solution. But what? *Think. Think. Think.*

"I was afraid you'd say that." Stone ran his fingers through his curls. "The only other option is for me to move in with you."

An image of what that would look like instantly formed. *Nope. Nope, nope, nope.* "What's your backup plan? You said you always have a backup plan?"

He blinked. "That was my backup plan."

"Oh. Surely, you can handle the threat without completely disrupting our lives. Like what if I added additional locks to my door, and a security system, one that includes cameras?"

"That's something we can work toward, but until it's in place and approved by Ms. Birdie, you and I are stuck together," Stone asserted, his tone leaving zilch room for argument.

Sophie sighed. Time to switch gears. Figure out who'd made the threat. "It's probably Antonio. The idiot's way of making sure if I do happen to have a backup copy of the image of him, I never share it."

"Do you have a backup copy?"

"No."

He nodded. "He is the obvious suspect. Which is a little too easy from where I stand, but I'll investigate the possibility as soon as I get your word you won't leave your office until I return to pick you up and take you home."

If it wasn't Antonio, then who? Some weirdo who had heard about her mission? But why? "How long will you be?"

"Not long. Do you have plans? A date?"

"Of course I don't have a date. I'm supposed to be your girlfriend for the foreseeable future."

"Right. Right," he said, sounding distracted.

"I don't like to leave Poppie unattended for more than three or four hours. Sometimes he gets confused if I'm not there to anchor him. I planned to head home by three."

Stone glanced at his watch. "I can make that work. I need to go home, grab a go bag, and fill my partners in on the situation. They can dig into the threat while I get what we need to make your place more secure. Until then, stay put."

"Deal," Sophie said. "And Stone, thanks for understanding."

"No problem. It's what I've been hired to do."

"Speaking of that, Poppie will think my boyfriend has moved in with me. You're going to have to sell the sweet guy persona. I refuse to allow him to worry one moment that I've fallen for the wrong type of guy again or that my life is in danger."

"Sweet guy. Got it. Anything else?"

"Don't be too sweet. I don't want his heart to be crushed when we split."

"What's considered too sweet?"

"Roses. Daisies are fine. You can cook but try not to look too efficient. And no nicknames. He's a sucker for nicknames. Sort of like I am with grand gestures."

"Got it."

"And you're going to have to come up with a good reason why it's been two months since our last date."

LISA WELLS

Chapter 16

Sophie fumbled with her keys in a rush to get inside her apartment before Poppie realized she was home. As the key slipped from her grasp and clattered to the floor, she bent to retrieve it, only to feel Stone's hand brush against hers as he reached for it too. At that exact moment, the hallway lights flickered.

"That's weird," Sophie murmured, straightening up, a shiver of unease trickling down her spine.

Stone's expression tightened, a hint of concern—or was it something else?—flashing in his eyes. "Stay here a moment," he instructed, his voice carrying an edge of command she wasn't used to. "I'll check for danger."

Sophie raised an eyebrow, glancing at the now fine lights. If there was any danger, wouldn't it be out here where the lights were flickering? Then again, this was an old building where half the tenants enjoyed rent-controlled living. Buildings like these weren't known for fine living conditions. "Okay." She placed her hand on his shoulder, so she could lean in and whisper the rest of her comment. "But hurry up. I don't want Poppie to see me out here with you."

Again, the lights flickered once and stopped.

Stone turned sharply, causing her hand to fall away. She watched as he scouted the empty hallway, his profile one of wariness. Was there more to his concern? His usual calm was tinged with a strain she hadn't noticed before. Like a man grappling—not with danger—but instead a shadow. One only he could see.

"Scream if you need me," Stone said before pulling his weapon and cautiously entering her apartment. Moments later, when Sophie heard noises from Poppie's apartment across the hall, she scurried into her apartment, shutting the door tightly behind her.

Stone emerged from the bedroom, glaring at her. "What the hell, Sophie? I hadn't given the all clear."

"I'll do better next time," she whispered, not wanting Poppie to hear her.

"Why are we whispering?" Stone asked, moving with stealth quickness to stand next to her.

She placed her finger to her lips. "Because I haven't figured out what to tell Poppie yet. He always knows I'm lying, and I hate doing that to him."

"Then let's tell him the truth."

"We can't. It would cause him to worry. Knowing Poppie, he'd try to guard both our places while we're at work, and that could end badly."

Stone ran a hand over his five o'clock shadow, the sound of flesh against bristle incredibly intimate in the tiny space. "Then we'll tell him I'm your boyfriend. If he asks where I've been since he last saw me, I'll tell him away on assignment. Once we've found out who has threatened you, I'll explain to Poppie why we fabricated a relationship."

Lying to Poppie hurt Sophie's soul. He was her person. The one she could always count on. To not be honest felt disrespectful. But then again, getting him hurt by telling him the truth wasn't a great option either. "Okay, but you've really got to sell the whole boyfriend act. I'm telling you, he can smell a lie."

"Deal. Where should I put my bag?" He pointed to her couch where he'd dropped a military-issued duffel.

True to his word, when Stone had returned to *Naked Runway*, he had transformed into the part of her boyfriend. According to him, Isabella had been briefed on the situation and had assembled a wardrobe for him, complete with a calendar which told him what to wear every day.

Sophie led him to her bedroom and pointed to an empty corner. "You can put it there for now. I've never had a guy live with me, so I'll need to clear out some closet space and a dresser drawer for you."

"I can live out of a suitcase; it's standard practice when I'm on assignment." He glanced around the room, and his gaze landed on a pile of children's books stacked on her desk. The entire collection of Junie B. Jones.

"Those look a little young for your tastes?" he teased.

"I have a monetized YouTube account where I read bedtime stories to children every night. We're currently making our way through those. They were my favorite growing up."

"Monetized?"

"I get a cut of the advertising money that is spent on my page."

"Smart. I bet you're good at reading them. You have a personality for bringing book characters alive. Hell, I feel like Miles is a friend after just one evening of our discussing his character." He continued his exploration of her room and stopped scanning when he saw the painting on the wall above her bed. "'Never settle for less than the fairytale,'" Stone read aloud.

"My mom painted the sentence right before she brought me home from the hospital as an infant. I just haven't had the heart to paint over it," she took a seat on the bed.

He glanced down at her. "Were her and your dad living the fairytale before their deaths?"

"I like to think so, but I don't remember much." She picked up her pillow and hugged it. "How often do you go on assignments that require you to move in with a person?"

"Not often anymore. Our focus doesn't usually require it, although we spend plenty of time staking out locations, waiting for the bad guys to slip up."

"Focus?" She really didn't know that much about him outside of his part ownership in a security business with his brothers.

"We retrieve children who have been kidnapped by their noncustodial parents."

She squeezed the pillow tighter. The thought of a child being kidnapped made her ill. "Is that a common occurrence?"

He sat down next to her, noticeably careful not to touch her in the process. "You'd be surprised. Especially where one parent has dual citizenship."

She scooted back and leaned against the wall. "Is it dangerous? Do you often find yourself under fire?"

He turned to see her better. "We usually manage without gunfire, but once in a while, things get sketchy and—"

A soft knock interrupted him, the sound abrupt in the quiet apartment.

"And so it begins," Sophie muttered, quickly rising to answer the door.

He caught her arm, pressing a finger to his lips, then tiptoed to the door to peer through the peephole. "It's Poppie," he said in a normal tone.

"I knew that already. I know the sound of his knock." Sophie went to the door but turned back to look at him before opening it. "Get ready to sell this." She turned back, twisted the knob, and opened the door. "Hi Poppie. Have you had a good day?"

"It's been busy." He pushed past her and came to a stop when he saw Stone. "Damn glad you got rid of that wig. Now you look like a man I can have a drink with. Do you drink? Where in the hell have you been for two months?"

"Work took me away. I've missed Sophie like crazy, and I've been known to enjoy a good whiskey now and then," Stone replied.

"Got any with you?" Poppie asked, not looking even a little suspicious.

"Poppie, remember what the doctor said about alcohol and your new meds," Sophie reminded him gently.

Poppie swore like a sailor. "Damn doctors stripping away all my vices—first they come for my sex life, now my booze. What's next, no weed?"

Stone came and stood next to Sophie.

The movement distracted Poppie from his rant. "Didn't expect to see you back here, buddy," he said, before focusing his gaze on Sophie and frowning. "Were you expecting him back?"

Sophie's heart skipped a beat, her palms dampening as she searched for the right words, feeling the weight of Poppie's attention. "Like he said, work called him away."

Stone extended a hand to Poppie, his smile easy. "Nice to see you again, sir. Sophie speaks very highly of you."

As Poppie shook Stone's hand, Sophie watched their interaction closely, her nerves strung tighter than the tension in a romance novel's black moment. "There was a bit of a mishap at his place...plumbing disaster, and so

I told him he could bunk here until his water is back on," she blurted, the words rushing out before she could think them through.

Poppie's bushy white eyebrows shot up. "Plumbing, huh? That's rough. Good thing you met a girl with a big heart. Not many would be that generous. If you haven't noticed, her place ain't hardly big enough for one, let alone two."

Sophie laughed, hoping it didn't sound as forced to their ears as it did to hers. "What are friends for, right? And anyway, it'll be fun having a nice guy around for a change. A palate cleanser, you might say."

"Damn straight," Poppie replied, his gaze shifting between Sophie and Stone. "Well, I guess that means you'll be staying for dinner. Sophie's making enchiladas."

"That's what I heard," Stone replied, with a warm smile that Sophie found surprisingly genuine. "I've offered to help."

As Poppie settled on the couch, Sophie and Stone shared a quick, conspiratorial glance before moving to the kitchen, which Poppie could completely view.

"That didn't go too bad," Sophie whispered as she began pulling ingredients from cabinets. "I was afraid he'd be rougher on you. He can be overly protective."

"I like him," Stone whispered back, his closeness sending a shiver down her spine. "I predict we'll be best friends by the time I'm ready to pack my bags and go back to my own place."

As they moved around the kitchen preparing dinner, the air between Sophie and Stone crackled like a secret on the verge of being spilled. Sophie reached for the salt at the same moment Stone did, their fingers brushing against each other. The moment they touched, the kitchen lights flickered briefly, casting a quick shadow over the room.

"Whoa, what was that?" Poppie called over the sound of *Wheel of Fortune*. "You two got too many things going at once in there?"

"Must be," Stone called out, only a slight frown creasing his brows. A quick, almost imperceptible reaction. His eyes scanned the room briefly, reminding her why he was here. She was in danger.

Poppie chuckled. "Well, just make sure you don't start any fires with all that static. I'm too old to be running out of burning buildings."

Sophie swallowed hard, her mind racing with concerns. Who was behind the threat? Were they causing the lighting issues? Would something sinister happen tonight? The idea made her knees weak.

"You okay?" Stone asked. "You've gone white."

"I will be. I'm just still processing."

Dinner proceeded with light conversation and laughter, but Sophie remained acutely aware of Stone's presence across the table and the threat lurking in her future.

As they cleared the dishes after their meal, their hands touched again, passing a serving spoon, and once more, a subtle flicker danced through the lights. This time, Stone's frown was more pronounced, and Sophie caught it immediately.

"Is my stalker playing with me? Is that why the lights keep doing that?" she asked quietly, her voice tinged with concern as Poppie recounted tales from his youth, oblivious to their exchange.

Stone met her gaze, his features softening. "It's nothing to worry about, Sophie. You're mine. I protect what's mine."

Mine. There was that term again. The romance booklover in her wanted to read something into his continued use of it. Something alpha-delicious. Common sense said it had been spoken more along the line of, "You're my assignment." That kind of *mine*.

Nevertheless, hearing him say *mine* wasn't awful.

Ugh. She clearly needed to do more work on her psyche to rid it of its toxic desire for that sort of book boyfriend to materialize in her life.

"Promise?" she asked Stone.

"Promise," he said without hesitation.

Chapter 17

T hree hours later, Stone stepped out onto the balcony, the brisk air contrasting sharply with the steam that wafted from the bathroom. He quickly dialed Clarabelle, his connection to a world beyond the ordinary.

"Wasn't expecting to get a ring from you this evening," Clarabelle said instead of hello. "What's troubling you?"

Now that Clarabelle was back in their lives, he and his brothers had a routine. Each of them was assigned two nights a week to call and check on her, making sure she hadn't crossed over without a goodbye. On Sundays, they either ate dinner together, if Clarabelle was nearby, or they did a Zoom chat after dinner.

"My magic is still glitching," Stone told her.

Several years ago, Stone and his brothers had discovered that Clarabelle had been an honest-to-goodness fairy godmother when she was alive. Then, when she had died, she'd gotten stuck in the second veil due to unfinished business.

They had been her unfinished business.

She'd had plans to train them to become Fairy Godfathers, but had died before she got around to rocking their world with her secret. Because Fairy Godmothers were on the verge of becoming extinct, Clarabelle had been granted time in the second veil to finish her unfinished business.

Now, Clarabelle was a Magical ghost, and even though her unfinished business had been accomplished, she'd finagled a way to stay longer in the second veil. The details of the persuading were not up for discussion.

"Oh, fiddle-faddle," Clarabelle said. "Tell me everything." Her voice was calm, which told him his news wasn't unexpected. "Is it your wand? Is it refusing to behave?" she asked.

"So far, so good with Bravo Baton." His wand was currently tucked away in his go bag. The last time he had tried to conjure something with it, he'd succeeded. "It's Sophie. Shit is still happening every time we touch."

Clarabelle tsked. "The same kind of shit? Or new shit?"

He chuckled at her use of swear words. As a rule, she disdained the little fuckers. "Most recently, I got this surge of energy I couldn't control, and the lights flickered."

Sophie had no idea just how right she'd been the other night when she'd told him control was his fatal flaw. But not in the way she assumed. Magic in the hands of a person not in control could become fatal. Thus, staying in control was essential.

Clarabelle's response to his dilemma was silence. Not a good sign.

He'd hoped for a laugh and a pithy comment about how magic just sometimes had to wiggle and scratch its backside. "Mom?" he prompted.

"And is it your injured hand you're touching Sophie with when this happens?" she finally inquired.

He leaned against the railing and stared up at the full moon. "Not always."

"Hmm. What a kettle of worms that presents."

"What?" Stone asked.

"It appears the spell I cast to heal your wound didn't take."

"Then this can be fixed. You can recast your spell?"

"No. That's not possible. It was a one-and-done type of spell."

"I'm not sure I understand what my wound has to do with anything. I was under the impression all my prior glitches were because of the damage done to my wand. That's why every spell I tried to cast went sideways."

"It wasn't a bad impression to live under," Clarabelle mused. "Unfortunately, we were wrong."

He closed his eyes. "Do you have any new theories on the problem?" During the two and a half months he had taken off before reconvening as Sophie's bodyguard, he'd been under the care of Clarabelle, who had *reset* his magic...so to speak.

And while that was taking place, she had also obtained the address of Zuberi the Enchanter, a wand wizard in Africa. Bravo Baton had been sent to him to fix. The black and gold wand had been blown in half by a bullet, and Clarabelle had been unable to put it back together with her own magic.

"It sounds like when the bullet went through your wand and grazed your finger," Clarabelle said, "the magic in your wand formed a new conduit through your injury. It's rare but not unheard of for magic to seek out a new balance in this way. Zuberi and I were under the assumption it still maintained all its magic."

Stone sighed. "You're going to have to explain this in layman's terms."

"It's possible that the original magic from your wand now resides inside of you, and it is resonating with Sophie," Clarabelle said. "Is she by any chance a Magical? Like a fairy?"

"Not that I'm aware of." Stone glanced inside Sophie's apartment making sure she hadn't exited the bathroom. This was not a conversation he wanted her to overhear. "I mean, she's quite fanciful in her approach to life, and would definitely make a much better fairy godmother than the guys and I have, but—"

"Nonsense," Clarabelle snapped. "Making the three of you fairy godfathers was the best thing I've done in this realm. You boys will be great once you're not so green. Magic takes effort and practice, just like getting all those muscles the lot of you like to flex took time and patience and work."

Stone's hand clenched around the phone. He abhorred being green. "If the original magic now resides in me, how is Bravo Baton still able to conjure?"

"The most likely answer is it's not. You're the one doing the magic, Bravo is now simply a prop."

The information tasted sour. "You're saying I got my wand assassinated?"

"Possibly. Another theory, one I find fascinating and will research, is that Zuberi filled it with new, more powerful, magic."

Stone recalled the note that had been included in the box holding Bravo Baton when it had been returned to him:

I trust this finds you well. In your hands, you will find your faithful companion rejuvenated and ready for new adventures. May it serve you with the strength of a lion and wisdom of an ancient baobab.

Handle it with care, for it holds the spirit of the savannah and power of the mountains.

The last line now took on a whole other message. One that leaned toward Clarabelle's second option for his wand. "Let's get back to my wand's original magic."

"I couldn't agree more aggressively. Let's stay focused on the current delectable dilemma," Clarabelle said.

"It is your theory that Bravo Baton's original magic now lives inside of me," Stone said, speaking slowly as he wrapped his brain around the thought. "And it thinks Sophie and I should...be together?"

"Aren't you just the cutest thing, being so whimsical?" Clarabelle gave off a soft laugh that sounded exactly like what a Fairy Godmother's laugh should sound like. Light and happy.

One he and his brothers needed to find a manly version of, so they didn't initially frighten their new clients upon first meeting. Especially the younger ones. Their last assignment, the one they'd learned about at Sunday night's dinner—the one Ryder had described as complicated—had been to help a woman survive finding out her best friend had a social media account where all she did was make fun of her. A best friend she was about to give a kidney to.

"I do believe Sophie, and her love of all things romantic, is rubbing off on you," Clarabelle continued.

"Mom, answer my question, please."

"Oh. Yes. That," Clarabelle said. "What was the question again?"

"Do you believe that my magic thinks Sophie and I should be together?" Stone repeated.

"Dear, magic doesn't think. But it does sense and align with powerful energies. If it reacts around Sophie, it could mean your paths are deeply intertwined."

He rubbed his temples with his free hand. "Like soul mates?"

"Possibly, but honestly, it is also feasible that the two of you have a nonromantic connection. All the glitching suggests is that it's a significant bond," Clarabelle explained. "The nature of that bond is up to the two of you to figure out."

Relief hit him like a cold blast of winter air. "If it's up to me, then nope. Nothing to see here. Just two adults thrown together by circumstances."

"Well, there you have it. You've answered your own question."

Stone's sixth sense told him Clarabelle had capitulated too easily. "But what if it does mean a relationship?" He stood and paced. "I'm here to protect her, not to get involved. Not to mention, I'm not at all interested in love. I'm a forever bachelor." While he now freely admitted to himself he was besotted with Sophie, his reason for remaining single remained more valid than ever. He wasn't husband material.

"Magic doesn't give two cents about your multitude of nots," Clarabelle said sharply, a sure sign she still wasn't in the mood to accept the fact that all three of her boys were confirmed forever bachelors.

"You're saying, I won't have a choice?" Stone asked. "That it can make me fall in love with Sophie?"

"Of course it can't make you. You have free will," Clarabelle said. "I mean, if it was possible to use magic to make you fall in love, I would have done it by now. So much easier than—" She stopped abruptly.

"Than what?"

"If you don't want to fall in love, I suggest you remain vigilant," Clarabelle said, not answering his question. "Keep your emotions in check. Stay out of situations that give you an opportunity to fall in love."

"Like moving in with Sophie?" he said ruefully.

"Exactly like that," Clarabelle said.

"Fuck."

Clarabelle tsked. "If I've told you once I've told you a hundred times, Fairy Godpersons don't curse."

"My apologies. It's just that as of this evening, I am living with Sophie."

There was a long pause. "What, may I ask, precipitated this change in your address?"

"She's had a viable threat against her. Until it is neutralized, we will be together twenty-four hours a day."

"Well. That is a big pickle," Clarabelle said, sounding way too cheerful. "On the food-for-thought side concerning your magic, there's a slight chance that what is going on is a test of your worthiness to continue having your powers. You did, after all, allow your wand to be injured, which resulted in it losing its original magic."

"Fu...fiddle sticks," Stone said, trying out Clarabelle's favorite curse word.

"Much better, dear."

"Do you think I should turn in my wand and get out of the fairy godfather business?"

More tsking. "Did I not tell you during boot camp that there is no leaving the business?"

"You did not."

"Anyway, what's at stake is the magnitude of your wand's new power. I've never known of a wand that had to be sent off to be fixed. Only time will tell if it holds new magic. And if it does, is it greater, or greatly less than what you were given upon completion of bootcamp?"

"You're saying I'm at risk of having a limp wand?"

Clarabelle chuckled. "It's possible. But before you get all caught up in what-ifs, just remember that what happened to your wand was not a result of neglect. The powers-that-be will take that into consideration."

"Who exactly are the powers-that-be?" She had mentioned the council a few times over the last month but had refused to tell him who served on the committee.

"That is not something I wish to discuss," she said primly. "The only thing that's important from this point forward is for you to remember that you control your actions, not the magic. What you do or do not do with Sophie during your time of forced proximity is your call. Your decisions cannot be blamed on your magic."

"In other words, I'm to keep it in my pants."

"Yes. Your penis should stay in your pants."

He groaned. That was never a phrase you wanted to hear your mother say. "I'm worried that all these glitches will bring danger to Sophie. Perhaps I should hand the job off to Ryder."

"Nonsense. You are a professional," Clarabelle said. "Focus on the job. The rest will sort itself out in due time."

Stone sighed. "I've got to get off here. I love you. Good night."

Stone hung up the phone and lingered on the balcony a bit longer, sweeping his gaze over the street Sophie lived on. What if magic *could* force two people together? What if he had no choice but to fall in love with Sophie, and her him? Would that be so terrible?

It would be for her. She'd made it abundantly clear he wasn't her type. And she deserved someone who lived a safe existence.

He turned to head back inside and caught sight of Sophie emerging from the bedroom. She was clad in short pajamas that showcased her long, slim legs, an image that momentarily scattered his thoughts.

"The shower's all yours," she said, her voice light as she opened the balcony doors wider and leaned casually against one. "I took a quick one, so there should be plenty of hot water left. Tomorrow, you can go first. I'll make up the couch while you're showering."

Stone edged past her, careful not to make any contact that might spark another unintended magical display, and glanced over his shoulder at the couch—it was barely five feet long. "Don't bother setting it up. I'll make a pallet on the floor."

"It's no bother at all, and I was planning on taking the couch and letting you have the bed," Sophie said, her tone both firm and accommodating.

"That's not happening on my watch," Stone replied.

"Because you're a gentleman and a gentleman wouldn't kick a lady out of her bed?" she asked.

About to agree, he recalled his need to cut any romantic notions off at the head. Both hers and his. "Because all the entries to the apartment are out here in the living room. Otherwise, I'd take that bed in a minute. I'll sleep on the floor. I've slept on plenty of hard surfaces in my life."

Not waiting for a rebuttal, he retreated to the bedroom, closing the door behind him. A groan escaped him as he leaned against it for a moment, his mind replaying the sight of her pajamas adorned with scenes from Cinderella.

Good God, even her sleepwear is whimsical.

A reluctant smile tugged at his lips. The juxtaposition of her quirky attire and his grim resolve underscored the stark contrasts in their worlds—a fairytale and a battlefield.

Chapter 18

The rich aroma of sizzling bacon and the gentle hiss of eggs coaxed Sophie out of sleep. Stretching languidly, she slipped into her house shoes and padded softly toward the kitchen, drawn by the comforting scents that now filled her small apartment.

As she rounded the corner, Sophie caught sight of Stone by the stove, dressed not in his usual attire but in what could only be described as his *boyfriend outfit*—a well-fitted T-shirt paired with a cozy cardigan that somehow cemented his role as the ideal cinnamon roll hero. Isabella had done superbly pulling together a quick wardrobe for him.

"Morning," Stone said, his back still turned as he focused on the eggs. "Hope you're hungry."

"Starving," Sophie replied, her voice carrying a hint of the confusion she felt. When exactly had he changed? His go-bag was still in her bedroom. Had he been in there? Had he watched her sleep? The idea made her skin tingle. She couldn't recall a time her skin had ever tingled. Weird.

She took a seat at the kitchen table, her gaze lingering on him. He was managing to appear every bit the part of a perfect partner, which only reminded her more of their differences.

Remember, he's no longer your type. You have a new type. An improved type. A type who doesn't hurt the one they love. A type so sweet authors no longer feel the need to have a breakup scene in a book when the hero is one of these types.

Stone placed plates heaped with breakfast on the table and finally sat down opposite her. "So, what's on the agenda today?" he asked, picking up his fork.

Sophie bit her lip, considering how to approach the topic. "Well, we're visiting the cinnamon roll guy I told you about—the one from my list."

"The one you wrote a note about? 'Do not fall in love?'" Stone raised his eyebrow in a teasing fashion.

Sophie chuckled, a blush heating her cheeks. "Yeah, that one."

"Then his nomination came from a named source?" he asked, before taking a bite.

"It came from Jenna Carter, an employee at *Naked Runway*. I've never met her, but I was told she's the editor of the lifestyle section. According to Isabella, Jenna has a keen eye for genuine people and stories that resonate deeply with the magazine's audience."

"And why did Jenna nominate the dude?" Stone asked.

"I don't know all the details, but basically, she was touched by his story and community spirit when she met him while on an assignment."

Stoned eyeballed her like she had a sign on her forehead that said *liar*. "So, what you're not saying is that they dated, it didn't work out, but she thinks he'll be perfect for another woman."

Sophie tried to look offended that he thought she'd lie by omission. She had simply not felt that part of the story was relevant. "Most of the nominees for this category have been made by exes."

"Poor schmuck is now going to be labeled with this cinnamon roll nonsense and seriously hurt his chances of keeping his dude card at the local bar where he hangs out."

"Oh, whatever," she snapped. "Being a nice guy is the new James Bond. Women find them hot and lovable. It's the perfect combination."

He snorted. "It's a safe bet he won't ask you to prove we're a couple by kissing me."

"Exactly." Sophie pushed around her eggs with her fork, the memory of that kiss leaving her all prickly. "Next time someone demands we kiss, I vote we just leave. No book hero would demand such of a couple."

Stone cocked his head. "I bet one of those billionaire horndogs you plan to interview would. I mean if it were me, and I was feeling ornery, I'd demand a kiss. Not to prove some guy's your boyfriend, but to prove I could take you from him if I wanted."

She wrinkled her nose. "Not all rich guys are assholes."

"But we're not talking about all of them. We're talking about the ones you labeled players. They would."

"Fine. Yes. They would. Bottom line, I'm done kissing any man during an interview."

He shrugged. "Smart."

As they continued eating, the light banter could not entirely mask the tension that had her neck in knots.

Sophie was acutely aware her life was in danger. Stone was not her boyfriend; he was her protector, and she had one month to find nine more book boyfriend candidates who were not only willing to be interviewed but also to stay single until after their feature was posted, not to mention participate in a bachelor's auction.

Finishing her meal, Sophie cleared her throat. "I made you another shirt to wear today. Something that should help sell the boyfriend image even more."

Stone's smile was one of good-natured reluctance. "I'm almost afraid to ask what it says."

"You'll see. It's perfect for today," Sophie assured him with a playful wink. How weird was it that mixed in with all her apprehension, she still managed a healthy dose of excitement? Exhilaration for the task at hand. She got to spend the day looking for breathing book boyfriends. And excited to do so in the company of Stone. He intrigued her mind.

"If you say so," Stone replied. "If the poor schmuck passes the initial gut-check test, what kind of questions do you plan to ask?"

"I've created a new and improved boyfriend questionnaire." She picked up her juice and took a sip. "Do you want to take it?"

He sat his napkin on the table. "Why not?"

Sophie flipped open her notebook to a fresh page, her pen poised and ready. "Okay, let's start easy. What does a perfect day look like for you?"

Stone considered the question, his brow furrowing. "A perfect day? It starts with no alarms. Then, maybe a long run in the early morning quiet when the city's still asleep. After that, just a calm day—no surprises. Time to read something that isn't a mission report or a romance novel, and maybe dinner at a place where no one knows my name or asks any questions. Simple and uneventful."

Sophie noted his answer and chose not to comment on the romance novel dig. "All right, what do you value most in a relationship?"

"Efficiency," Stone replied almost immediately, then chuckled at her look of horror. "Kidding. Trust, I guess. In my line of work, trust is everything. You can't really get close to someone if you're always wondering if they're hiding something or lying to you. And I need someone I trust without hesitation. Even the slightest hesitation will have me bailing."

Sophie filed away that response. She'd ponder it more later. "What are you passionate about?"

"That's a tough one," Stone admitted, rubbing the back of his neck. "I used to be passionate about a lot of things. Now? It's more about making sure I do my job well. Protecting people who need it, ensuring that what needs to happen happens. It's not about passion; it's about duty."

Sophie wrote down his answers, her smile waning slightly. How sad not to have a passion.

She had lots of them. "Last question: Describe your ideal partner."

Stone's gaze drifted past Sophie as he appeared to consider his words. "That would be a waste of time, because she doesn't exist."

"Pretend she does. Describe her," Sophie persisted, intrigued by the sureness in his voice.

He shrugged. "Someone who understands my life, the unpredictability of it, and the weight of what I do. They'd need to be strong—not just physically but emotionally. Someone who can watch me walk out the door every day knowing I might not come home. Someone who doesn't need constant reassurance or can't handle being alone sometimes. Someone who would never blurt out another's secret." He gave her a rueful smile. "As I said, my perfect woman doesn't exist in reality. She's a fairytale. Which is why I'm a confirmed bachelor."

Sophie snorted.

"What?"

"It's nothing."

"It sounded like something," he persisted.

"It's just if I had a million for every time you've felt the need to remind me you're a bachelor for life, I'd be able to buy up 5th Avenue by now."

He grimaced. "I'm sorry. I didn't realize I was doing that."

She closed her notebook. "No big deal. It's not like I'm secretly vying for your heart. Why don't I go grab that T-shirt for you?"

"Wait." He reached out as if to touch her but then withdrew his hand. "What is your passion?"

Out of all the questions he could have asked her to bring a smile to her heart, it was that one. "That's easy. The pursuit of happiness. The one thing the death of my parents taught me is that life is short. Take chances. Pursue the impossible. Embrace life—messiness and all."

He nodded as if saying *good one*. But he said nothing, so she hopped up.

"Let me go change, and we can get our day started."

Fifteen minutes later, she emerged from the bedroom. She wore an orange T-shirt that said *Chapter One*. "This one's for you," she said, tossing him his.

He glanced at it and laughed before slipping into the bedroom to change, not even bothering to argue.

"I like it when you do my bidding so easily," she called out.

"Don't get used to it," he hollered back. "I don't have a gooey middle. I'm steel through and through."

And therein lay the problem. As she'd mentioned in one of their conversations. Men could be molded into perfect book boyfriend material, but they had to want to change. Unfortunately, those made of steel seldom did. "That's really too bad," she whispered to the closed door. He wouldn't need to change much. He'd just need to be willing to risk loving someone.

Chapter 19

The soft chime of the bell above the door greeted Stone and Sophie as they stepped into Graham's Corner, located in Tribeca. Stone immediately glanced around for all viable exits. He found two. He positioned himself so that his back was not to either of them.

Then he surveyed the warmly lit bookstore, taking in the cozy reading nooks scattered between the shelves. The charming, homey atmosphere felt oddly out of place in the upscale neighborhood—a stark contrast to the location of their first book boyfriend quest.

A man with tousled brown hair and warm, inviting eyes looked up from behind the counter. "I'm Oliver," he introduced himself, shaking their hands with a warmth that matched his smile. "Jenna sent you, right? She mentioned something about a book-boyfriend project. I'm flattered to be considered."

Sophie's face lit up. "Yes, that's right. Jenna thinks you're a perfect fit for what we call a Cinnamon Roll Hero—kind, empathetic, and community-focused. Anyway, I'm getting ahead of myself. I'm Sophie, and this is my boyfriend, Stone."

For some strange reason, Stone found himself puffing out his chest like a proud peacock when Sophie introduced him as her boyfriend. Then he reminded himself he wasn't and that Oliver Graham, with a well-groomed beard and a friendly smile, wearing a soft cardigan that seemed designed to reinforce his image as the quintessential Cinnamon Roll Hero, could be under the right circumstances.

"It is so nice to meet both of you. Care for a tour of my pride and joy?"

Oliver led them through the two-story bookstore, sharing stories about his community projects and his late wife's legacy. The air was filled with the musty, comforting scent of old books and a faint trace of a burning vanilla candle.

Stone couldn't help but notice how Sophie hung onto Oliver's every word, like she was listening to a captivating storyteller weaving a spellbinding tale. Everything about her body language displayed genuine interest, admiration, and awe. And why not awe? This was the man of her fantasies. Oliver was not just fulfilling the role of Sophie's preferred hero trope—he appeared to be setting a new standard for all who followed.

A twinge of something Stone couldn't quite place zapped him like a high-powered taser. The zap caused a puzzle piece to click into place in his mind, one that crowded up against his self-esteem, rubbing it the wrong way.

Oliver Graham was the type of man worthy of Sophie E. Clark. The guy was genuine, caring, rooted in the community, and clearly still receptive to finding new happiness despite his past loss. And more than anything, he appeared to be an open book. A guy with no big secrets hidden in the basement just waiting to blow up Sophie's life.

Stone should encourage Sophie not to feature Oliver but pursue him instead. That would be good for her and good for Stone. He couldn't accidentally fall in love with a woman mooning over another right under his nose night after night.

After their tour of the bookstore, Oliver led them to his office, a small but inviting space filled with personal touches: photographs of his wife, a shelf of first editions, and a large window that looked out over the bustling street. He gestured for Sophie and Stone to take a seat across from his desk, which was neatly organized except for a stack of children's books slated for the next community reading hour.

Sophie opened her notebook, her professional demeanor slipping into place as she prepared to go through her list of questions. The same ones she'd asked Stone this morning.

"Oliver, I have a set of questions I will ask everyone I feature in the column. They will help readers to get a better sense of who you really are beyond just what I observe."

Oliver nodded, a hint of amusement in his eyes. "I'm unreserved. Ask away."

Sophie pulled a pen from her purse. "First question: What does a perfect day look like for you?"

Oliver leaned back, his gaze thoughtful. "A perfect day starts with opening the shop early, maybe finding a moment to read a chapter or two of whatever book I'm into at the moment. Then, I'd spend the day interacting with customers, helping them find books they'll love. In the evening, I'd close and head to one of the local community centers where I volunteer, maybe help with an art class, or organize a book donation. Finally, I'd end the day at home, cooking a nice meal and unwinding with some jazz music."

Sophie sighed appreciatively. "That sounds wonderful. Next question: What do you value most in a relationship?"

Oliver's answer was immediate, his voice warm and sincere. "Honesty and compassion. I believe a relationship should be built on a foundation of trust, where both people feel safe to share their true selves without judgment. I'm not big on getting to know someone only to find out months later they have a huge secret they didn't bother sharing. If you have a secret, I want to know it. I won't tell anyone, but I want the right to know up front if I should give you my heart or not. Some secrets are deal-breakers, and that's why people keep them a secret." He trailed off, and he gave a sheepish grin. "Sorry. I'll get off my soapbox."

Stone shifted uncomfortably in his chair, his gaze fixed on Oliver. It was like the guy knew Stone had a secret he'd not yet shared and was passing judgment on Stone while trying to warn Sophie.

Damn. Was Oliver right? Should he tell Sophie? Of course he shouldn't. They weren't really an item. But if they were...

"And what's one thing you're passionate about?" Sophie asked.

"I'm passionate about giving back," Oliver responded. "Whether it's through the bookstore or my work with local charities, I feel it's important to contribute positively to the community that has given me so much. It's my way of keeping my late wife's spirit alive; she was deeply committed to volunteering."

Stone made a mental note to discover how Oliver's wife had died.

Sophie nodded, visibly moved. "That's admirable. Last question: Describe your ideal partner."

Oliver paused, considering his words carefully. "My ideal partner would be someone kind-hearted and supportive, someone who shares a passion for making a difference and values quiet evenings as much as lively gatherings. Someone who understands the joy of a good book and the simple pleasure of a cup of coffee shared in good company."

As he spoke, Sophie leaned in as if totally caught up in his words.

Stone watched the exchange, a knot forming in his stomach. Oliver's answers weren't just hero-worthy—they were a direct echo of Sophie's own values and desires.

The interview concluded with Oliver's gracious thanks and an invitation to return anytime.

As they stepped out of Oliver's bookstore, Stone glanced down at his T-shirt emblazoned with *To Be Continued*. A counterpart to her own that said *Chapter One*. He found himself not resenting the implication that he was a part of her forward journey. Not today. The sense of belonging, even if it was just a façade crafted for the sake of their undercover act, felt surprisingly comfortable. Like an extra blanket on a cold stakeout, wrapped around his carefully guarded heart, making him wish it could be real.

As they walked, Stone caught his reflection in a shop window. The cardigan and tee ensemble he wore was supposed to mimic Oliver's style, a part of the whole *boyfriend* image Sophie wanted to project. He eyed his image critically.

Oliver, with his genuine warmth and effortless charm, had worn the look naturally, embodying the role with grace. Oliver didn't just wear the clothes; he seemed to live them, weaving each thread with the same care he extended to everyone around him.

Stone, on the other hand, wore the outfit simply because Sophie wished it, the fabric feeling more like a costume than a second skin. He was a fraud. A battle-weary knight awkwardly disguised as a poet, trying to fit into her world.

Sophie deserved a guy like Oliver, a man whose life wasn't as shadowed and complicated as his. A man who didn't have secrets that could potentially be nonstarters. A man she could kiss goodbye to go to work and feel quite confident he'd return...unharmed.

Stone's gaze shifted to Sophie, who was animatedly discussing Oliver's answers to her questions. He watched her, admiring her energy. She was so fiercely dedicated to her quest for the perfect story, the perfect hero, yet oblivious to the complexities she wove into his life with each step they took.

In her *Chapter One* T-shirt, she seemed ready to begin a new venture. As the man currently wearing *To Be Continued* on his chest, he couldn't help but wonder just how the in-between chapters would unfold. Was he a subplot, and it was Oliver who would become the central thread in the tapestry of her life? Or was Oliver nothing more than a complication they would overcome?

Later, as they sat at a small café table, surrounded by the quiet hum of conversations, Stone decided it was time to test the waters.

"Sophie," he began, while she was still scribbling down notes, "have you ever thought that maybe some stories are meant to be lived, not just written about?"

Sophie looked up, her expression curious. "What do you mean?"

"I mean Oliver," Stone forced himself to say. "He's exactly the kind of man you describe wanting. But if you put him out there as this ideal book boyfriend, you're opening his world to every other single woman in Manhattan. Why not keep him for yourself and find another to share with the masses?"

Once, when he'd been very young, Clarabelle had taken him and his brothers to church. The preacher had spoken about birds, and how if you loved them, you let them go. If they never came back, they were never yours to begin with. This was him letting Sophie go. Pushing her toward a guy worthy to be called a book boyfriend hero.

Sophie paused, her pen hovering over her notebook. "That reminds me, I forgot to ask him if he would be willing to participate in the bachelor auction should he be chosen for one of my columns."

"All the more reason not to choose him for a feature," Stone pushed.

Sophie's brow furrowed. "Well, he is awfully yummy. But what if I didn't choose him and then he didn't even ask me out on a date? What a waste that would be."

"But what if he did, and you hit it off, and you found your fairytale ending?"

"Hmm," she replied, obviously chewing on the thought.

Stone watched her face as she imagined a life with Oliver. "He is everything you want in a man...right?"

"Maybe," she said, surprising him with her indecision. "Maybe not."

His hands fisted in frustration. "What do you mean not? I thought you knew what you wanted."

"I did. I do." She sighed as if he'd just asked her to explain quantum physics. "I don't know. It's complex."

Her sudden uncertainty rubbed him the wrong way. Now was not the time for her to be hesitant. "And yet you've insisted I look the part of your idea of the perfect man. As in, you knew what you wanted in a guy, and you demanded your way or the highway."

"I am not a demander. I am a suggestion-er. And no offense, but you've not mastered the ways of a cinnamon roll."

"Says who? I've seen myself in a mirror."

"Sure, you've got the clothes, but not the right attitude, or the easy-going body language, nor the low-key energy. You are way more a wrong-side-of-the-tracks guy than a cinnamon roll."

"Considering I'm a brat abandoned at a fire station—because my birth mom decided three boys were too much trouble to raise—and then trapped in the foster system for five years, there's no big surprise in that revelation."

A slow smile tugged her lips, confusing the hell out of him.

"What?" He'd said nothing that would make a normal person smile.

"Sorry. Your story is tragic."

"Then why the smile?"

She wrinkled her nose. "Did I ever tell you, Stone Blackthorn, in my fantasies—my naughty ones—I like my guys with a tragic backstory?"

He clamped down on his back molars to keep from speaking. Women. They were as unpredictable as his current magic situation.

Chapter 20

One week later, a week in which Stone had started acting uber-professional toward Sophie, she sat at the corner bar down the street from her apartment with Donna.

"Thanks for meeting me at the last minute," Sophie said, her voice betraying some of her turmoil.

Stone sat at a table across the room, scanning the surroundings with professional vigilance and occasionally staring at her. She knew this because every time she checked on him, their gazes met.

On the one hand, she was reassured knowing he took his job so seriously. On the other, it was a bit much. Her apartment had become a fortress. She now had a front door camera. This allowed her to, via an app on her phone, look to see who was there without placing her body in front of the door to check the peephole.

Also, the front door now possessed a triple lock system, and the patio doors were double locked with a bully stick in the sliders. Her place had a state-of-the-art alarm, and Poppie's place had been outfitted the same way.

"Tell me what's going on and don't leave out any of the details," Donna said.

"I'm in a real reading slump," Sophie confessed. "Ever since I started hunting for real-life boyfriends for the column, my usual reads just don't captivate me anymore. It's like I can't dive into any story."

"Maybe you should try a different genre for a while."

"Like what?"

"A thriller, maybe? Something edgy and intense to shake things up," Donna suggested, her eyes lighting up with the idea. "It could be a refreshing change from the usual romance and might just jolt your system."

"Hmm. That's a great idea," Sophie mused. "And maybe I could rope Stone into reading it, too. It might give us something more substantial to talk about during our mostly silent meals."

"I take it things are still strained?" Donna asked.

"I miss our fun, flirtatious conversations. Lately, he's been determined to keep me at arm's length. He even tried to get me to ask one of my interviewees out on a date instead of featuring the candidate in a column."

"Interesting."

"Maybe from where you sit. From where I sit, it's annoying."

Donna leaned forward, placed her elbows on the table, and cupped her chin in her hands. "What happened right before this switch in him? Can you pinpoint the moment he went quiet?"

Sophie thought. "It was right after I confessed to him that my preferred fantasy trope guy is a guy like him."

"The plot thickens," Donna said.

"How?" Sophie asked.

"He's showing signs of a guy who is scared and is in retreat mode."

"If he's afraid of anything, it's that I'm going to fall in love with him, and he doesn't want to have to deal with that."

"If that's the case, the guy's an idiot. You'd be the best thing that ever happened to him." Donna glanced Stone's way and waved.

He jerked his chin upward in response.

Sophie's phone vibrated against the wooden bar. She swiftly answered the unknown number. "Hello. This is Sophie E. Clark. May I ask who's calling?" She hoped it was one of the prospective book boyfriends, ready to confirm an interview. Another step forward in her quest.

Silence greeted her. "Hello. Can you hear me?" Sophie repeated, frustration creeping into her voice. The lack of response was annoying, given her tight schedule.

Nothing.

She glanced down, the screen dark and unresponsive. "Must have hit the *off* button by mistake," she muttered, though a niggle of doubt lingered—had she charged it last night? Shrugging the whole thing off, she refocused on Donna. "Sorry about that. Now, where were we?"

"You're going to change your reading habits so you can find common ground with a guy who has changed the way he dresses to please you but doesn't like you in a boyfriend way."

"His new wardrobe was necessary for him to fit in during my interviews. It has nothing to do with him secretly trying to impress me, if that's what you're implying."

"If you say so."

"I do."

Donna leaned in. "Speaking of fitting in, do you have candidates for all your boyfriend tropes? More specifically, do you have one on board who is willing to spill his secret to the woman who buys him at auction?"

Sophie groaned. "I'm still in search of that unicorn. I didn't really think it through when I added it as one of my boyfriend tropes. Real guys don't just give up their secrets for a good cause. But it's too late to unring that boyfriend-trope bell, so I'm searching high and low for one."

"What's your backup if he doesn't materialize?" Donna asked. "What trope will you use instead?"

"Backup plans imply doubt," Sophie replied. "I refuse to harbor that stuff. I'll find him, you just watch." Her confidence was as much a shield as it was a spur driving her forward against the odds. Just as those who'd doubted her ability to make a living daydreaming had spurred her into proving them wrong.

Sophie's phone buzzed again, breaking her train of thought. She grabbed it, hoping for a connection this time. "Hello, you're speaking with Sophie E. Clark. To whom am I speaking?"

There was a brief silence, then nothing. Frustrated, Sophie tapped her phone, checking the signal. Dead again. "My off button must be trigger-happy." A flush of irritation, joy riding right beneath her skin, made the room seem suddenly hot. She pulled at her shirt collar for air. "They'll call back if it's important. Now, where were we?" She resisted an urge to glance Stone's way.

Donna tilted her head thoughtfully. "We were discussing the idea of you stepping outside your comfort zone with a thriller."

"I have always been a bit intrigued with the genre. I mean, what's not to love about a category that inspires James Bond-like characters?"

"It's interesting you should say that," Donna said. "I can't help but wonder if maybe, just maybe, there's a deeper lesson here."

"Lesson?"

"Perhaps the unexpected—like Stone—could end up being what you really need, not just in your reading choices but in life."

Sophie blinked, taken aback by Donna's insight. She swirled the ice in her drink, considering. "You mean to suggest that someone as different as Stone might actually be good for me other than as a one-night stand?"

"Yes, exactly." Donna's voice rose with enthusiasm. "Think about it. Stone might be from a different world, but he's shown dedication, he adapts quickly, and clearly, he cares about your safety. Aren't those qualities valuable?"

Sophie chewed on her bottom lip, her gaze drifting toward Stone. He was now quietly speaking with the waiter, likely about security logistics, but his posture was relaxed, and there was a gentleness to his demeanor that she hadn't noticed before. "Maybe," she conceded softly to Donna, "but it's not like he's interested in the things I am. Our worlds barely connect. Heck, he goes out of the way to make sure we never touch."

"Sophie, maybe it's not about shared hobbies or even similar pasts. Maybe it's about balance, about what you can learn from each other," Donna argued gently, reaching out to touch Sophie's hand. "You're always writing about these ideal traits in your columns, but real relationships—those are built on complementing each other, not mirroring."

The idea settled over Sophie like a soft shadow, intriguing yet intimidating. "I suppose you have a point. But how do I even begin to explore that? It's not like I can just start treating him as a potential...anything. He's here for a job."

"Well..." Donna grinned before sipping her drink. "Maybe start small. Share that thriller with him. See how he reacts, not just to the genre shift but to the idea of the two of you sharing something he's interested in."

Sophie considered this, her mind racing with possibilities. The last time she'd tried to test the waters with him by asking him to meet for dinner, he'd shut her down hard. What if he did that again? The alternative was to continue to endure silent dinners with him. "I'll think about it. It would be nice to once again discuss something deeper than our next meal."

As they wrapped up their drinks, Sophie's phone rang once more. Instead of raising it to her ear, she pushed the button to put the call on speaker. No way would she risk hanging up on whoever it was a third time. "Hello."

"Is this Sophie?" a female voice asked.

"It is. And you are?"

"It doesn't matter. I'm calling to tell you to stay away from Oliver."

The line went dead.

"That was rude," Sophie said, frowning.

Donna nodded. "Really rude. Do you think it's a jealous girlfriend he failed to mention?"

Sophie peeked at Stone, who happened to be glancing at them, his brow knitted as if he instinctively knew something unsettling had just happened. She gave him a small shake of her head so he wouldn't come over.

He ignored her body language and approached. "Everything okay?"

"Not really," Donna answered. "Some weird chick just called Sophie and told her to stay the hell away from Oliver."

"Give me your phone," Stone said in a tone just barely above freezing.

"This is not necessary," Sophie said, as she handed it over.

"I'll be the judge of that." He held her phone up to her face to unlock.

"I'm telling you, it's no big deal. Some girl likes Oliver and doesn't want him featured."

"Considering you've been threatened, I can't ignore anything out of the usual." He pushed a call button on his own phone. "Hey, Montgomery, I need you to trace a number."

"Listen, hon, I've got an early morning tomorrow. I better scoot," Donna said. "Give me a call tomorrow and let me know what Oliver has to say about this new development."

"You've got it. Thanks for hanging out. I needed the girl time."

"Remember what we talked about," Donna said. "I can't wait to see how that plays out." She winked at Sophie and then sauntered away.

"Are you sure?" Stone was talking into the phone.

Sophie finished her drink while she waited for Stone to hang up.

When he did, his scowl was in full force. "The phone was a burner. Jealous girlfriends don't usually go so far as to buy a burner phone to make a threat."

"Sometimes they do."

"Most of the time they don't." Stone caught the attention of the bartender. "Check, please."

Chapter 21

Stone waited until Sophie was asleep before pulling out his laptop and digging into Oliver's background. The dim light from the screen cast shadows in the living room, mirroring the unease in his heart. It didn't take much effort to discover that Oliver had recently been on a couple of dates with a supermodel during fashion week.

Other than that, his profile was low. He'd lost his wife and unborn child due to pregnancy complications three years ago. Stone's fingers paused over the keyboard, a pang of unexpected sympathy piercing through his professional detachment. He could only imagine the weight of that kind of loss, the void that would never fully close. Was that why Oliver was open to the adventure Sophie had tossed his way? Had he come out of his tragedy with a lesson learned—one that proved life was fleeting, and a person should embrace the now instead of waiting for the later? The same lesson Sophie had learned from the loss of her parents?

In complete contrast, Stone had taken a stab at love once, had been burned, and shut his heart down forever.

Which of them had the right approach?

He continued reading.

Oliver had inherited the bookstore from his grandfather. He was an only child. He volunteered in a half-dozen organizations, one of which was where he and the supermodel had met. Stone rubbed his jawline. As much as he wanted to dislike Oliver, he couldn't ignore the man's dedication to others, the genuine goodness that seemed to flow through every aspect of his life.

Stone leaned back and ran a hand through his hair. His emotions were a tangled mess of jealousy, admiration, and a strange sense of begrudging respect. The man he wanted to see as a rival was becoming increasingly complex, challenging the simple narrative Stone had constructed of cinnamon roll heroes to keep his own feelings in check.

Finding nothing alarming, he shifted his focus to the model. That's where things got interesting. She had no prior arrests, but her name appeared in some posts accusing her of bullying the girlfriends of her male friends if she didn't feel like they were good enough. If she'd felt the need to bully Sophie, did that mean Oliver had confessed to the supermodel he was interested in Sophie? And the woman had deemed Sophie not good enough?

In what world would Sophie be not good enough for any man? She was kind-hearted, optimistic, intelligent, and a hard worker. Cuter than any woman he'd ever known. And sexy as hell.

Stone's jaw tightened. He sent the information to his brothers, demanding they dig deeper. No way was he letting some pretentious model dim Sophie's brilliance. He was about to call it a night when his phone chirped. Clarabelle wanted to Facetime.

He accepted the call. "Hi, everything okay? It's late for you." He quietly let himself out onto the balcony, careful not to wake Sophie. The cool night air did little to soothe the fire in his chest, but seeing Clarabelle's face brought a semblance of calm.

"Sorry. Couldn't be helped. I've just gotten back from a meeting with the Grand High Enchanter of Fairy Affairs, Lady Seraphina, and I have fabulous news."

"The who?" Stone frowned.

"The Grand High Enchanter of Fairy Affairs."

"I've never heard you mention this person or this position in the Fairy Godmother organization."

"That's because Lady Seraphina took a ten-year leave of absence. But she's back, and she summoned me to her chambers."

He shrugged. Who was he to question the ways of the Fairy Godmother world? "Why were you summoned?"

"Zuberi, the wizard we sent your broken wand to, reported the incident to her. They are apparently lovers and are into kink."

Stone closed his eyes. Nope. He wasn't touching that one. "And why would Lady Seraphina care about my broken wand?"

Clarabelle tittered. "Because that's part of her job duties."

"And they are?"

"There are lots, but the one I'm calling about is she manages magical resources. And the news that yours was broken due to a bullet alarmed her. So, she sent for me, since I'm the one who trained you in the proper maintenance and protection of your wand."

"Did you get reprimanded because of my momentary lack of concentration?"

"That's not the point. The point is, after I explained what happened, I then proceeded to share with her the glitches you've been having with your magic, and how Sophie appears to make them worse. And then, I told her of my theory that she may be magical and that your magic from your wand is now inside of you and you don't want to fall in love and... Well, that about sums it up."

"Mom, what did she say? Have you been instructed to retrieve my wand and strip me of my title?"

"On the contrary, she gave me a spell to use on you. It will temporarily resolve your glitching. Actually, it will permanently resolve the matter unless..."

"Unless what?"

"Unless the two of you are meant to be."

"Why would it have that caveat?" Stone asked, sensing Clarabelle wasn't telling him everything.

"Because I asked her to."

He sighed. "I'd ask why, but I know why." He shook his head, trying to push down the conflicting emotions swirling inside him. "Go ahead, cast the spell. We'll let the hearts fall where they fall." The words slipped out easily. As if his heart had taken control and made a demand decision without bothering to confer with his brain.

He opened his mouth to retract but shut it. What if Sophie was the person he *was* meant to be with? Did he really want to turn his back on all that implied? Out of fear? Without exploring options? If a damn cinnamon roll hero could be brave enough to search for love after a loss, couldn't Stone at least be brave enough to keep his options open?

"That's my boy. I knew I hadn't raised a man afraid to feel. You'll see. Everything will turn out in a way that will be perfect."

Stone glanced back toward the house, where Sophie slept peacefully. Despite his reluctance to admit it, the thought of her had a way of sneaking into his decisions, making him wonder what it would be like to let his guard down, even just a little.

Chapter 22

The next evening, Stone pushed open the door of Graham's Corner with a sense of unease that had little to do with the mission—discovering if Oliver had a jealous girlfriend other than the supermodel—and everything to do with the magic that ran just beneath his skin. Something about the spell Clarabelle had cast upon him last night had him on full alert. Colors were brighter. Sounds were clearer. Sophie was...well...Sophie-er.

He took a step back. "After you," he said to Sophie.

"Why thank you," she quipped with a cute curtsy.

All the way over to the bookshop, he'd been careful not to make physical contact with Sophie. But once they were back at her place, he planned to touch her and see if the spell had worked. Until then, he just had to be careful.

"Sophie, Stone, great to see you both again." Oliver's warm greeting pulled Stone from his thoughts. "What has you dropping by? Are you in search of a book?"

"Actually, I am," Sophie said. "I've decided to read a thriller. Do you have any you recommend?"

Stone's gaze swung to Sophie, who was smiling brightly at Oliver. A pang of something—jealousy or concern?—fluttered in his chest. Ever since she'd told him of her fantasy man, he'd been off kilter. Despite his decision last night to let the heart fall where the heart fell, he'd decided that until this assignment was over, he would keep his emotions sealed off. This was a mission, and she was his assignment. He'd complete the mission.

"Which kind of thriller are you looking for?" Oliver asked.

Stone resisted an urge to remind her he read thrillers. Had she forgotten? He'd not forgotten a detail she'd ever shared with him about herself.

Sophie laughed. "I have no idea. This is one of those decisions I made while drinking with my best friend a couple of nights ago." She fluttered her lashes at him. "I shall have to throw myself on your mercy. What do you suggest?"

Stone glanced closer at Sophie. Was this her way of testing Oliver to see if he'd break and say he had a girlfriend? Or was she honest-to-goodness flirting with him?

"That's hard to say without knowing you a little better. You see there are historical thrillers, legal thrillers, medical thrillers, military thrillers, psychological thrillers, supernatural—"

"Darling, I know you're a little forgetful," Stone interrupted. "But I do read the genre. You could have just asked me for my suggestions. After all, as your boyfriend, I think I know your taste."

Sophie grinned. "And that's why I need more than one cup of coffee every day. Without my morning caffeine, my noon brain crashes harder than a hero in a romance novel realizing he's in love with the heroine."

Stone chuckled despite himself.

She gave him an impish look. "Stone, darling, which novel do you choose for me to burst my thriller cherry?"

Oliver coughed, his face going red. "Um. I think I'll leave you two to your search. When you're done, if you like, I'm hosting an afternoon of literary games. Feel free to stay and join us."

"That sounds like loads of fun." Sophie surprised Stone by tucking her hand into his elbow.

He immediately tensed, but she didn't appear to notice. Her touch was warm and disarming. And this time, there were no glitches. The spell had worked. Did that mean the magic didn't want them together, and so now it was up to him to make the decision unencumbered by forces outside of his control? If so, that was a good thing... right?

"Can we stay?" she asked, looking up at him. "Please?"

He managed a nod, though his mind raced. "Actually, it does sound interesting," Stone replied, recalling the real reason they'd dropped by. He glanced at Oliver. "Will your girlfriend be joining us?"

Oliver gave him a small frown. "I don't have a girlfriend. Isn't that why Sophie interviewed me for her column?"

"My bad. Sorry," Stone said, choosing not to mention the phone call. "It seems I've not had enough caffeine either." Until he knew more, he wouldn't tip his hand.

"Let's go get my thrills on," Sophie said to Stone, pulling him toward an aisle of books.

Once they were out of earshot of Oliver, she dropped her hand away and blew out a grumpy breath. "You see. He's single. The call was a crank. Don't you dare say one more thing to him that might make him back out. I mean he's so freaking perfect for the cinnamon roll hero. I'll not find a better one. I bet he gets the highest bid at auction."

"The sweet guys are that popular, are they?" Stone mused.

"They are," she said, full of sincerity.

He scratched his head. "All I know to say to that is...you haven't met the right un-nice guy. Let's go find you a book that will introduce you to a different type of man than you're used to reading about."

Twenty minutes later, they'd chosen three for her to read: a psychological thriller, a domestic thriller, and a supernatural thriller.

"You promised you've not read any of these?" Sophie asked. "I want to read them with you at the same time."

"I haven't. That's why we have two of each book. Now, shall we join in on the fun and games? We can scout out the crowd and see if there are any stalkerish women hanging around Oliver that he's blissfully unaware of."

"Oh yeah. Weird. I keep forgetting about that call." She laughed. "There's something about you that makes me a tiny bit more scattered than usual."

"Same," he said honestly.

As guests started trickling in, filling the bookstore with a buzz of anticipation, Stone stood in the corner and observed while Sophie got drawn into the preparations, helping Oliver arrange chairs and hand out game materials. He couldn't help but admire her energy and enthusiasm, even as he kept a watchful eye on the crowd, ready to step in if anything seemed off.

Sophie caught his eye across the room and waved him over. "Come on, Stone. You're on my team."

For a moment, Stone allowed himself to be pulled into the spirit of the event, his usual reservations fading slightly in the glow of Sophie's enthusiasm. As they joined a group of laughing participants, Stone felt the edges of his world expand—a bit of magic that had nothing to do with spells or fairy godfathers, but everything to do with the unpredictable joy of human connection.

He wondered if, when this was over, he really could let himself experience the fall.

LISA WELLS

Chapter 23

Sophie fumbled with her keys, giggling at her own clumsiness as the world swayed just a bit too much. It was well past midnight by the time they had returned to her apartment, fresh from the buzz of the book party and a spontaneous trip to the nearby bar. Though she had indulged a little more than she should have, Stone remained ever professional, clear-eyed, and alert.

"Thanks," she said as Stone unlocked the door and stepped inside to flick on the light, casting a warm glow into the otherwise dark apartment. She teetered in after him, leaning slightly to one side.

"For what?" Stone turned to face her with a bemused expression.

"For all the thingies you've added that make mine and Poppie's apartments safer. And for being my pretend book boyfriend tonight. And for wearing my T-shirts." She slurred slightly, her words tumbling out in a rush. "I sold a gazillion at the party."

He raised his brows, his surprise evident. "You did? When?"

"All those women whispering at me while you were chatting with the guys. They wanted to know about your shirt, and one thing led to another..." Sophie swayed as she spoke, animated despite her tipsiness. "Next thing I knew, I'd given out all my business cards, and my phone blew up with messages saying I'd just made a sale."

"I'm happy for you," Stone said, his voice warm and not even a little slurred. He had managed the evening without overindulging, his professionalism unyielding. "Believe it or not, some of the guys even asked me about it. They thought wearing one of your creations to a bar would be a great conversation starter with women. They might be on to something."

Sophie giggled, a sound that filled the small entryway. "What? Are you going to buy some for when you're no longer my book boyfriend, in the hopes they'll help you with your pickup game?"

"Now, you're just putting words in my mouth." He chuckled, leading her through the doorway and locking the door behind them. "But, just for kicks, what is your website where you sell them? I should probably check it out...for security reasons."

She giggled. She seemed to be doing a lot of giggling. "I bet you can't guess."

He nodded. "I bet I can't either."

"Find Your Book Boyfriend Dot Com."

"Yep. That wasn't ever going to be my guess." Stone said, his lips twitching.

The sound of a knock caused Sophie to jump. She swirled around, opened the app on her phone, and saw Poppie, his usual mischievous grin in place.

Unlocking the door, she greeted him with a warm smile. "Poppie. What are you doing up so late?"

"I was watching *Die Hard* reruns and heard a bunch of high-pitched giggling. Reminded me of when you were young. I couldn't resist checking in on my favorite girl," Poppie said as he stepped inside, his eyes twinkling. He looked over at Stone and nodded in approval. "Seems like you're good for my girl. I can't recall the last time I heard her laugh like the days of her youth. Back before she had things to worry about. What all have you young'uns been doing?"

Sophie led Poppie into the living room. "We just came back from a book event that spilled over into a bar event."

She glanced at Stone, who gave her the most uncomplicated smile she'd ever gotten out of him. It was as if in this very moment, he'd let every last one of his guards down and was allowing her to see him for who he really was.

"You know what, Poppie, you might be right." She winked at Stone before turning to her grandfather. "I do feel a little less stressed having Stone in my life. It's like he's taken on all my demons so I can just enjoy this current journey of being a professional daydreamer."

"I think you might have found a good one this time, Sophie," he said, walking in and settling into an armchair.

As if in agreement, Sophie and Stone took a seat on the couch.

Poppie's gaze flitted between them. "Stone, did Sophie ever tell you about that time her no-good ex-boyfriend reported me as a danger to myself?"

"You've got to be fucking kidding me," Stone said. "What kind of assholes have you dated?"

"Poppie, maybe tonight isn't a good time to regale Stone with all of my past mistakes," Sophie said.

"Nonsense. You two live together and all—it's time he gets to hear some of the bad with the good." Poppie tapped his chin. "It happened when my Sophie had gone out of town on a girl's trip with the other officers in that book club she's so fond of. What's it called again?"

"Book Boyfriend Connoisseurs Club," Sophie replied.

"Right. Right. Anyway, unbeknownst to me, she asked that boyfriend to stay at her place, under the pretext she was expecting a delivery she didn't want to miss, but it was really so he could keep an eye on me. She thinks just because I'm old, it means I'm feeble."

"Not feeble, just health impaired," Sophie said. "It was right after you had that spell, and I was worried. I had no idea that asshole would do what he did."

Poppie waved a dismissive hand. "Ah, I know your heart was in the right place." He refocused on Stone. "There I was, taken away for a seventy-two-hour observation because I defended Sophie's honor with a slingshot."

"Her honor?" Stone asked. "Did I temporarily fall asleep and miss part of the story?"

Poppie glanced at him blankly. "How the blazes should I know if you snoozed?"

Sophie laid a hand on Stone's arm. "I think the part you fell asleep on is the part where my ex tried to sneak another woman into my apartment, and Poppie caught him." Poppie used to be the best storyteller ever, but lately, he skipped parts without realizing what he'd done.

"Now stay awake because the next part is what Sophie likes to call the black moment of this story."

"I'm listening," Stone said.

"That damn idiot called the cops. They locked me up in a damn hospital for seventy-two hours because they thought I was a danger to myself and others, and Sophie didn't have cell service, so they had no one to release me to."

"You're kidding," Stone said.

"The only one I was a danger to was that fool who laughed at me when I aimed my slingshot at him. That rock hit him between the eyes, it did."

"Good for you," Stone said. "Sounds like someone needs to have a chat with that young man."

"Nah. He's not worth going to jail over," Poppie said. "Besides, Sophie hasn't given me specifics, but she assures me she took care of the matter in her own way." He winked at Sophie.

Sophie smiled, though the memory brought back a rush of protective feelings. "Of course I did. No one messes with my Poppie."

Poppie's eyes filled with an unspoken gratitude that warmed Sophie's heart.

"How about we change the subject to something not such a buzzkill?" Sophie said.

"I'll do you one better," Poppie said. "I'll get out of here and let you young folks get back to your evening. Don't stay up too late, Sophie."

After seeing Poppie out, Sophie turned to Stone with a grin. "Sorry about that. He does love to tell a story. He's just not quite as adept at it as he used to be because his memory comes and goes. When I was little, he would read me bedtime stories. In fact, it was him who bought me my first Junie B. Jones book." The memory filled her with a warm, nostalgic comfort.

Stone nodded. "Tell me more about how you took care of the idiot you dated."

"Oh God. He's in the past, and that's where he's going to stay." She jumped up and walked to the table where she'd dropped the bag containing their new books. "How about we decide which one of these we want to read first?"

Sophie playfully tossed the books onto the couch next to Stone and to their surprise, a loud crack sounded as one of the couch legs buckled under the weight. Sophie burst into laughter, almost doubling over when Stone went sideways with the couch and ended up cattywampus, the books on top of him. The vase full of fresh flowers on the end table tumbled, spilling water onto his bedding, rolled up and tucked next to the couch.

"You think this is funny, do you?" he said, a grin on his face as he struggled to stand.

She giggled one more time. "Ever since you came into my life, weird stuff has been happening non-stop."

"I have no idea what you mean," he said, glancing away from her and gathering the books.

"Don't tell me you haven't noticed."

Still not looking at her, he responded, "Noticed what?"

"Glitchy lighting, thunder with no clouds, downpours on sunny days, and now a couch that can't handle a few books?" Another fit of giggles swept through her.

Stone joined in the laughter, his eyes not quite crinkling at the corners. "Seems I'm a bit of a jinx."

Sophie, still snickering, nodded toward her bedroom. "Well, looks like we're going to have to share my bed. Strictly platonic, of course. There's no way I'm letting you sleep on wet blankets on the floor."

"They'll dry. I'll be fine"

"I won't sleep a wink wondering if they've dried yet. I've *barely* been sleeping a wink knowing you get up off the couch and make your bed on the floor every night after I retire to my bedroom."

"There's no need—"

"Stone, you're not going to win this argument. I promise I'm not after your honor."

"What makes you so sure I won't be after yours?" Stone asked.

"I'll build a wall of pillows between us. They will thwart all your non-cinnamon-roll-boyfriend-like ideas."

"Is your bed even big enough for the two of us?" he asked, sounding not quite like himself.

"It's a full. We'll be fine."

He swallowed hard enough she saw his Adam's apple convulse. "Strictly platonic?"

Sophie offered up her pinky. "I pinky promise that I do not have any intentions other than platonic ones toward you."

Stone's nostrils flared before he linked pinkies with her. "Tonight only. Tomorrow, I'll buy you a new couch. One long enough I can sleep on it."

She had a sudden desire to hug him but resisted. Instead, she settled with words she hoped were the equivalent of a big teddy bear hug. "Thanks for being here, Stone. It means a lot."

"Anytime, Sophie," came his soft reply, the night wrapping around them.

Chapter 24

Stone knew he wouldn't sleep next to Sophie in a bed barely big enough for one of them let alone two and a slew of pillows. Nevertheless, he played along. Arguing with a slightly tipsy Sophie wasn't a battle he wished to win tonight. Besides, this would be the perfect test for Clarabelle's spell. A spell he doubted had completely taken hold considering the broken couch. Either that... or... Well, he'd think about the *or* tomorrow.

While Sophie had disappeared into the bathroom to brush her teeth, he had changed into a pair of sweats and a T-shirt. One of his own, not one of hers. When the bathroom door creaked open, he couldn't help but glance over. Sophie stood framed in the doorway, the light casting her in a soft glow, clad in pink pajama bottoms and a matching T-shirt that read: *Dreaming of My Book Boyfriend.*

"Bathroom's all yours," she offered, her voice cheerful as she slipped under the covers.

"Wrong side. You'll need to sleep over there." He pointed to the other side of the pillows, heading toward the bathroom.

"But this is the side I always sleep on," she protested with a hint of pout in her voice.

"Yes, but it's the closest to the door. You'll be the first target if someone bursts in here with guns blazing...unless you're quick enough to grab your own and fire back," he reasoned, half-jokingly.

She huffed. "Fine, but I'll have to read to fall asleep on that side of the bed."

"Not a problem. Why don't we both start one of the thrillers we picked out?"

By the time he returned, Sophie was propped up on pillows, the covers pulled up under her armpits, a book lying next to her, and another on his pillow.

He crawled in beside her, the bed dipping as he did, but thankfully not breaking. He glanced at the title of the book she'd chosen. It was a paranormal thriller. "Good choice."

"Want to take turns reading out loud?"

"Sure," he replied, not hating the idea.

Sophie flipped the book to the first page and began reading. Her voice was light and airy.

After a few pages, she paused. "Do you believe in paranormal things?"

Stone's eyes, previously closed as he listened, snapped them open. The book raised for reading prevented him from seeing her expression. Was she serious or just playful? He took a moment, choosing his words with care. "I think there's a lot we don't understand about the world. What about you?" he asked, shifting slightly to face her more directly.

She plucked away one of the pillows between them and rolled onto her side, meeting his gaze earnestly. "Honestly, I think Mom and Dad visit me sometimes. More so when I was little, but now and then, I see a flash of light when it's dark, and I feel like it's them, just checking in on me."

"Are they here now?" Stone asked, his tone gentle, not wanting to dismiss her beliefs.

She shook her head slightly. "If they are, I don't feel them tonight. What about you? Ever felt like you had angels or ghosts or something watching over you?"

Stone hesitated. It would be the perfect moment to share his secret, but the timing wasn't right...not yet. None of the conditions were in place for him to spill. He and Sophie weren't a couple, and no one had said *I love you*, and he wasn't even sure if he could trust her. She had told him Ziggy's secret without a hint of remorse. And had mentioned she had a blurting problem. "It's getting late, and tomorrow you have three interviews lined up. We should probably try to get some sleep."

Sophie wasn't having it. "No way, mister. I told you my deepest secret. You've got to give something back. That's how friendships work."

"Only, we're not exactly friends," he reminded her gently.

Sophie's brow furrowed. "Oh. I thought we were. Don't you like me?"

"I do, Sophie, but I'm here to protect you. Being friends—that can complicate things."

"In that case, I fire you. I'll let Ms. Birdie know first thing in the morning."

"You can't fire me. She'd think you're being impulsive. You don't want her to think that, do you?"

Sophie yawned, her playfulness fading as sleep beckoned. "Maybe not tonight. But, Stone, we're both adults. We can consent to a fling that doesn't have to be all tied up in your rules of conduct. Life is short. If you find someone that makes you happy, why not explore that happiness while it lasts? It's not like I'm ever going to forget you're a bachelor for life and fall in love with you. We could just have fun."

Her words made him sad. "I—"

"Don't say no. Just think about it. And in the morning, we can discuss it and another idea I have. Maybe one of my best ideas ever."

"Good night, princess," Stone said, smiling as Sophie drifted off to sleep.

He, on the other hand, did not sleep. He laid awake, contemplating the fine line he was walking—between his duty and the unexpected bond forming between them. How much more time could he spend around her without falling? And did he even want to keep from falling?

Chapter 25

Sophie awoke with the first lazy rays of sunlight filtering through the curtains, casting a warm glow across the room. As she blinked the sleep from her eyes, she realized the barriers of pillows they had set up the night before were gone. Instead, she found herself entwined with Stone, their bodies molded together in an unintentional embrace that felt surprisingly right.

She lay there for a moment, savoring the warmth and safety his presence offered, her mind replaying the vulnerable conversation they'd had before sleep had overtaken them. The memory of her half-serious suggestion about exploring happiness together lingered in her thoughts, mixed with the uncertainty of his silent response.

"Stone," she whispered, hesitant yet needing to know where he stood. He stirred next to her, his eyes slowly opening to meet hers.

"Good morning," he murmured, his voice rough with sleep.

Sophie took a deep breath, bolstered by the clarity that morning brought. "About last night—"

"I remember," Stone interrupted gently, his hand reaching up to tuck a curl behind her ear. "You suggested we reconsider the rules."

Sophie nodded; her gaze locked on his. "I did. And... I also mentioned another idea, something that might be one of my best ideas ever. But first, I need to know, after our talk, do you believe it's possible? For us to explore what this is?" Her voice was soft, her inside all vulnerable and exposed.

Stone's expression was thoughtful, his usual guarded demeanor tempered by the night's knocking down of walls. "Sophie, I—" He paused, his gaze dropping to where their hands were linked between them. "I like you. But I'm not the type of man you should want to get involved with. Oliver would be a much better choice."

Her heart tightened. "Why would you say that?" she pressed, needing to understand his hesitation.

"Because, ..." He sighed, his gaze meeting hers again, this time with an intensity that took her breath away. "People with lives like mine... We don't just get to have the fairytale. There's always a cost."

Sophie's resolve hardened; she wouldn't let him retreat. "Maybe the right man is someone who doesn't think he's right but is willing to try and figure out a path forward, for the right reasons."

Stone's face softened, the hint of a smile playing on his lips. "Even if I were the kind of guy who would do that, we've established that I'm not your type."

Her heart fluttered at his words, the possibility of *what could be* suddenly seeming within reach. "Not completely true. If you recall, I told you that in my fantasies you're exactly my type of man."

"And what book boyfriend trope do heroes with tragic backstory fall under?"

"Any of them."

"Why would a generic hero with no trope be your fantasy choice?"

Heat filled her cheeks, but she didn't shy away from responding truthfully. "Because heroes with tragic backstory are often excellent dirty talkers."

"What I hear you saying is you fantasize about men like me—not because we're perfect for you—but because in real life you've never had a man tell you, 'Get down on your knees and—'"

"I'm not going to apologize for what turns me on," she snapped.

"Nor should you. But the ability to talk dirty to a woman isn't something one builds a forever relationship upon. It's more of a torrid fling asset. Which I'm—"

"Can I kiss you?" she interrupted before he said something that ruined her mood. "You see, before I woke up, I had a dream that my mom was talking to me about how conflicted I am where you're concerned. And in my dream, she said I'd know you're the right guy if you bend your rules for me and for me alone. I figure a kiss is the biggest rule I can get you to bend right now."

Stone's smile turned tender, genuine. "We've already bent that rule, or did you forget?"

"Yes, but I want to bend it here, where no one is watching, and it's being bent for discovery purposes that I hold very dear. You'd be doing me a huge favor."

He groaned. "Has any man ever managed to tell you no while looking at you freshly awake after a night spent in your bed?"

"Nope," she said with as much assurance as she could manage considering he was the first she'd ever asked a special favor of.

"We haven't even brushed our teeth," he said.

She reached around and opened the top drawer of her bedside table and pulled out a pack of Listerine breath strips. She snapped open the container, pulled three out, handed them to him, and then plopped three in her mouth. "A professional daydreamer is always prepared," she quipped. "Now, can we kiss?"

"I can't see the harm in kissing you one more time... If it means that much to you."

"You're the best." She scrambled onto her knees and leaned across him, lowering her face until their lips touched. And before she could decide tongue or no tongue, he yanked her down and deepened the kiss.

Sparks and heat consumed her. Like her skin was alive with magic. She shuddered at the sensation.

There was tongue.

When she was certain her pulse couldn't beat any wilder, he growled against her mouth and fisted his hand in her hair. Who knew a girl's pulse could push into that gear?

The kiss exceeded even her wildest hopes. The fierce, desperate vibes of this might-be-our-last-so-let's-make-it-a-good-one were off the chart.

She was so lost in all the new sensations kissing him presented, she didn't notice he'd shifted until he was suddenly on top.

His lips left hers to drop soft kisses on her forehead, her eyelids, her cheeks.

"Stone, I—"

"Don't say it," he growled and captured her lips again, preventing her from speaking.

She arched into him, grinding against his erection.

He stilled, moved his lips to her ear and spoke. "Don't."

In that moment, Sophie's spinning brain told her two things. One, she felt safe in his arms. Two, she wanted them both naked. "But I want to," she practically whined.

Somewhere in a faraway place, a phone rang.

"Fuck," Stone said, causing her to startle.

Realizing the phone wasn't far away but instead was in her bedroom, she stilled. It rang again, and she realized it was Stone's. That's why he was cursing. "Don't answer," she pleaded.

He briefly dropped his forehead to hers and then reached for the noisemaker, keeping her firmly under him. "What?" he snapped.

There was a moment of silence, and then he swore. "Fucking hell." He disconnected from the call, and sat up, his breathing still heavy.

Sophie waited for him to say something. When he didn't, she asked, "Is everything okay?"

He glanced at her as if he'd forgotten she was even there and shook his head. "It was my brother, Ryder. They know who threatened you. I must go."

"Why not just let the police handle it?" Sophie asked, immediately worried. "You're injured. I thought you were benched from heavy security duty."

Her concern caused his already dark expression to grow darker. "This." He made an open-palmed gesture toward her. "This is why I'll never get married. You and I aren't even a couple, and you're stressed to the point of having red splotches all over your neck at the idea of my leaving to go and do my job."

She was amazed at the level of ugliness in his tone. One would have thought she'd just admitted to adultery or something. "Don't," she exclaimed, and then paused, noticing the weariness in his eyes. "Don't do that to me," she finished quietly.

"Do what to you?" he asked, looking genuinely puzzled.

"Shut me down for showing concern. I have news for you—you could be going across the street to pick up our hairless cat at the pet beauty parlor, and I'd be a little concerned that a piano might fall on you between here and there. It doesn't mean I want to shuck the whole idea of our exploring us...especially now that I'm assuming you'll no longer be shadowing me twenty-four hours a day."

He reached out and gently cupped her jaw. "Sophie, I'll never be book boyfriend material. Don't fantasize about a forever with us. Any exploration we might engage in will always have an expiration date."

She bit her lip and nodded. He wasn't saying anything he hadn't already said a thousand times. It wasn't his fault if her heart hadn't been listening. "We'll talk later. I'm sure you need to go." Maybe, just maybe, his heart hadn't been listening either.

What kind of professional daydreamer would she be if she didn't hope?

He grunted and glanced at his watch. "The guy's in another state. I'll be back tomorrow afternoon. Please promise me you'll cancel all your interviews for today."

Much to Sophie's relief, he didn't wait for her to make the promise.

Chapter 26

Sophie had prepared meticulously for today's interviews. Opting for a touch of nostalgia, she'd donned a retro ensemble: a T-shirt emblazoned with *Dreamer at Work*, paired with flared bell-bottom pants and chunky platform shoes. She figured the standout outfit would make her a memorable sight—enough so that any would-be kidnapper might think twice.

Despite Stone's explicit wishes that she refrain from conducting interviews during his absence, Sophie had ultimately discarded his request. Mainly because of his offhand remark, as he'd left her apartment, about possibly not returning soon. Who knew how long securing a replacement for him might take? Moreover, the excitement of uncovering new book-boyfriend possibilities was too enticing to postpone. Plus, she was on a deadline. Yes. That's the one she would lead with should he demand an explanation upon his return. Which he would because he was the broody sort who wouldn't appreciate his wishes being ignored.

Besides, it wasn't like any of today's interviews posed potential threats. They'd all been nominated by people who either worked at *Naked Runway* or were known by someone who worked there.

Now she sat in the reception area of a funky start-up company, waiting to meet a guy who mirrored the hero from Claire Kingsley's novel, *Falling for My Enemy.*

"Mr. Drool will see you now," the receptionist announced with a straight face.

Sophie couldn't suppress a snicker. The surname was just too perfect for a prospective living, breathing book boyfriend. As she stood to approach the office, the door swung open.

"Hi," greeted a man with a crooked grin that instantly charmed her. "I'm Howie Drool, and you must be Sophie E. Clark, the woman who got my name by accident."

Sophie shook his hand. "Not by accident. You were nominated, and trust me, the nominator was vetted."

He gestured for her to take a seat in a chair across from his sleek, minimalist desk, then circled around to sit himself. "May I ask who put my name in the hat for this—farce?"

"I'm afraid that is confidential," Sophie replied, deciding not to be insulted, "If we told certain candidates who nominated them, it might not go over so well for the person."

"I see. Well, I understand someone thinks that I'm *book boyfriend* material," Howie remarked, his tone mixed with amusement and disbelief. "Beyond that, my receptionist seemed to be in the dark."

Sophie leaned forward. "You see, here's the deal—I'm featuring men who embody the essence of literary romantic heroes for my upcoming columns in *Naked Runway*. You've been flagged as a hot nerd archetype." Her voice was tinged with an eagerness she couldn't quite conceal.

"A hot nerd?" Howie echoed, arching his eyebrows as if the concept was utterly foreign. "I'm pretty sure that's a joke. Sorry to say, someone's playing you."

"Oh, I don't think so. You're smart, right?" Sophie challenged, tilting her head.

"Well, I do own this place," he conceded, a flicker of pride passing through his eyes.

"And I can vouch you're cute. So, the only other thing left to know is—are you single?"

He sighed, a hint of resignation in his expression. "It appears that way."

Sophie forced a smile, her mind drifting back to Stone. Despite her resolve to push forward, the uncertainty of his return lingered, making her feel more alone than she cared to admit. The thrill of the interview was tainted by a gnawing sense of abandonment. She couldn't shake the feeling that she was dancing on the edge of something fragile, and without Stone's steady presence, it felt dangerously close to breaking.

Sophie caught a glimpse of something deeper, a hint of sadness in Howie's eyes, suggesting a recent heartbreak. "Would you be open to staying single until the end of the year? And quite possibly participating in a bachelor's auction for charity?"

"You want me to agree to be auctioned off?" Howie asked, his tone laced with skepticism, his eyes reflecting total horror at the idea.

"It's for a fantastic cause—Childhood Cancer Research."

Howie scratched the back of his neck. "Damn. How about I just donate a large sum instead?"

"Or you could embrace a bit of adventure and do both. Who knows, maybe you'll find the love of your life in the process," Sophie suggested, twinkling with happiness because she knew she had another book boyfriend on the hook.

He scoffed, shaking his head. "That would be a long shot. My idiosyncrasies seem to be a bit much for women to handle."

"Somehow, I doubt that's true for every woman," Sophie countered, challenging his self-deprecation. "It sounds like you've just been focusing on the wrong women. Trust me, there are plenty out there who are searching for their very own nerd in shining armor."

"Are you one of them?" Howie asked.

"I am single, if that's what you're asking," Sophie replied, maintaining a professional tone that would have made Stone proud. "But my contract explicitly states I cannot date any of the men I feature, at least not until after the auction is over."

"If I agree to participate, will you then tell me who nominated me?" he queried, leaning forward slightly.

"Sorry, no. But I have the feeling it's someone who really cares about you and wants to see you happy."

"That would be my mother," Howie remarked, a resigned chuckle escaping him.

Sophie laughed. "How about I get a photo first, and then I'll interview you?"

One hour later, Sophie found herself in the bustling lobby of her next interview location.

"Hi, I'm here to see Mr. Orvil," she announced to the receptionist. "I'm—"

"Sophie E. Clark, President of Book Boyfriend Connoisseurs," chirped the receptionist, a perky redhead with an infectious smile. "I'm Taylor. I'm a huge fan of yours. I belong to the club but haven't made it to a meeting yet. Every time I plan to go, he"—she nodded toward a stern-looking closed door— "invents some urgent task that absolutely requires me to work late."

"Hi, Taylor, it's great to meet a fellow club member. I really do hope you can make it to our next meeting. I'll look forward to seeing you there," Sophie replied warmly.

Taylor leaned closer. "Before I tell him you're here," she said in a low conspiratorial whisper, "I just need to know...you're not going to tell him I nominated him for the Bosshole Book Boyfriend hero, are you?" Her eyes darted nervously toward the same closed door.

Sophie made a motion of zipping her lips. "Mum's the word."

"Okay. Here's the scoop: he's undeniably sexy, pays fabulously, and is super generous at Christmas. Loves his mom, too—all signs of a redeemable guy. But as a boss... Well, he's pretty much a classic bosshole. For instance, he barks orders like a crusty drill sergeant, he's grumpier than any cat I've ever owned, and he expects me to purchase gifts for his revolving door of women," Taylor finished in a tone of resignation.

Sophie grinned. "Sounds like he is a perfect candidate for the boyfriend trope."

Taylor's expression brightened. "I was bummed to miss the club meeting where you discussed the rom-com with that trope. I had so much I could have added to the conversation."

"We should definitely talk book boyfriends over a drink sometime then," Sophie offered. "I'm always game for a book chat."

"Thanks. I'd love that," Taylor replied, her eyes grateful. "Back to my bosshole dilemma, though. I'm just filling in for his regular admin, who must have been a saint because nothing I do ever meets the mark. She's on a year's sabbatical, and here I am, six months deep in this madness. My neighbor pushed me to apply for this job—never again will I take career advice from an eighty-year-old, that's for sure."

**

Twenty minutes later, Sophie was sitting in Orvil's office, wrapping up her conversation with him. He turned out to be surprisingly charming and genuinely funny, a far cry from the bosshole persona Taylor had described.

He had burst into laughter when Sophie revealed the category under which he had been nominated and quickly surmised that it must have been his newest hire who put his name forward. Sophie maintained her professionalism, neither confirming nor denying his guess, which only seemed to amuse him further.

He not only agreed to be featured in her column but expressed a commitment to improving his management style and participating in the auction.

"Guess it's a good wake-up call, isn't it?" he'd joked during their conversation.

Sophie found herself genuinely liking him; his self-awareness and easy-going humor were disarming. By the end of their meeting, it was clear that Orvil was more than willing to embrace the challenge, promising to strive for a less basshole-like reputation.

The last interview of the day took Sophie to an unlikely venue—a gritty biker bar in the East Village, known for its rough charm and secretive patrons. The person she was meeting reportedly had a secret so compelling that the nominator thought it was high time it was shared with the world. Sophie herself was in the dark about the nature of the secret, which added an element of suspense to the task.

As she pushed open the heavy door of the bar at two in the afternoon, the sound of a bell echoed sharply through the air.

"Not open yet," a gruff voice announced from somewhere within the dimly lit interior.

"I'm not here to drink," Sophie responded, scanning the shadows to locate the source of the voice.

Her question was quickly answered when a man stepped out from a hallway, his presence commanding immediate attention. He could have been a character straight from the thriller she and Stone had been reading, with tattoos covering every visible inch of his skin, including his bald head, creating a striking montage of ink and muscle.

"What can I do for you?" he asked, his tone guarded. "You seem a bit lost."

"Umm. I'm here to speak to a Connor Jenkins," Sophie stated, trying to sound more confident than she felt.

"My friends call me Con," he said, his eyes narrowing slightly as he sized her up. "Since you're not a friend yet, you can call me Jenks. It helps me keep my friends and...acquaintances...separate."

"Fair enough," Sophie replied, offering a small smile. "I hope before I leave, you might consider me more friend than foe."

"I'm listening," he said, folding his arms.

Sophie smiled prettily, eager to make a good impression. "My name is Sophie E. Clark, and I'm a professional daydreamer."

He grunted out a laugh. "Ain't nobody ever told me that was a job option when I was growing up. If they had, I might have chosen a different career path than... Well, the one I ended up on."

Someone who uses the words *career path* in a sentence couldn't be all bad. "I'm currently writing feature stories about gentlemen who have been nominated as swoon-worthy, breathing book boyfriends." Sophie's gut told her that to get him to say yes, she'd really have to emphasize the romantic allure of being nominated. Appeal to his male ego. "Someone thinks you're super cute."

"Cute is a fighting word where I come from," Jenks retorted. "You didn't just walk into my bar to pick a fight, did you?"

"Or sexy," Sophie corrected quickly. "They probably thought of you as sexy, which is definitely more fitting for a biker than cute."

"Let me save you some time. I've sworn off romance. And I ain't interested in associating with a fluff piece who calls herself a professional daydreamer. No offense," Jenks said dismissively.

"Some taken," Sophie replied, keeping her tone calm and professional while not being a pushover. "Is there any way I can persuade you to reconsider? The person who nominated you mentioned that you were both book boyfriend-worthy and harboring a secret that needed to be shared."

"What the fuck did you say?" Jenks snapped, his demeanor shifting instantly.

"I said, whoever nominated you mentioned you have a secret that needs to be told," Sophie repeated, sensing the sudden escalation. "Not a bad secret. More like a secret that gets in the way of romance blooming."

"Who the fuck told you that?" he demanded, swiftly pulling a gun from behind the counter and aiming it squarely at her.

Sophie squeaked, stepping back and groping for the door handle. "I genuinely have no idea. I only show up to do the interviews based on the nominations."

"Well, here's what we're gonna do," Jenks growled, his voice low and threatening. "You're gonna walk out of here alive because I like your gumption walking into a biker bar alone wearing that. But if I so much as hear a whisper about my secret getting out, I'll hold you personally responsible. You do not want to be on my enemy list, darling."

"That's fair," Sophie managed to say, her voice trembling. "But I promise, if your secret does get out, it won't be from me. I don't even know what it is. If I did, I might have reconsidered this visit because it seems like it's a doozy."

He chuckled darkly. "Doesn't matter if you know or not. Now get out, before I change my mind."

Sophie didn't need to be told twice. She turned and fled, not stopping until she was safely out of the bar and several blocks away. Gasping for breath, shaking from adrenaline, she very much regretted not having Stone by her side today. What had she been thinking, asking a man like Jenks to agree to tell his secret? A smart person would have taken one look, known he was bad news, and spewed something about having the wrong address.

As Sophie continued to distance herself from the bar, the tension from her encounter clung to her like a skunk fart. She could still feel the chill from his threat and the seriousness of the situation.

How had his name been allowed to stay on her list of men to interview? Someone at *Naked Runway* must have messed up. Must have thought he was attached to someone reliable, but he obviously was not.

Her phone vibrated with an incoming call. For a terrifying moment, she thought it might be Jenks. When she saw it was Stone, a wave of relief washed over her, almost bringing tears to her eyes. "Stone." Her voice sounded more unsteady than she intended, betraying the fear still coursing through her veins.

"Tell me you're not doing what I think you're doing," Stone replied bluntly, his voice a lifeline she desperately clung to.

"I wasn't expecting you back this early," she said, sounding guilty as charged, her heart pounding.

"What have you done?" The weight of his disappointment was palpable, cutting through her like a knife.

"I decided to cross off a few of the interviews I needed to do. And before you say anything, I chose the ones I knew wouldn't put me in harm's way." Her voice wavered, the memory of Jenks's threat still fresh.

Silence, the kind that nobody likes, greeted her. The kind that makes you glad you're not enduring it in person, but it still felt suffocating.

"I never promised I wouldn't," she blurted, when she couldn't stand it any longer, desperation creeping into her tone.

"I'm sending you an address. Meet me there." His tone held no room for argument, his concern wrapping around her like a protective shield.

She glanced at her watch. "When?"

"Now."

Chapter 27

The elevator door slid open, and Sophie spotted Stone standing by the railing, his posture rigid and radiating tension. Sensing the storm of emotions brewing within him, she hesitated before clearing her throat to get his attention. Perhaps, taking the time to go home, shower, and change before coming hadn't been one of her best ever decisions.

He remained still, his gaze fixed on the horizon. Was he doing this on purpose? Making her feel anxious as a way of punishing her for not following his rules? If that was the problem, he was just going to have to get over it.

Glancing around, she realized he'd had her meet him in a secluded rooftop garden. Interesting choice. Surely, he wasn't so furious that he would contemplate something drastic. The thought settled for a second before being discarded as silly. She blamed it on the thriller she was reading, where that was exactly the kind of thing the villain would have done.

In the real world, it was much too pretty of a night to be murdered, especially by one's security detail.

Deciding she'd had enough of the silent treatment, she spoke. "This place is lovely."

Stone turned, his gaze dipping to the word *Dreamer* printed across her chest, his brows furrowing as if the simple, optimistic word somehow read as a provocation rather than an aspiration.

Choosing not to ignite the argument he seemed poised to begin, Sophie opted for neutral ground. "Is this place open to everyone, or do you know someone who lives here?" Pulling up her I'm-not-scared-of-the-big-bad-wolf panties, she stepped fully through the doorway.

The building was nestled in a swanky part of Manhattan, where affluence and prestige were prerequisites for residency. It was the kind of place where deep pockets met influential connections, each apartment a testament to both wealth and well-curated social references.

"You went on another interview," Stone said by way of greeting, his voice matching the icy sharpness in his eyes. "Even though I expressly told you to wait."

Sophie took a breath. She was her own person. He wasn't her boss. In fact, he sort of worked for her, not the other way around. "I did," she said unapologetically. "I thought—"

"What?" Stone snapped, cutting her off, his frustration palpable in the thick air between them. "You thought it was okay to just ignore the danger?"

She stuck her chin in the air. "Obviously, I was right since I'm here, unharmed."

"And you think that makes you right?" Stone's voice was incredulous. "At best, it makes you lucky. Do you realize how reckless your decision was?"

Sophie's patience unraveled. Exasperated, she gestured toward him. "This—this right here is why I prefer guys like Miles. Sweet guys. Guys who don't try to bully everyone around them." She regretted the words the moment she spouted them. She'd never convince Stone he was her type if she kept saying the opposite, even if saying the opposite helped save her pride.

"I'm not trying to intimidate—I'm trying to educate." His voice dripped with a tone that sounded uncomfortably pompous.

"I am not a child," Sophie snapped, no longer regretting her earlier word choice. "I'm perfectly capable of handling interviews with individuals who have been thoroughly vetted by *Naked Runway*. Just because you've built a career around dealing with dangerous people doesn't mean everyone in the world poses a threat. This project was meant to be enjoyable, and it is—when you're not looming over it, casting a shadow over everything I do."

"What if we hadn't captured the douchebag? What if he'd slipped through our perimeters and come after you while you were out there in the city without your damn security detail?"

She rolled her eyes. Imaginary worries were a waste of good energy. "Nothing happened, Stone. Two out of the three interviews went beautifully. The men are excited about becoming book boyfriends."

"And the third?" he pressed, eyes narrowing slightly, searching her face for any sign of trouble she might be hiding.

She held his gaze. There was no way she would reveal that the third man had pulled a gun on her. It would only escalate his fears and provoke an even bigger overreaction on his part. "Nice enough guy, but he wasn't interested in spilling his secret for the cause."

"What kind of secret?"

"I don't know," she answered honestly. "He clammed up before sharing anything."

Stone pinched the bridge of his nose as if his level of exasperation had reached its pinnacle. "Do you even want to know who was after you?"

"Was it the guy from the garage?"

"No."

"My ex-boyfriend?" she asked in a mostly light tone.

"No." This time the no came out more explosive.

Stone's one-syllable responses were grating on her nerves. "Are you sure? Because I did put his name on a do-not-date-ever list and mentioned his, uh, shortcomings in the bedroom. He's the petty type who might want to settle a score.

Finally, Stone gave her the briefest hint of a smile, a glint in his eyes. "Trust me, he won't be bothering you again."

"What the hell does that mean?" A shiver went through Sophie—a cocktail of fear tinged with an undeniable thrill.

"Let's just say we had a conversation the day after Poppie first mentioned him."

"Are you freaking kidding me?" She balled her hands into fists and plopped them on her hips. "I handled him. I didn't need you stepping in."

"I simply made sure he understood the situation clearly," Stone said in a flat tone.

"You made sure?" Sophie retorted. "For your information, I didn't need you to rescue me." Gah. She wished Poppie had never mentioned how gullible she'd been when it came to her ex.

Stone's expression hardened slightly. "I just provided him a little...extra incentive to keep his distance"

"Please tell me you didn't hit him. That's so barbaric and not at all like the cinnamon roll hero you promised you'd be."

His eyes narrowed. "I didn't lay a hand on him, but I did make it abundantly clear that if he ever came sniffing around you again, my fist would be the last thing he saw before his teeth met the back of his skull."

"Unbelievable. You are the most unbook-like boyfriend I could have ever had the misfortune to be paired with."

"That's because there's nothing sweet or soft about me," Stone bit out. "If you insist on labeling me as a book boyfriend, try dark alpha."

"Who introduced you to that type?" Sophie asked, half curious, half annoyed, half jealous he'd been talking book boyfriends with someone other than her. And yes, she knew that was one too many halves, but it was what it was.

Stone smirked slightly. "Let's just say, I've been doing my own research. Turns out there's a whole spectrum of book boyfriend tropes you've conveniently never mentioned."

Sophie sighed. "That's because my column is focusing on those types most prevalent in romantic comedies—those that charm with a touch of vulnerability. Not...whatever you're embodying."

"I'm perfectly happy knowing my tragic backstory fits right in as a dark romance hero," Stone said.

She scoffed, more to bruise his ego than out of disbelief. "You do realize those characters are aggressive lovers, rarely play by the rules, and often tread on the dark side of the law, right?"

"I'm well aware."

"And you're trying to tell me that's you?"

Stone looked her straight in the eye. "I don't know why you didn't see that from the start."

She studied him, a sudden realization dawning on her. He was trying to scare her off. Trying to keep her at arm's length. As if he thought she was on the verge of falling for him, and he wanted to avoid that at all costs.

The fact he was right pissed her off. The realization bruised her pride. Well, she had news for him—she didn't go around leaving her heart at the feet of men who didn't want it. She snatched that organ up and crammed it back into her chest where it belonged, all while glaring at Stone. What an ass.

"You'd make a lousy dark hero," she practically shouted, suddenly in the mood for a fight. "Sure, you're tough on the outside. Your job demands it. But inside, you're a stickler for rules. Hell, that's why you're mad. I didn't play by your rules. Newsflash, alpha types don't give a damn about rules."

"You're mistaken if you think my actions are governed by them," he countered with a steely edge.

"Prove it," Sophie dared, her eyes locked on his.

His nostrils flared. "How exactly would you have me do that?"

"I don't know." She shrugged, her voice casual but her mind racing. "You're the alpha. Figure it out."

"You won't like my choice." His voice was a low growl. Like he was a caged animal being toyed with.

Sophie ignored the danger signs and flashed him a mischievous smile. "How about you prove it by breaking your rule to never get involved with a client?"

He closed the distance between them, his presence hot and overwhelming. "You're playing with fire," he warned, his voice a dangerous whisper.

"Fraud much?" she taunted lightly, challenging his self-control and the very rules he clung to.

Stone grabbed her shoulders, and for a heart-stopping moment, they stood locked in a silent standoff under the dark sky, his breath shallow, her heartbeat thundering in her ears like a frantic drum.

"If you're smart, you'll tell me to stop. Right now. This moment." His voice was rough with restrained intensity.

Sophie met his gaze unflinchingly. Just because he wasn't worthy of her heart didn't mean she didn't want to finish what they'd started this morning. "You're bluffing."

With a low groan, he pressed her back against the railing of the rooftop garden, the lights of Manhattan twinkling like distant stars. *Whose* roof garden she couldn't be sure and didn't really care. All that mattered was the darkness enveloping them, the solitude of their high-rise retreat, and the raw intensity in his eyes as he promised she'd just poked a bear. A bear who vowed to prove her wrong.

Sophie tried to drum up a little concern and found none existed. The truth was she wasn't a bit sorry at the idea of Stone schooling her in such a way.

"I don't bluff," he warned, his voice a rough whisper that brushed against her skin just before his hands cradled her face. Then, his lips assaulted hers in a kiss that caused her whole body to wake up with fiery need. A kiss that shouted resisting was a waste of time. *Like that was going to happen.* She'd waited her whole life to be kissed like this.

Sophie raised her hands and allowed her fingers to trace the contours of his chest until they rested at the nape of his neck; then she danced them over his newly shaven head.

She paused, a flicker of curiosity about his choice to return to being bald. Part of being her cinnamon roll hero boyfriend was having hair.

His hips pressed against hers, snapping her back to the heated moment at hand.

After years of devouring romance novels where the tortured hero surrenders to his deepest urges for the forbidden woman, Sophie was finally experiencing it in reality. Every bad boy decision she'd ever made had been with the hopes of this deliciousness. Of feeling the hard evidence of a man's arousal pressed against her, signaling that his need had him twisted up in delicious torment. And finally—*fi-*

nally—she'd found a bad boy who actually delivered on the fictional hype.

His tongue dove into her mouth, and she released a moan so primal it rippled through her, sending a shiver of anticipation spiraling down to her core. His hands traced a path from her face to her shirt, his touch electrifying. He pulled back just enough to catch a glance at the word she'd emblazoned there in hot pink, then flashed her a wicked grin. "The next shirt I wear of yours better scream *alpha*."

Before she could even nod, his lips claimed hers once more, fervent and insistent. His hands charted a tantalizing path down her chest to the hem of her shirt, slipping beneath the fabric with a boldness that sent her pulse racing. They ascended her stomach in a slow, seductive crawl until they found their destination, cupping her breasts through the delicate lace of her bra, lingering there in a bold, possessive hold. Squeezing.

Sophie's fingers itched to explore just as brazenly. She reached for his belt. Her hands, slightly clumsy in their eagerness, fumbled. With a low chuckle, he stepped back and undid it himself. With a few swift movements, he stripped down to his boxers and then stood proudly before her.

Holy fairytale endings. The tip of his cock, poking out of his boxers in a most delightful display of readiness, met all her book boyfriend fantasies...and then some. "The epitome of Victorian-faint-worthy yumminess," she managed to murmur, causing him to laugh.

Before Sophie could mirror his daring undress, he swept her back into his arms, his movements decisive as he steered them to a secluded wall away from the ledge. With a swift tug, he peeled her shirt over her head, his fingers deftly unhooking her bra clasp. The cool wall at her back contrasted with the heat of his urgent touch, sending shivers of anticipation down her spine.

As she let her hands drift down, her bra slipped from her shoulders and fluttered to the floor, his eyes following its descent before returning to hers.

"Magnificent," he murmured, reverently. His voice thick with awe, painting a vivid portrait of an alpha on the verge of losing control.

A playful breeze teased around her neck, coaxing a shiver from her. She drew him in closer, craving his warmth, and was instantly rewarded by the firm press of his chest against hers.

Sophie had always been a sucker for a romance where the man was carved with six-pack abs and possessed the rough touch of chest hair. This was her first actual encounter with such a man who had both.

And don't even get her started on the muscles that bulged in his biceps. The only thing missing, the thing that would crown him the ultimate alpha—tattoos. Which surprised her, considering he'd been a Navy SEAL.

His hands ventured between them, catching the hem of her skirt, coaxing it upward inch by tantalizing inch. His fingers grazed her thighs, urging gently until she parted them further, an unspoken invitation.

His lips met hers again, this time soft and teasing, his teeth nibbling at her bottom lip as his fingers traced lazy, provocative patterns on her inner thigh.

She leaned into him, aching to feel the hard press of his erection. But he held her back.

"Not yet." His restrained voice heightened her anticipation, stirring a delicious mix of frustration and excitement within her.

This wasn't just any kiss; this was a kiss from Stone—Stone, whom she'd needled until he'd lost control and broken his rule of engagement.

Given that he was a man who'd proudly proclaimed he'd mastered self-will, he would greatly regret this in the aftermath. Not that she felt bad about shoving him off his own stance—after all, hadn't she declared his fatal flaw to be that of an unwillingness to lose control? She'd done him a favor by pushing him until he broke. Until he admitted that sometimes he had to hand over the reins and become vulnerable.

It was the only way he would ever be the hero of his own love story.

But she'd save that to think about for another day. Right now, all that mattered was the commanding way he claimed her in his arms, promising a mastery she had only read about.

His fingers shifted slowly up her thighs, sending a surge of desire pulsing through her, igniting her senses as though she was caught in a thunderstorm and every nerve became a live wire.

When his fingers halted just a whisper away from caressing her needy flesh, she groaned. "Touch me," she ordered, in a breathless command.

He complied, and a sharp hiss of approval escaped her as his fingers met her eager clit.

His low chuckle vibrated against her skin. "If you like that, you're really going to like this." He dropped to his knees and gently raised her skirt, sending waves of keenness rippling through her belly.

At that moment, Sophie's world turned vibrantly sensory. The sweet scent of night flowers mingled with the crispness of the evening air, and the aroma of his skin—a deep and compelling mix of dark rum and the distant smokiness of a bonfire.

As he lowered himself to his knees, Sophie couldn't help but sigh in eager approval of his next move. She braced her hands against the cool wall, her entire being silently screaming for him to continue, her need mounting with each breath.

He glanced up at her, his gaze intense, and for a fleeting moment, Sophie thought he was going to ask for permission.

She waited, the word *yes* already forming on her lips.

Instead, his eyes took on a smolder. "I hope you're not too attached to these." His fingers teased the flimsy scrap of material at her hip.

Before she could even process his words or muster a response, he tugged sharply. The fabric gave way as if it were mere tissue, and suddenly, her panties lay in a soft heap around her ankles. The swift, bold move left her breathless, her heart racing from the thrilling alpha-like action.

Only to be followed by an even more thrilling move, his mouth pressing to her mound. Over the roar in her head, she somehow heard him say, "Sophie," in a husky, gruff utterance that ignited a primal surge of feminine power.

His tongue worked relentlessly, his hands gripping her ass, anchoring her in place, dictating a maddening slow rhythm. Each languid stroke was so exquisitely torturous that Sophie thought she might die from despair.

"Quicker," she managed to gasp out, barely audible.

"What's the rush?" he teased, his voice a low rumble against her.

"Someone might come before I do and that would be fatal," she replied, her voice betraying her desperateness.

"No one's going to interrupt us," he reassured her.

"I've never had sex on a rooftop," she confessed breathlessly.

"That's because you've never been with a true alpha." He rose to his full height. "Don't move."

His order both challenged and thrilled her.

Through half-closed lashes, Sophie watched him stride to his discarded pants, his movements purposeful. He retrieved a condom from his wallet and then turned to face her, his every action heightening the tension between them.

While she held her breath in anticipation, he stepped out of his boxers and kicked them away. The movement caused her breath to whoosh out only to get sucked back in as she watched him deftly roll the condom on his magnificent cock. "That's going to take some getting used to," she murmured, her eyes glued to it as he approached her.

"Turn around and place your hands on the wall," he ordered.

Like a good little girl, she silently added to his demand. As she pressed her palms against the cool, rough surface and waited, every book-boyfriend-loving ounce of her hoped like hell his next words would be dirty. Dirty. Dirty.

"Spread your legs," he ordered, "and don't make a sound unless I give you permission."

She smiled as she spread them. What exactly would he do to a good little girl who disobeyed a command? Perhaps she—

He was behind her in an instant, his lips finding the sensitive curve of her neck, his teeth grazing her skin in a sharp nip causing all thoughts to flutter away. "You were very naughty today." His words came out growly with an undertone of something she couldn't quite decipher.

She swallowed hard but said nothing.

He palmed her ass, gave it a sharp squeeze and then slapped it.

She yelped.

He slapped it again. "I said no sound."

She bit her tongue to keep from verbally responding, but her body was singing yes, yes, yes.

Much to her delight, his fingers expertly sought her, parting her with practiced ease, as he positioned himself teasingly at her entrance. His shaft brushed against her, the contact electrifying, sending waves of near-unbearable pleasure through her, threatening to undo her completely before they even truly began.

She moaned.

He stilled. "Sophie, did you hear me say no sound?"

"I did."

"And yet, you continue to make them. I have half a mind to make you suck me off and then send you on your way unsatisfied."

Would he do that? "Please don't?"

"Please don't tell you to get down on your knees and suck my dick like a good little girl?" he asked. "Or don't send you away like a bad little one?" As he spoke, his thumb rubbed against her clit.

Sophie considered her answer the best she could what with being on the brink of an orgasm. "Please don't send me away unsatisfied."

His thumb slowed its movement.

She whimpered. No one had ever edged her before.

"If you don't want me to stop, what exactly do you want me to do?" He positioned his shaft at her opening.

"Fuck me now, punish me later."

He responded with a low, husky rumble of laughter, and then complied, entering her slowly. "Tell me if it hurts."

"Only in the very best way," she said breathlessly.

He circled one hand around her, his thumb once again finding and deliciously teasing her clit, moving with a rhythm that could only be described as a masterpiece.

Just as she teetered on the brink of losing control, he pulled back.

"Damn it," she exclaimed. "I was about to come."

"I know," he said, spinning her around to face him, scooping her into his arms, and carrying her inside. "I want to see your eyes the first time I make you orgasm." He didn't pause until they reached a massive bed, where he gently dropped her onto a soft mattress.

In an instant, he was over her again, his presence commanding as she opened her legs to welcome him back. Wrapping them around him, she anchored her feet at the ankles. "I'm not letting you go until I get what I want."

"As you wish, princess," he responded. "But later, we'll talk punishment." With those words, he entered her.

She and Stone found a primal rhythm, their movements now frenzied as they chased their climaxes. Amid guttural growls, and *oh my Gods*, and *fuck that feels goods*, their skin grew slick with sweat, and the air around them became charged with the heat of the union and, if she wasn't mistaken, sparkles.

"You have no fucking idea how much I've wanted this," Stone growled. "To drive out any notion that I could be your sweet, leading man in some romantic tale."

"Sweet guys are the ones women marry, but bad boys like you are perfect for moments like this," she replied, a raw honesty in her voice. It was a belief she had always held. The reason she'd dated her ex. But now, as the words left her lips, they struck a chord deep within her, causing her heart to jolt with a terrifying intensity. She no longer believed that to be true. Men like Stone were also marriage material.

"Smart. Fucking smart. Never marry a man like me." Stone's response was laced with a hard edge of realism.

Her body tensed, her mind racing. No. Not smart. Profoundly mistaken. "But—" she started, her protest caught in the vortex of her swirling emotions and the undeniable connection that tethered her to him in that charged moment.

"No buts, princess," Stone whispered, his voice a commanding velvet before his lips crashed into hers, silencing any further protests. His hand moved with certainty between them, finding her clit and pinching sharply, the unexpected intensity sending her spiraling into oblivion. Her world fractured into blissful shards as waves of ecstasy overwhelmed her, her entire being consumed by the powerful release that rocked through her, shuddering in the wake of the most intense orgasm she'd ever had.

At the same moment, Stone stilled, his own climax mirroring hers, a shared storm of release that left them both breathless.

"Holy book boyfriend," Sophie whispered in awe. Never had she ever been...so fulfilled.

"Alpha book boyfriend," he corrected with a chuckle.

As their exhausted breaths mingled in the quiet aftermath, he gently slid off her, drawing her into the crook of his chest.

"Sophie?" he murmured, propping himself up on one elbow to gently brush the hair from her face, a soft tenderness replacing the earlier fervor. "We need to talk."

"Hmm," she managed, still lost in the haze of their shared enjoyment.

"The guy who threatened you—it was someone from my past," Stone began. His voice was burdened with a weight she hadn't heard before. "Years ago, we clashed, and he never forgot it. He heard about us on Isabella's podcast and saw a chance to strike where it would hurt me the most...by targeting you. A woman he believed was the love of my life."

The heavy implication of his words lingered in the air, casting a pall over the room.

Sophie, her bones still rubbery with happiness, struggled to prop herself up on one elbow, as her brain scrambled to make sense of what he had said. "You caught him?"

He nodded solemnly. "Yes."

"It's over, then?" She wanted to make sure she'd understood.

Again, he nodded.

"I see. You knew the threat was over, and yet you chose to scold me for simply continuing my life in your absence. Why?" She didn't wait for his answer. She knew the answer. "Because it meant you couldn't control me, and God forbid the great Stone Blackthorn doesn't have complete control over every aspect of his life, even his client."

"You've got it wrong," Stone shot back. "The past twelve hours have been my fucking worst nightmare. Every quiet hope I've ever harbored—that I could somehow have both love and a career—has been shattered. His decision to target you just confirms it. My life, my career, it's too dangerous for—"

"For what? For someone to love you," Sophie interjected. "You think you have the right to make that choice for yourself and the woman you fall in love with and who loves you back?"

"Do you love me?" he asked, looking startled.

Nope. This was not how she was going to admit that to him. Hell, she'd not even admitted it to herself. "Are you still my bodyguard?"

"I resigned six hours ago."

"Unbelievable," she muttered. "You didn't even talk to me first."

"I made the decision that was best for all concerned."

She sat up and scrambled off the bed. "No. No, you didn't. Your decision was not what was best for me. You're nothing but a coward hiding behind *what ifs*. Not a hero. And until you figure that out, you'll never be book-boyfriend material. I don't care how good you fuck."

Chapter 28

S tone watched Sophie dress, words failing him as he strived to see the situation through her eyes. Only he couldn't. She lived life like a story written in a book, a story guaranteed to have a happy ending.

That wasn't reality.

When she grabbed her purse and turned toward the door, he blurted, "Can we at least talk?" He had to try one more time to make her see sense. To make her understand he was right.

She stilled. "About what?"

The question hung in the air, while he waited for her to turn. He wanted to see her face during this conversation. And give himself time to think of the right words. Somehow, he didn't think she'd respond well to, 'You're wrong, you know.'

Only she didn't make eye contact. Instead, her gaze swept over the sleek, modern décor. "I take it we're at your place?"

"Of course," he said in frustration.

"There must be more money in security than I'd imagined," she commented. "No wonder you didn't blink twice before ditching me as a client."

Stone suppressed a sigh. If only he could tell her about the real perks of being a fairy godfather. His home, much like many other aspects of his life, was a reward for his unseen duties—duties that required him to keep secrets even from those he completely trusted. Like Sophie.

In the past twenty-four hours, he'd done a lot of wistful thinking about things he wished could be but couldn't. And he had drilled down on the why behind the desires. During that introspection, he had concluded several things, he did trust Sophie on the big stuff. She might be a little flaky on how she approached her day-to-day life. But under that was someone solid. Someone he wanted to give his heart to but couldn't. For her sake.

"So, what did you want to talk about?" She spoke in a nonchalant tone, her expression guarded.

"About your perception of me," he said honestly.

She studied him. "I thought I made that pretty clear."

"If love was in the cards for me, I'd choose you. I hope you know that."

"Right, and I have an ocean-side property in Arizona," she said, her voice dripping with sarcasm.

"You don't believe me?" How could he prove to her he would? Wasn't that just something you had to take at a person's word?

She wrapped her arms around her middle. "Stone, how could you choose a future with someone whose middle name you don't even know?"

She was right. He had no idea what the E. stood for. Why hadn't he asked? "I know your message. That has to count for something."

"My message?" Sophie asked, looking confused, which was much better than disinterest or disdain.

He walked over to her and tugged at her arms until she loosened the hold she had on herself, allowing him to grasp her hands. "Yes, the billboard that is Sophie E. Clark."

She furrowed her brows. "What exactly does my billboard say?"

"Professional Daydreamer at Work."

"Oh. That." She stepped back, slipping her hands from his, and headed to the door.

"What do you mean?"

She stood with her hand on the knob. "It's just... I've found it's not a trait that inspires a lover to want more. It's a trait that inspires him to want something temporary."

"Then you've been with the wrong men."

"Are you saying you want more from me than date, sex, rinse, repeat, until you tire of me and fade away?"

"You've stirred me to want more," Stone countered, only realizing the mistake of his words when he saw hope flitter across her face, brightening her eyes. Sure, he knew she could handle his secret, but that didn't remove his dangerous lifestyle. Didn't remove the fact that someone who hated him had gone after her. He'd be a fucking asshole to entice her to love him. "Sophie—"

"Then you've decided to chase the fairytale," she said, all smiles. "To forget all your fears?" She took a step toward him.

He held out a hand, not to stop her from coming to him, but to stop her from getting her hopes up. "I said I want the more... I just can't see how to get that *more* given my career constraints."

"So, what you're really saying is you'd like to enjoy *now* with me but not *later*?" Her gaze was sharp, seeking truth.

"It's the best I have to offer." Hell. He was going to lose her, but that was a price he was willing to pay if it meant her heart never broke as a result of emotional choices he made now.

She snorted. "You know what, your offer is romantic in a fleeting sort of way."

His chest tightened. "I—"

"Let me finish," she demanded. "It's romantic like a single page torn from a lovely story. But I'm a woman who has committed to never settling for less than the fairytale. The fairytale is forever. The love that comes with my dreams continues after death. It has no expiration date."

"Sophie, I'm a bachelor for life."

"Oh, God yes. You've made that abundantly clear. Just as I've made abundantly clear that I'm a romantic forever. That's why I'm going to say thanks for the offer. But I'm good. I'm going to keep my options open for a man who can promise me a tomorrow if our hearts decide they love one another," she spoke softly, yet oh-so-fucking-firmly.

He opened his mouth to argue, to change her mind, but shut it. A pang of anguish shot through him, an ache so deep it felt like his chest was caving in. He was doing this to protect her, to keep her safe. But God, the thought of not having her by his side, of seeing her with someone else who could give her the future she wanted, tore at him like nothing else ever had.

Every fiber of his being screamed to pull her into his arms, to beg her to stay, but he couldn't. She deserved her happy ever after. Her fairytale ending. Even if it meant his own heart would shatter into a thousand irreparable pieces.

The misery settled in his bones, a cold unyielding presence that he knew would haunt him long after she walked away. But this was for her. He was giving her a future One without the fear of the boogeyman appearing around every corner.

He walked to her and pulled her into a kiss. When they parted, he placed his lips next to her ear and whispered, "Anyone who can make a living daydreaming should never settle for less than the fairytale." He pulled back and gave her a sad smile. "You should go home now."

Chapter 29

Ninety-two days later, Stone opened the front door, saw his mom and siblings, and tried to shut the door in their faces.

He knew an intervention when he saw one, and he wasn't in the mood.

Tonight marked another month since Sophie had walked out of his life. And, as he had with the prior two anniversary months, he planned to get drunk.

Three months of pure hell. Three months in which he'd operated on autopilot. "If you guys are here to cheer me up, that ship has fucking sailed."

"Language." Clarabelle twirled her wand in the air, and the next thing Stone knew, he had a bar of soap in his mouth.

He spat it out and glared at her. "You used to count to three before you did that."

"You used to be a child who needed guidance, not tough love."

"Let me guess," Stone said caustically, his attention on his brothers. "The lot of you have shown up uninvited to tell me to stop pouting and get back out there and get laid?"

Ryder, the middle of Clarabelle's three adopted sons, held out a hand to Montgomery, who was the oldest. "I told you that's what he'd think."

Montgomery passed money to Ryder.

"Dang it, dude," Montgomery said to Stone. "I thought for sure you were smart enough to know the answer to your problem without our having to interfere."

Stone did know the answer. But getting over someone like Sophie E. Clark was easier said than accomplished. "Are you saying this," Stone asked Montgomery as he motioned toward the other two, "wasn't your idea?"

"Hel...heck no," Montgomery said. "I've got better things to do on a Friday night than—"

Ryder elbowed Montgomery. "Dude. We're a family. Family breaks dates and shows up to kick each other's asses when asses need kicking."

Clarabelle raised her wand. "Language—"

"No offense, Mom," Ryder said, "but sometimes a guy's got to cuss."

She pursed her lips but lowered her wand.

"Could we just skip the pleasantries and get to the point of why you're all here?" Stone grumbled. "I've got a date with Jack later." He glanced toward an empty Jack Daniel's bottle and frowned. When had he finished it?

"Stone, if you miss one more monthly meeting, the elders will have no choice but to relieve you of your wand. Is that what you want?" Clarabelle asked.

"They can do that?" Stone frowned. "I thought once a fairy godfather, always a fairy godfather." He drained the beer in his hand and tossed it toward the pile of other cans by the couch.

"Oh, you'll still be one," Clarabelle said. "Just not one with powers. You'll be a figurehead only."

"Fuck that," Stone said. "If I can't have a wand, I'm not keeping the title."

"That's why we're here," Ryder interjected. "Do you want out?"

"Out of the magic business?" Stone asked.

"Out of it all." Montgomery clarified. "Out of security, out of magic, out of all the things that have been your steadfast reasons for why you couldn't pursue Sophie."

Stone sighed. "I'm not turning my back on my family for a woman. Even if I have fallen for the girl. We're the three musketeers, abandoned by family once, but never again."

They all smiled. Except him. Stone didn't smile.

"We've got a plan," Clarabelle said.

"The kind that's going to require groveling on your part," Ryder said. "But we're pretty sure you can pull it off if you put your heart into it."

"What your brothers are trying to say is we've figured out a way for all of you to have your cake and marry it too."

For the first time in three months, Stone found himself harboring hope. "I'm listening."

"Before we go any further, do you love Sophie?" Clarabelle asked.

"I do." Stone had no idea how that had happened. He'd been so careful not to get emotionally involved with her. But despite all his efforts, she'd stolen his heart.

"Do you trust Sophie?" Ryder asked.

"Absolutely."

"Then here's the plan," Montgomery said. "You're going to go up on the auction block as one of her book boyfriends. If she loves you, she will move heaven and earth to win you at auction."

Stone made a buzzer noise. "She doesn't have money to spare. There's no way she could bid even if she wanted to."

"Darling, I have spoken with Ms. Birdie, and we have come to an agreement," Clarabelle said, not looking him in the eyes.

"What kind of agreement?" Stone asked, suspicious.

"With Ms. Birdie's help, Sophie will be able to bid on you at auction."

"How?"

"Sophie will participate in the silent auction. She will offer a bundle of all her T-shirt designs. Ms. Birdie will offer to match the highest bid and give that money to Sophie. You are going to covertly be the highest bidder."

"Me?"

"Your bid will be outrageous," Clarabelle said. "So incredible that Sophie won't even think twice about worries she can't afford to spend money bidding on you. Her only thought when you're up on the stage will be if she wants to win you at auction."

"And Ms. Birdie has approved this idea?" Stone asked.

Clarabelle nodded. "The only thing we can't control is the choice Sophie makes when she sees you on stage."

Stone ran a hand over his beard. "Trust me when I say she won't want to. The last thing I said to her was I'm a bachelor for life and you should leave now."

"You're such a moron," Montgomery said. "I can't believe we're related."

"Fuck off," Stone sneered.

Clarabelle made a tsking noise, but Stone's mouth stayed free of soap.

"You're right, she won't want to," Clarabelle said sharply. "But you're going to show up in the hopes that she does anyway."

"And which book boyfriend trope am I to represent? If it's the damn cinnamon roll, you can count me out. She'll know that's bullshit."

"You'll go up there," Clarabelle snapped, "and be whatever it takes to win back the woman of your heart."

He opened his mouth to argue and shut it. When she got that look in her eyes, there was no getting around her will. Mightier than Stone had tried and failed. "Yes, ma'am."

"As it turns out, her book boyfriend with a secret—that he would reveal to the highest bidder—backed out," Clarabelle said.

"Backed out or was asked to be a no-show?" Stone asked, smelling a rat.

"Do not take that tone of voice with me, young man," Clarabelle said.

He sighed. "I wasn't aware Sophie had found such a book boyfriend." Who had it been, and who had she taken with her to the interview for protection?

"She did, and he's perfectly lovely, so stop scowling," Clarabelle ordered.

"I'm not scowling. I'm thinking."

"Well, stop it. It's going to give you wrinkles."

He forced himself to have no expression. "Better?"

She nodded. "As I was saying, you will take his place. Once Sophie wins you at auction, you will tell her you are a fairy godfather. If that doesn't cause her to run, you've been cleared to offer her a job as a Fairytale Coordinator for you and the boys. It's been preapproved by the Grand High Enchanter of Fairy Affairs."

"How did you pull that off?"

"Let's just say we have theories about Sophie that coincide."

Stone went on full alert. "You're saying I can tell her my secret without her saying I love you first?"

"Yes," they all said in unison.

"But what if she's not great at keeping secrets?" he forced himself to ask, because accidental telling of secrets can and do happen. And he wanted to know the outcome should that occur. Protecting her was still his focus. When they'd all been sworn in as Fairy Godfathers, there'd been a strong emphasis on the need to keep what they did out of the limelight. According to Clarabelle, if the wrong group of people learned of their existence, bad things could and would happen to the magic in the world.

Clarabelle smiled sadly and patted him on the cheek. "For starters, if she tells your secret, both of your memories of each other will be erased."

There was no world in which he'd want to exist where he didn't remember someone as perfect as Sophie E. Clark. "Starters?"

"Darling, stop borrowing worries. Now is the time to embrace possibilities. Go for the gold. Grab your own fairytale ending."

"In other words, grow a pair," Montgomery said.

"Man up," Ryder added.

"Indeed, indeed," Clarabelle said, causing both of his brothers to double over in laughter.

Stone let the ribbing slide. His gut told him Sophie could keep an important secret, especially if she knew the consequences of letting it slip. Which meant there was nothing stopping him from saying yes to offering Sophie a fantastical job. The realization caused him to laugh.

Hell, he had no idea what he and his brothers would do with a Fairytale Coordinator—mostly because he didn't know what one of those did—but it didn't take a sober genius to know Sophie would love the title. He could just imagine the T-shirts she would design for all of them to wear. "I'm in."

"We thought you might be," Ryder said, clapping him on the shoulder.

Montgomery puffed out his chest. "It was my idea, and I came up with the title."

"Suck up," Ryder jibed.

Clarabelle made a tutting noise at her boys.

Reality—a bully who'd been hiding in the fucking shadows like a coward—chose that moment to jump out and sucker punch Stone, wiping the grin from his face and the joy from his heart. "Your plan doesn't keep Sophie emotionally or physically safe. As much as I like your plan, I'd rather die alone and unhappy than to be the reason one hair on her head is ever hurt." Which is why he'd spent the last three months miserable.

"That's the beauty of the plan, "Clarabelle said. "She'll be protected by fairy magic. The same as any Fairy Godperson."

"Why all the hoopla? Why can't I just go to her tonight, and tell her?" Stone asked.

"Because Sophie deserves a grand gesture," Clarabelle said.

Fuck. "What am I supposed to do for a grand gesture?"

"You're getting up on that stage—all in the hopes the girl you love will bid on you—will be your grand gesture," Clarabelle said. "It's lowkey, and she might not get it at first, but when she does, it will seal the deal."

"Are you sure she'll get it? Because I don't," Stone said.

Clarabelle gave him a sad shake of her head. "Darling, the mere fact you don't is why you need that girl in your life. If I recall, you mentioned she once said your fatal flaw was your unwillingness to ever lose control. Thus, your getting up on that stage, hoping for a certain outcome, but having no control over the actual way it turns out, is you losing control for her."

"He always was the dumb butt in the group," Ryder said, under his breath.

Stone flipped him the bird. "And if that's not enough?" he asked Clarabelle.

"Honey, I have faith you'll figure that one out when the time is right."

"The way I see it, there's an eighty-eight percent chance she's going to tell you to go hump yourself," Montgomery added.

"The math genius is right," Stone replied. "Sophie won't know what I'm hoping for when she sees me on that stage, so she won't see it as a grand gesture."

"As I said, darling," Clarabelle said. "She probably won't see it as a grand gesture until it's all over, and that's okay."

"If she doesn't see it as one, why would she bid on me?" Stone asked.

"Because she loves you," Clarabelle said.

"Yeah, keep up, bro," Ryder added. "Weren't you paying attention at the beginning?"

"Why would Ms. Birdie be willing to get involved in any of this, let alone match the highest bid on Sophie's product?" Stone asked.

Clarabelle's cheeks went deep pink. "Because she's a lovely person."

Stone studied her. "The two of you are in fucking matchmaking cahoots, aren't—"

A bar of soap in his mouth kept him from finishing.

"That is for me to know, and you to never find out," Clarabelle said primly.

Chapter 30

Three months had passed since Sophie had told Stone she wanted more out of their relationship—a connection beyond their fake-couple adventures. During that time, she had tried to find the joy in living the life of a professional daydreamer, but the magic had started to wane.

Book boyfriends no longer sparked her the way they had. While they were great as a fantasy, they were unobtainable outside of the page. Sure, she'd scouted real-life versions of men who fit the mold of playboys to grumpy billionaires, from heartthrob celebs to those fixer-upper types you just can't help but root for, but none fit the bill of a man with dark secrets nor a man with a murky past willing to bare his soul to a lucky auction winner. And Frankie was breathing down her neck to finish the lineup.

Just as Sophie was cataloging another dud, Ms. Birdie fluttered into the doorway of Sophie's cluttered office, a smirk playing on her lips.

"Do you have a minute to chat?" Ms. Birdie asked.

Sophie beamed up at her, pushing aside a stack of romance novels. "For you, always." In the past three months, they'd formed a bond. One that started the day Ms. Birdie walked in on Sophie crying and Sophie had spilled her heartache to the woman.

Mischief twinkled in Ms. Birdie's blue eyes. "Still hunting for a bachelor with a secret?"

"I am," Sophie admitted, her interest piqued. "Desperately."

"Darling, I've got just the man. He's ready to drop a bombshell on whoever takes him home from the auction."

"Really? Who?" Sophie asked, her heart skipping beats.

Ms. Birdie's smile widened. "I'm afraid I'm not allowed to say. At the auction, he'll be introduced as Mr. X, cloaked in mystery—and quite literally wearing a disguise."

Sophie felt like she'd just stepped into the pages of a best-selling romance. "Do you know his secret?"

Ms. Birdie nodded, her eyes gleaming. "And before you ask, no, I can't tell you that, either. But trust me when I say he is book boyfriend perfect."

A niggle of suspicion weaseled its way into Sophie's brain. "And he's willing to reveal his bombshell secret to some random stranger who happens to have deep pockets at the ball?"

It went against all common sense for a man to do that. Even a cinnamon roll book boyfriend willing to sacrifice a secret for a good cause would have to have reservations.

"It won't be a free-for-all—there are a few loopholes to jump through," Ms. Birdie assured her. "First, they'll need a clean slate on a background check and agree to seal their lips with a nondisclosure."

Sophie's suspicions eased. "Makes me wish I was sitting on a pile of cash to throw in the ring for him."

Ms. Birdie's laughter filled the room. "Keep dreaming big, Sophie. One day, you'll have that and much, much more."

A wave of optimism washed over Sophie at Ms. Birdie's words. "Guess I'll need his measurements. Need to know what size of superhero cape—er, I mean T-shirt—to tailor for our mysterious Mr. X."

"An extra-large should do quite nicely for him," Ms. Birdie said. "He's quite the specimen—broad shoulders, muscle to spare."

"Yummy. He sounds like a perfect book boyfriend."

"Speaking of which," Ms. Birdie said, her tone now serious. "Have you and Stone had a chance to catch up recently?"

Sophie's mood shifted as she turned to shuffle through the cardboard cutouts of literary heroes. "There's nothing left for us to say."

"Darling, I'm not one to interfere in another's love life," Ms. Birdie said, walking up behind Sophie and placing a hand on her shoulder. "But take it from a woman who's seen her fair share of romances bloom into a garden of happiness, you and Stone were well matched."

"I don't know how you can say that." Sophie turned. "There's nothing sweet about him."

"And you think that's a problem because you're sweet and romantic and very much a pink girl?"

A *pink girl*. Sophie pondered the descriptor. It implied girly-girl, which some would take offense at...but Sophie kind of liked it. She'd never pretended to be anything other than pink. She loved being someone who embraced the romantic side of life. And pink was her favorite color. And...oh yeah, Ms. Birdie was waiting for a response. "Yes, I'm a pink girl, and he's a thundercloud."

Ms. Birdie smiled like she had a secret, but instead of revealing it, she said, "And what of all those novels you've read? Are there none of them where the hero and heroine are night and day but still complete each other?"

Sophie nodded. "I love good opposites-attract romances."

"See there. Maybe Stone needs a little pink added to his life and, no offense, but maybe a thundercloud every now and then would help keep you from floating away on a dream cloud and missing all the messy wonderfulness of living."

Sophie gave a strained smile. "Your points are great. But honestly, I've experimented twice with dating guys outside of my comfort zone—and both times, it backfired."

"Once was a disaster, true," Ms. Birdie conceded with a nod. "But the second time wasn't about incompatibility—it was just... complicated"

Ugh. Complicated. It was Sophie's newest disliked word. "An insurmountable complication, more like."

"Funny things about complications," Ms. Birdie said in a conspiratorial tone. "They have a funny way of resolving themselves over time."

Nope. Nope, nope, nope. "Not all of them."

"Suppose this one did—where do you stand with Stone?" Ms. Birdie asked. "What are your feelings toward him?"

Sophie sighed. Dwelling on her feelings was a waste of time. Theirs was not a complication that would untangle itself. Then again, perhaps if she talked about her feelings, it would help her to untie the knot in her heart. "Just between us? I'm head over heels for him...and so is Poppie. And Stone is the first man Poppie's ever taken a liking to."

"Excellent." Ms. Birdie beamed. "Now, are there any other glitches in your delightful book boyfriend tropes that I may assist you in smoothing out?"

Sophie hesitated. "Well, there's Frankie. She's threatened to sue me for breach of contract if I don't deliver on a man with a sketchy past."

"I'll handle Frankie," Ms. Birdie declared. "As it happens, I believe I may have just the solution for that too."

"Has anyone ever told you you're better than a fairy godmother?" Sophie said.

"Not better than, but I have been called one on occasion," Ms. Birdie said. As she reached the doorway, she paused, her gaze returning to Sophie. "Before I go, could you clarify the design on these shirts?" She waved at the

T-shirts draped over each cardboard cutout. On the front were the words: *And then he said...* "What's the story there?"

Sophie grinned. "That's part of the fun for the auction. Each bachelor will read a line of dialogue—those breath-stealing, swoon-worthy lines from the romance novels they represent."

Ms. Birdie's expression brightened with understanding. "They'll read the line in the book where they declare their undying love for the heroine?"

Sophie shook her head. "Umm. They'll read a line from a moment of passion in the book. I got the idea from a TikTok trend. Where readers show their lovers a sentence and ask them to read it out loud. The kind of lines that tend to make women go weak in the knees."

"Oh my. That sounds rather exciting," Ms. Birdie admitted with a thoughtful nod. "It will certainly make for a memorable auction."

Sophie laughed. "I predict it will drive up the bids beyond your wildest hopes."

"I do believe you may be right," Ms. Birdie said, approval in her voice. "We've had quite the influx of twenty-somethings not only buying tickets but using their parents' unlimited platinum cards to open a line of credit for bidding. In fact, we sold out in just under one hour."

Sophie grinned. "An unlimited credit card. I can't even imagine owning one of those."

"I most certainly did not have access to one at that age," Ms. Birdie said. "I predict it's going to be quite the night. Oh, and Sophie, I'd like to have a table at the silent auction featuring your T-shirts. Are you interested?"

Sophie's stomach fluttered with excitement, and forgetting herself, she threw her arms around Ms. Birdie in a hug. "Yes. Absolutely, yes."

"Excellent," Ms. Birdie said, once she managed to disentangle herself from Sophie.

After Ms. Birdie left, Sophie turned and spoke to her cardboard cutouts. Up until today, they had been her sounding board for all her emotional upheavals over Stone. "You heard the woman. No time to worry about my heart. We have a table to plan for the silent auction."

Chapter 31

The night of the auction unfurled with a whirlwind of glitter and glamour; the paparazzi snapping photos of all who entered the event.

Sophie had brought Poppie as her plus one. Thanks to *Naked Runway*'s Glam Team, the two of them were holding their own in the elite setting.

Sophie radiated starlit grace in a midnight blue gown that cascaded down her frame; its fabric, which caught the light with her every movement, was sprinkled with crystals that mimicked a clear night sky. Her hair was swept up in an elegant twist, and delicate diamond earrings—her mom's—peeked through to add just the right touch of sophistication.

Poppie, ever the dapper counterpart, was decked out in a tailored charcoal suit that complemented Sophie's look perfectly. His tie matched the deep blue of her dress, and his smile was as bright as the polished cufflinks at his wrist. Instead of his walker, he sported a posh cane.

The moment they had arrived, Poppie had been whisked away by Ms. Birdie. The dear had someone he simply must meet that instant.

Sophie made her way backstage to check on her book boyfriends.

Isabella stopped her before she got a peek behind the curtain. "Sorry, darling. No one who isn't walking the stage is allowed to enter."

"Oh, but I wanted to check on my guys," Sophie said.

"They're fine." Isabella paused to make a note on the clipboard she held. "Go have fun. Rub elbows with Manhattan's wealthiest."

"If you insist." Sophie turned and made her way toward the sea of haute couture. Never had she ever walked among so much awesomeness. The gowns, the shoes, the hair, the makeup, the purses, the men. It was the perfect opportunity to make connections for her next adventure...whatever that turned out to be.

"For a professional daydreamer, you clean up quite nicely," drawled an all-too-familiar voice, causing her pulse to quicken and her breath to catch.

She slowly turned and laid eyes on Stone—the epitome of suave—clad in a tuxedo that hugged his frame with the kind of precision that could only be referred to as sinful. Or, as Sophie had read in a book recently, it hugged his frame like a dirty dream.

"I didn't expect to see you tonight," she said.

"You look breathtaking."

The memory of their last encounter—the night she'd thought he'd lost all control and broken a golden rule for her but hadn't, the night he reminded her he was a bachelor forever—made its way to the surface, and her smile vanished. "Why are you here?"

He pointed to his earpiece, a sleek black curve against his chiseled jaw. "I'm on duty. Ms. Birdie insisted on heightened security. Seems she expects the excitement to notch up to the rowdy side tonight...thanks to you and one of your brilliant ideas."

Then again, why should she spend even one minute of tonight upset? There'd be time tomorrow, and all the tomorrows to follow, for her to recall she didn't much care for Stone anymore. Tonight was for happiness. She let her smile return, and a laugh bubbled up from her throat as her eyes took in the eclectic mix of guests. "That's the hope."

Ms. Birdie had described the guest list as a fresh, vibrant crop of potential donors, almost vampiric in their youthful zest for new experiences.

Amid the glittering crowd, Sophie had already spotted at least five highly powerful influencers. The air around them crackled with the electric anticipation of the night's bidding frenzy.

"Would you like to grab a drink after this all wraps up?" Stone asked, snapping her back to the present.

The proposition tempted her, momentarily drawing her thoughts away from the bustling crowd. She glanced at Poppie, her steadfast date, who was currently engrossed in conversation with an elegantly dressed elderly woman. The socialite's white-gloved hand rested gently on Poppie's arm, and he looked utterly charmed. "I can't," Sophie replied. "It would be unseemly to ditch my date for a man who's already ditched me once, don't you agree?"

Stone's response was a stiff nod. "Fair enough." He turned and melted back into the crowd of partygoers.

Sophie sighed. "You could have at least tried to change my mind," she muttered. Needing a moment to regroup, she made her way to the silent auction, where it wouldn't be so crowded. Much to her delight, Ms. Birdie had insisted on adding a note to Sophie's T-shirt table informing bidders that their donation would go to charity, and Ms. Birdie would give a matching amount to the upcoming entrepreneur who'd designed the shirts—Sophie E. Clark.

Sophie had resisted the offer, but Ms. Birdie had insisted, saying it was the least she could do for the person who'd caused ticket sales for the annual charity auction to sell out in record time.

"Darling, there you are," Ms. Birdie said, materializing beside Sophie with her usual flair. "Have you taken a peek at any of the bids on your lovely contributions?"

"Not yet. I can't imagine they'll be all that popular, but it's wonderful exposure." Sophie let her gaze drift over the items—or in some cases, small replicas of the actual item—displayed on row after row of tables. Ms. Birdie had managed to get trips, boats, jewelry, cars, and so much more donated for her silent auction. "Hopefully, I'll get a few sales down the road."

Ms. Birdie harrumphed. "Nice had nothing to do with it. I believe in rewarding those who bring me good fortune. Now, go and look. I do believe you'll be pleasantly surprised—you might even decide you can afford to bid on one of your book boyfriends after all."

"That would allow me to return some of your generosity back to your charity," Sophie mused. "Not that I believe any of the men will go for an amount equivalent to whatever nice bid someone made on my behalf."

"And that's why you deserve all the happiness the world has to offer," Ms. Birdie declared. "You have a good heart. And darling, just know, if you see a bid, it's not a mistake." With that comment, Ms. Birdie linked arms with a dashing gentleman. "I do believe I know just the item you should bid on this evening," she whispered to him, guiding him toward a table laden with jewelry.

Chapter 32

Sophie's heart raced with a mix of awe and anxiety as she navigated through the labyrinth of silent auction tables, each more lavish than the last. She'd known the auction had a reputation for being high stakes—the kind of event that raised an obscene amount of money for its designated charity.

But she'd had no idea what obscene meant until now. People in attendance were generous beyond reason. It was as if the attendees had stumbled upon a forest of money trees. Or more plausible, they were all moonlighting as counterfeiters.

The one-upmanship among the bidders was a thing of beauty. Full pages of bids and the auction had barely started.

Yet, nothing had prepared her for the moment she spotted the bid on the bundle of T-shirt designs from her online store. The initial bid—a staggering five-figure sum—had quickly ballooned into the realms of six figures. Would Ms. Birdie match that kind of money? Surely not. But if she did, that would be life changing. And Sophie wouldn't be a professional daydreamer if she didn't pause and consider what those changes would look like.

Three hundred and fifty thousand—yes, that was the current bid—could whisk her and Poppie into a more upscale neighborhood. And provide Poppie with financial relief. And, if they were frugal, Sophie could take her time exploring her next adventure. After all, one couldn't be a professional daydreamer all their life.

"What has you wearing a shit-eating grin?" Poppie's voice cut through her reverie, pulling her back to the present.

"Shush," she hissed playfully, her eyes darting around. "You can't use that kind of language here—" She paused, studying him more closely. "Wait a minute. You're glowing like someone who just had a decade peeled off their life. What happened?"

"I asked first," Poppie countered with a smirk.

Their light banter was abruptly interrupted as a voice over the PA system filled the air, silencing the room. "Ladies and gentlemen, the bidding on tonight's Book Boyfriends will begin in fifteen minutes. If you've not yet retrieved a number, please do so immediately."

The room thrummed with anticipation, and Sophie felt it—a pulsing, brilliant energy that promised an unforgettable evening. Tonight, fortunes would be spent in the blink of an eye, all in the name of a charity. And somewhere in that whirlwind, Sophie would try and capture some of that magic.

"Darling," Ms. Birdie declared, reappearing at Sophie's side. "I took you at your word that you would vigorously bid on a book boyfriend and thus give back a slice of the fortune you're raking in from your products." Her voice was a blend of amusement and pride as she handed Sophie a bidding paddle. "I must admit, I had no clear idea your success would be quite so spectacular. I'm rather proud of myself for initiating this."

Sophie accepted the paddle. "Then you're not upset it's going to cost you so much out of pocket? I could secretly reimburse you."

"Absolute nonsense," Ms. Birdie waved her off with a flourish of her hand. "One should never gamble more than they can afford to lose, nor shy away from backing a worthy cause. I'm more than ready to write a hefty check. But now that you've come into your own windfall, I find myself quite eager to nudge you to do the same. After all, it's not every night that one enters a gala with a modest sum in their account and leaves as a multi-millionaire."

"Wait. What?" Sophie said. She must have misheard. "I just looked, and the last bid was at three hundred and fifty thousand."

"Oh darling, that was the last bid on the first page of bids. You didn't look at the bids on the next page or the next. Trust me, when I say multi, I mean more than a couple."

Sophie gasped, the sound barely a whisper as a wave of lightheadedness swept over her. "How many more?"

"Many, many multis," Ms. Birdie said.

"I can't let you match that." Sophie reached out and snagged a glass of champagne from the tray of a waitperson passing by. "Are you even capable of matching that?" She took a large gulp.

"Yes, darling. I'm quite capable." Ms. Birdie smiled serenely. "And I most certainly will match the amount."

Sophie fanned herself with her bidding paddle. "I can't even imagine." She glanced around for a place to sit. For the first time in her life, she thought she really might faint.

"The only thing I ask of you is that you enjoy your newfound wealth and pay it forward," Ms.

Birdie said, taking her by the arm, leading her to the bidding area, and finding her a seat.

"Ladies and gentlemen, our first book boyfriend of the evening is striding right out of the pages of *Aggie the Horrible versus Max the Pompous Ass*." Isabella's voice boomed over the speakers. "Please put your hands together for our very own charismatic Bosshole, Max, also known as Dillon Brax."

The crowd erupted into applause as a tall figure stepped into the spotlight. His confident gait and smoldering gaze embodied the beloved character to perfection.

"Enjoy," Ms. Birdie demanded. "And remember, you can afford to buy one."

In a daze, Sophie nodded, clutching the bidding paddle, feeling the energy of the room around her. The fictional world she had so often escaped to was coming alive before her eyes, and now, thanks to Ms. Birdie's clever push, she was a player in this serious game. She downed the rest of her champagne and sat the flute under her chair.

"Ladies and gentlemen, prepare your paddles. Let's open the floor and see who will have the pleasure of this charming man's company. Shall we start the bidding at five thousand? Do I hear five thousand? Step right up, don't be shy—this is a once-in-a-lifetime opportunity."

When no one immediately jumped in, Sophie heard herself saying, "We won't know what he's worth until we've heard him read his line from the book *Aggie the Horrible Versus Max the Pompous Ass*."

Isabella laughed. "You're so right. Pardon my blunder." She glanced at the bachelor on the stage. "Dillon, could you please read the line written on the index card handed to you before you walked onto the stage."

Dillon glanced at the card and then directed his gaze to the audience. "'Stop or prepare to be punished.'" His voice was low, growly, and toe-curling.

Sophie swallowed. Damn. "Five thousand."

"Do I hear six?" Isabella asked.

"Fifty," someone said, causing Sophie to gasp. Dear slum lords, who could afford to spend that on a date?

"Fifty-three," another said.

Five minutes later, Isabella said, "Sold for sixty-two thousand."

Sophie nearly fell out of her chair, and it wasn't because of the guzzled champagne. Her book boyfriend idea had netted the charity sixty-two thousand dollars. And there were eleven more bachelors to go. She tried to do quick math on how much that would add up to if they all went for a similar amount. It was a lot.

Obviously, the ladies of Manhattan loved themselves a good bachelor auction. Either that or they just really liked a man who could deliver a naughty line in a tone that caused their imaginations to think very wicked thoughts.

"And now, ladies and gentlemen, please welcome our next heart-stopping hero, the man who will sweeten your day just like your favorite morning pastry. Straight from the pages of Emily Henry's delightful novel *Funny Story*, here's Miles...a.k.a., Oliver, our cinnamon roll hero. He's as sweet and comforting as they come, ready to win your hearts with his charm and kindness. Let's hear Oliver read his line from the book."

Oliver raised the card, silently scanned the line, blushed, cleared his throat, and read. "'I know we said no sex, but can I touch you?'"

As Oliver delivered his line straight from the pages of *Funny Story* with an irresistible blend of charm and sincerity, she couldn't help but be swept away by his performance. The moment he finished, she started the applause with rapid-fire clapping of one palm against her paddle, all while doing a quick scan of the crowd to see how the other women were responding.

Her gaze unexpectedly locked with Stone's. His expression was a stark contrast to the lively atmosphere. He was scowling, his eyes intense and seemingly fixed upon her. The connection was startling, igniting a flurry of questions. What could have possibly soured his mood on such a thrilling night? Surely, not her declining his drink offer. He couldn't really have expected her to say yes.

Sophie tore her gaze away from his and refocused on Oliver.

"Shall we open the bid at six thousand?" Isabella said.

"Six." Sophie held up her paddle.

"Do I hear six-two?"

A woman from the very back of the crowd clearly said, "Twenty-five thousand." It was a voice Sophie recognized. It was the voice from the phone. The one who'd told her to stand down.

Sophie barely hesitated before saying, "Twenty-seven."

"Thirty," the woman replied.

"Forty-five," a different person shouted.

Sophie looked closely at Oliver as she continued bidding on him. She was looking for a sign, any sign of who he wanted to win the bid. When she finally got a hint, a huge smile from him at a certain bid, Sophie stopped. Oliver wanted the woman from the threatening phone call to win him at auction. Interesting. Should she warn him? Or did they know one another already?

"Darling, why aren't you bidding?" Ms. Birdie said, coming up next to her.

"My gut tells me he wants the other woman to win."

"You my dear, are too nice. If you want a man, go after him."

"Oh, I will if that man ever comes along."

"He will. You'll see. He will. Now, be a doll and stop being so nice. You've got deep pockets. Don't make me regret taking you under my wing." She handed Sophie another glass of champagne.

"Got it. I won't." Deep pockets? Holy Book Boyfriend, that was going to take some getting used to.

Chapter 33

Two hours into the auction, out of sight from the crowd, Stone stood slightly to the side of the stage, adjusting his mask, while the bachelor ahead of him was auctioned off. Each round of applause frayed his nerves. Who was he kidding? *Frayed* didn't do the situation justice. His nerves were jumpy as fuck—a new experience for him.

He normally approached the unknown cool and calculating. Hell, he'd stared into the face of death on more than one occasion and never broken a sweat. But now, the murmur of the audience, a constant roar, reminded him of the sea—relentless and unforgiving.

He ran his damp hands over his thighs. The nerves weren't from fear. Instead, they were directly related to the pounding of his heart. A heart fully aware of the gravity of the moment. Agreeing to be up on the stage involved much more than getting auctioned off for a good cause.

It was the precursor to his confession. A confession of love but also a confession of identity. An identity that could be a deal breaker just as it had been with the last woman he'd thought could handle the truth. If Sophie said no to embracing a similar identity, then his love confession would not be made. And considering she'd turned down his invite to have a drink after the event, what were the odds she'd move heaven and earth to win him at auction?

It didn't take a genius to figure out the answer.

He shoved the thought on its ass. Nothing good would come from worrying. There had been a hundred dominos stacked to get him to this point, and now one of them had been pushed. Only a coward turned and fled just because winning suddenly didn't look plausible.

From his concealed vantage point, Stone observed as the book-boyfriend bachelor known for his murky past effortlessly won over the crowd. The man's smile and gestures were perfectly crafted to charm, and Stone wondered if the guy had used his good looks to lure Sophie during their interview. Had he asked her to save a date for after the conclusion of the auction? Was that the real reason she'd turned down his offer?

Of course, he'd had the same damn thought with every bachelor who'd been on the stage tonight. And why wouldn't he? Had she interviewed him, he would have asked her out, rules be damned. It didn't help that Sophie had enthusiastically bid on every last one of them.

Another animated cheer from the audience drew a curse from Stone. The bids were happening at a lively pace. With each new bid, applause and laughter followed. This because the bachelor in question was giving them a spectacular show, dancing and flirting from a distance. It was like watching a masterclass in appeal and allure. Stone wasn't surprised by the bachelors' ability to fascinate. That's how guys like him were able to skirt the rules and live on the edges of the law.

A jaw-dropping offer reverberated through the hall, and the crowd went quiet.

"Sold," Isabella said, clanging her gavel on her podium.

Stone's gaze narrowed slightly as he recognized the figure who had placed the winning bid—it was Frankie, *Naked Runway*'s formidable editor-in-chief. A familiar prickling sensation crept up his spine. There was something unsettling about her, a certain sharpness in her demeanor that hinted at deeper, unseen motives. Though he couldn't quite pinpoint the source of his unease, his instincts screamed that a secret was there, lurking beneath her polished exterior.

He'd mentioned his concern to Ms. Birdie, who'd brushed him off and said she was on top of it.

"You're up next," Ziggy said. The magazine's fashion editor was tonight's behind-the-scenes manager, making sure the book boyfriends were on time for their big moment. "You ready to out-stud the last stud?"

"That guy will be a damn hard act to follow," Stone said.

Ziggy tittered. "That's what she said."

Stone scowled, causing Ziggy to titter again.

Resisting the urge to continue to wear his feelings on his sleeve, Stone instead straightened his bow tie and took a deep, steadying breath. While the rest of the crowd wouldn't recognize him, he'd gone with one of Isabella's cinnamon roll ensembles—other than the mask—in the hopes Sophie would.

"Let's do this," he said to Ziggy.

Stone quietly rehearsed the pivotal line he'd been given to deliver. It was a line spoken by the beloved hero to his heroine—a line that gave Sophie her fantasy's desire.

"Go," Ziggy ordered. "You're on."

As Stone stepped onto the stage, the crowd's applause washed over him like a tidal wave of sound, causing his steps to momentarily falter. Fuck. What if this was a mistake? He peered through the narrow slits of his mask, scanning the faces for Sophie's. She'd moved. No longer in the same spot she'd been in all night.

Relief washed through him when he finally located her.

There she was, Sophie E. Clark, the woman whose relentlessly optimistic outlook on life had effortlessly capsized his world. Only she wasn't smiling at the new bachelor on the stage. Instead, her face was an impenetrable mask, her eyes sharp and searching, roaming over his disguised form as if trying to decide if she knew him.

"And now, ladies and gentlemen, our final and most enigmatic book boyfriend of the evening," Isabella said. "Please welcome Penny Reid's Alex from *Love Hacked*. Tonight, he's known simply as Mr. X.

"Like Alex, Mr. X harbors a secret—a secret he's willing to disclose exclusively to the highest bidder. A secret so compelling, he's offering a money-back guarantee if you're not thoroughly intrigued." Isabella pivoted toward

Stone. "Mr. X, if you would, please share your *then he said* line?"

Stone didn't glance at his cue card. His gaze locked with Sophie's as he leaned into the microphone. "I'm going to touch you how I like, whenever I like, and you're going to let me," he declared, his voice a mix of command and vulnerability and truth.

Sophie blinked, the swift motion breaking their connection for a fraction of a second. When her eyes opened again, recognition—sharp and profound and angry—flared within them.

Panic swept through Stone. Recognizing him wasn't supposed to make her angry. This was a grand gesture. They were supposed to make a person swoon. But the look in Sophie's eyes told the story of a woman who wanted to commit murder.

"The bid on Mr. X is starting at..." Isabella's voice rang out, echoing through the charged atmosphere of the auction hall, and cutting through the *fuck, fuck, fuck* fog in Stone's head.

So much fuck fog that Stone was barely aware of the numbers flying around like buzzards. His focus was entirely on Sophie. A woman who most certainly wasn't bidding on him.

Her eyes, usually so warm and inviting, were sharp and piercing, slicing through the distance between them with an intensity that seemed almost tangible. If she didn't see his presence on the stage as a grand gesture, how did she view it?

Like an invasion of the finale of her professional daydreamer gig?

Was his being on the stage marring her happiness?

Of course it was. This had been a mistake. A massive mistake. She didn't see his presence as him becoming vulnerable. She saw it as him mocking her hard work.

His grand gesture was a grand wreck.

And if Sophie didn't bid, someone else would win. Someone expecting a giant-ass secret out of him. Why the hell hadn't they all devised a backup secret?

Wait. He had a backup plan. A different line he could have cited from the book. One that made him one hundred percent vulnerable.

Just as the auctioneer's voice signaled the bids were approaching their climax, Ms. Birdie glided gracefully next to Sophie and laid a hand on her arm. As if startled, Sophie flinched.

Stone held his breath as the two women exchanged a few hushed words.

"I have ninety-five going once... going twice ... and—"

"Wait," Stone said. He moved to Isabella. Took the microphone. Looked at Sophie. "I have one more line from the book *Love Hacked* that I'd like to recite, if that's okay with the audience."

He paused, swallowing hard.

Applause rang out.

Stone made eye contact with Sophie and slowly repeated his favorite line from Penny Reid's novel. "I don't want to learn how to live without you."

"One hundred." Sophie's voice rang out, her paddle slicing the air with decisive energy.

His chest heaved in relief. He glanced at Isabella, willing her to bring her gavel down.

She didn't. She couldn't. Because the bidders went wild.

"Do we have one ten?" Isabella asked.

"One twenty-five," came a shout from across the crowd. Not Sophie.

Silence fell over the room.

Stone's eyes locked with Sophie's, imploring her silently. Wishing he'd bid an even higher amount on her T-shirts. An amount so out-landishly outlandish it would obliterate her common sense that was no doubt telling her to stop bidding. That the money could be better spent elsewhere.

"One ninety-five," Sophie declared sharply, erupting the crowd with more excited chatter.

"Two hundred," rang out a new voice, cold and clear.

What the... Stone scanned the sea of faces, finally resting his gaze on a woman in the back. Her smile was tinged with an enigmatic allure. Why was she bidding on him?

"Two fifty," Sophie countered firmly, her paddle high in defiance.

"We have two fifty. Can I hear two seventy-five?" Isabella said, seizing on the sudden quiet.

Stone glanced at Isabella, appalled at the amount of money she was egging the bidders to spend.

Isabella didn't look the least bit guilty. Her eyes twinkled with the thrill of the auctioneer's chase.

"Two seventy-five," someone said, causing a new avalanche of bids.

Stone's heart pounded. He'd been a damn fool to put himself in this situation. Exposed, vulnerable, his future dangling on the strings of women drunk with champagne and unlimited bank balances.

"Two eighty," came the counter from the woman in black, her voice carrying a challenge.

Isabella smiled. "Ladies and gentlemen, we've got a real bidding war on our hands. How much are these fine participants willing to pay to uncover Mr. X's tantalizing secret? A man who did promise to reimburse you if you're not impressed with what he shares." She glanced at Stone and winked.

This seemed to shake loose the inhibitions of every last bidder in the room, and the bidding frenzy escalated.

As the bids soared, Stone's mind wandered back to his childhood in the orphanage, where even the most minor luxuries were out of reach. He remembered dreaming of simple pleasures—a lunch packed with Hostess Cupcakes, Oscar Mayer Lunchables, and name-brand sodas—things other children took for granted. He had been grateful at the orphanage for the meals provided, but they had been a stark reminder of what he didn't have.

It wasn't until Clarabelle had taken in him and his brothers that he had experienced the joy of choosing his school supplies and clothes, not those given out of charity. The luxury of choice had been a profound gift, yet here he was, witnessing his secret being auctioned off for sums he once couldn't even fathom.

"One million," Sophie said, her voice firm and resolute.

Stone blinked. Had he heard her correctly? That was half of the amount he'd bid on her silent auction bundle. This woman, who'd quit college and worked odd jobs to make ends meet for both herself and Poppie, was now giving up half of a windfall to buy him. Was it because she loved him? Or had she gotten carried away? Was she trying to keep the bidding going in the hopes of making ridiculous amounts of money for the charity? Was that what Ms. Birdie had talked to her about? Told her to bid when it looked like he was about to be sold. Was it a calculated risk on Ms. Birdie's part that someone would outbid Sophie?

It didn't matter. Sophie had bid on him. He'd worry about why later. Hell, he'd happily reimburse her.

No new bid rang out.

Isabella, looking as shocked as he felt, picked up her gavel. "Going once, going twice, and sold."

As the gavel slammed down, Stone's gaze found Sophie's. Her eyes were a little wild, his no doubt the same.

Applause burst forth like a storm, and Stone stood there, unsure what to do.

The indecision was fleeting because Isabella's voice reclaimed the room's attentiveness.

"Ladies and gentlemen, please direct your attention to the stage for one final spectacle."

The lights dimmed and then flared dramatically. During this time, Stone was helped off the stage by Ziggy.

"Let's welcome the authors whose works inspired this evening's auction." A line of women stepped through the curtain.

Stone swiveled, searching for Sophie, certain she'd come backstage to claim her prize. Well, if not certain, at least hopeful.

"... *Aggie the Horrible versus...*"

Behind him, he heard Isabella announcing authors and books.

"Emily Henry, *Funny Story*. J. J. Knight, *Single Dad on Top*. Lucy Score, *Things We Left Behind*. Lauren Layne, *Made in Manhattan*. Pippa Grant, *The Bride's Runaway Billionaire*."

Where was Sophie? With her credentials, she'd be able to come backstage if she wanted.

"Annika Martin, *Most Eligible Billionaire*, Emma Chase, *Tangled*, Claire Kingsley, *Falling For My Enemy*, Sara L. Hudson, *Anyone But The Billionaire*, and Penny Reid, *Love Hacked*. Let's give them all a round of applause."

The cheers were deafening, the atmosphere electric with admiration and excitement. Behind the authors, larger-than-life cardboard cutouts were placed, each depicting the fictional heroes whose personas had been brought to life that night.

Before Stone could go in search of Sophie, Ziggy shoved a T-shirt at him.

"We need to get this on you ASAP," Ziggy said as he removed Stone's tie and started unbuttoning his shirt.

Stone knocked his hands away. "I've got it." He quickly undressed and tugged the shirt over his head.

"Bachelors, please return to the stage and stand next to your cardboard cutout."

"That's your cue," Ziggy said when Stone didn't budge.

Each participant re-emerged onto the stage with waves. They were now wearing their *he said* T-shirts that Sophie had designed.

From where he stood, Stone couldn't see Sophie in the audience. Was she waiting backstage for him?

The crowd hooted and whistled, a cacophony of appreciation for the literary and the living embodiments of beloved characters.

Amidst the applause, Ms. Birdie took the microphone, her voice commanding the room. "And let us not forget the brilliant mind behind this year's theme, the talented Sophie E. Clark." The crowd clapped and that's when Stone finally saw the professional daydreamer herself as she was ushered onto the stage, a blush coloring her cheeks.

Unfortunately, once she took her place next to Ms. Birdie, all he could see of Sophie was her back.

Ms. Birdie continued, "Thanks to Sophie's innovative idea, between the silent auction and the bachelor auction, we've raised a tentative total of..." She paused, glancing down at the note handed to her, "An astonishing $8.9 million for our charity!"

Stone stepped away from his assigned spot and managed to position himself where he could see Sophie's profile.

Her smile was tentative as she stood beside Ms. Birdie. The audience's appreciation was palpable.

"Now ladies, if you purchased a bachelor, they will be in contact with you tomorrow to set up your date. Please stop by the cashier table and pick up your receipts for your purchases."

While Ms. Birdie continued to explain the finer details, Stone was swept along by the tide of bachelors leaving the stage. They were all apparently anxious to exit through the back door before being bombarded by the women who had not won them at auction.

Stone looked back, searching for Sophie, but his view was obscured by the moving bodies and shifting shadows. The next thing he knew he stood outside on the sidewalk. He turned to go back into the venue, but the door had locked.

"There they are," a woman shouted, and a gaggle of women rounded the corner and ran toward them.

"Hurry. Get in," one of the bachelors shouted at Stone.

Swallowing his frustration, Stone jumped into a limo right as the driver pulled out into traffic.

Sitting beside the single-dad bachelor, Stone pulled out his phone and texted Sophie.

Meet me on the rooftop. —Mr. X

LISA WELLS

Chapter 34

A charming limo driver dropped Sophie and Poppie off at their apartments a little after midnight. A lot had happened since they'd left to go to the bachelor ball—a life-changing lot. So much so that, as if by agreement, neither of them had spoken of it on the drive home.

Now Poppie, with his cane and tuxedo adding a distinguished touch to his weathered charm, offered Sophie his arm as they walked slowly toward their building. His cane tapped rhythmically against the pavement, echoing the silent excitement of the night.

It wasn't until they were standing in front of their respective doors that the silence was broken by Sophie, who had a sudden fit of giggles.

"You going to be able to get those under control, or should I call for help?" Poppie asked, eyeing her with amusement.

Sophie turned and leaned against her door, the cool surface grounding her well enough to get the giggles under control. "Am I dreaming?"

"If you are, so am I." Poppie shifted his weight on his cane. "We both heard Ms. Birdie say the same thing."

"What did we hear?" Sophie whispered, afraid to break the spell of the night.

"I don't know about you, but what I heard is a fancy designer approached her and wants to feature your boyfriend shirts during Fashion Week."

"Me, too." A grin slid through Sophie, spreading warmth and disbelief. "Poppie, I did it. I didn't settle for anything less than the fairytale. Mom would be so proud."

Poppie studied her with eyes full of affection, his weathered face softening with paternal pride. "Honey, she was proud of you from the day you were born. Tonight, though, she'd be extra happy for you. Her greatest wish was that you would live a life so full of fantastic moments that authors would write fairytales about you."

Sophie's laughter bubbled up again. She pushed off the door and hugged Poppie tightly. "Thank you for everything," she whispered, her voice thick with emotion.

Poppie patted her back gently, his cane tapping lightly against the ground. "You're welcome, darling. Now go get some rest. Tomorrow's a new day, full of more dreams to chase... And who knows, you might find more book boyfriend bachelors in need of being purchased at auction for crazy amounts of money." His tone only held humor, no admonishment.

Sophie wrapped her arms around herself and rubbed the goosebumps on her arms. "I did go a little overboard, didn't I?" She still couldn't believe she'd bid a million dollars on Stone. She hadn't meant to go that high, but then he'd spoken another line from the book. One he could only know if he'd read the book. A line she'd wanted to believe had been spoken for her alone, and she'd bid an amount that shut everyone up.

"Your momma always said you were special," Poppie said, wiping a tear from his cheek. "And boy, was she ever right."

Sophie twitched her nose to keep from crying at the amount of pride in his voice. "You know this means we can live anywhere in the city we want?"

"You can," Poppie said fiercely. "I'm staying right here. Can't wait to tell that blowhard landlord I can afford his rate hikes, and he's not getting his hands on my unit."

"Poppie," Sophie said quietly. "Life's too short to make decisions based on revenge."

"At your age, there's a lot of truth to that. At mine, not so much."

Sophie yawned, feeling the exhaustion of the evening finally catching up to her.

"You're tired. Get in there and go to bed. We'll talk about our choices tomorrow," Poppie said, his voice softening with concern.

"I'm holding you to that, right after I meet with Ms. Birdie in the morning. I should be home by noon." Ms. Birdie had asked Sophie to brunch tomorrow and promised to let Sophie know precisely how much money her items had brought at the auction.

"By the way, when are you going to collect on that secret you bought?" Poppie asked, swinging his door open and then turning to look at her. "Tonight might be as good a night as any. You could give him a call, ask him over."

Sophie furrowed her brows. "Not tonight. Tonight has been perfect, and I refuse to make any decision that might ruin that."

Poppie cocked his head. "Is it that, or are you just not ready to learn his secret? Learn what possessed him to get up there on that stage and save your bacon from the wrath of Frankie?"

Stone had done that.

"I need a moment to let everything sink in," she said to Poppie. "I want to enjoy this high without complicating it." *Complicated.* Man, how she hated that word. In today's world, it had become the get-out-of-jail-free card one used when they wanted out of a relationship.

"Fair enough," Poppie said. "Just don't wait too long. Sometimes, the magic fades if you let it idle until it runs out of gas."

"I promise I won't. Goodnight, Poppie."

"Goodnight, dear."

She watched him enter his apartment and listened for him to lock his doors.

She let herself into her apartment and triple-locked the door before leaning against the frame, closing her eyes, breathing deeply, and reliving the night's events—Ms. Birdie's generosity, the excitement of the auction, the designer, Stone's expression when he'd spoken his second line, and now the anticipation of uncovering Stone's secret.

Her instincts told her that while she'd already tumbled over the cusp and found herself amid something wonderfully significant and life-changing, there was another cusp in her near future. The nature of it, she couldn't be sure. But it had something to do with Stone's secret.

She pushed off the door and headed to her room. Why exactly had Stone asked her, before the auction began, to have a drink after the event? He'd given her no hint behind the request. Was it to tell her in private he couldn't live without her so he wouldn't have to do it publicly?

Then again, now that she thought about it, that line he recited could have been his way of saying I don't want to live without you as my friend...or as my reading buddy.

Or... any other stupid thing guys suggest after they've FUBARed the hell out of a relationship.

As she showered and changed into her pajamas, her mind raced through a list of possible reasons. Maybe he wanted to apologize, or perhaps he had some convoluted explanation that would just make everything more confusing. She knew she shouldn't dwell on it, but the questions kept coming.

She crawled into bed, pulled the covers up to her chin, and stared at the ceiling. Her mind drifting back to the way he'd looked when she'd won him, a mixture of hope and regret in his eyes. Despite everything, a part of her still felt a pull toward him, a magnetic force that made her heart flutter and her thoughts race.

Sophie sighed, turning on her side and hugging her pillow tightly. "Stupid boys," she muttered to herself. "Why do they always make things so complicated?"

She closed her eyes, inhaled, and exhaled until her spiraling thoughts dissipated. Tomorrow would come with its answers and decisions.

For now, she let herself sink into the comfort of sleep, a place where she could dream about fairytales, auctions, and the whisper of more fairytale endings to come.

Chapter 35

Stone stood on the rooftop, his eyes sweeping over the dimly lit space around him. The soft glow of the garden lights cast long shadows, creating an almost ethereal atmosphere. He checked the time again and then reread the message he had sent Sophie. He would like to think it was unlike her to leave him hanging.

But how in the hell would he know that, considering they hadn't dated...yet?

Here he was, ready to declare his love, and he'd never even asked her on an official date. The ludicrousness of it all formed a new knot of worry in his chest, tightening with every passing minute.

Clarabelle, who'd called him as soon as she'd gotten word the auction was over, had assured him it was all very romantic. The kind of thing movies were made of, or books were written about.

According to her, falling in love with your client was an age-old romance trope, and Sophie adored tropes.

According to Clarabelle, Sophie would see the magic in the whole situation.

Unfortunately, it appeared Clarabelle was wrong. Sophie wouldn't even meet with him to hear a secret she'd paid a million dollars to obtain.

The thought of trying to sleep was out.

The idea of going to work tomorrow and telling his brothers that he'd been blown off was repugnant.

The thought of never telling Sophie he loved her and wanted to spend his life with her was...not an option.

If ever there was a time for a backup plan, it was now.

With a determined nod, he pocketed his phone and headed back to the elevator.

If the professional daydreamer wouldn't come to him, he'd go to her. No more waiting around, hoping fate would cut him a break. He'd march straight to her apartment and lay it all on the line—starting with his secret life as a fairy godfather.

If that went well, or even if it didn't, he'd bare his soul and tell her he loved her.

And if that went well, or even if it didn't, he'd ask her to be his girlfriend and allow him the honor of earning her love.

Somewhere in this emotional rollercoaster, he'd pitch her the idea of becoming a fairy-tale coordinator for him and his brothers. It sounded ridiculous, but with Sophie, ridiculous had a way of turning magical.

Or maybe he should start with the love confession. Then drop the fairy godfather bombshell. And then... No. Hell. He needed to scrap the script, embrace the chaos, and, for the first time in his life, do things Sophie's way—wing it.

The cab ride to her apartment was a blur as his mind raced with thoughts of Sophie and their stilted conversation at the auction, and the myriads of expressions she'd shown him while bidding. Not one of them had been happy.

If those thoughts weren't heavy enough, he also worried about what if she didn't take his fairy godfather revelation well, and what if she didn't love him back?

He shook off the doubts. Tonight, he'd let go of control and leap into the unknown, heart first.

"You getting out, or what?" the cabbie said, cutting through his swirling what-ifs like a bullet through a bad guy.

Stone glanced at the exterior of her brick-faced building. Tall, narrow windows with white trim gave the building a quaint, almost storybook appearance...which suited Sophie to a capital T.

Inside that building was where he'd donned his first book boyfriend T-shirt. It's where he'd first kissed Sophie. It's where he'd met Poppie. It's where he'd fallen in love.

"Thanks for the lift," Stone said, hopping out of the cab.

The driver grunted and pulled away, tires squealing slightly on the asphalt.

Stone stepped inside the building and made his way to Sophie's front door. She'd changed the sign. Now it read: *Dreams do come true. Knock for your fairytale ending.*

If he and Sophie were to get married, what would their front door sign say? "Not if. When," he corrected his thoughts. After all, a man had to have hope before going into battle.

He rapped his knuckles against the door. The sound echoed in the quiet hallway, and he winced, not wanting to wake up Poppie. When she didn't answer, he knocked again. He waited, ears straining for any sign of movement from within. He glanced at his watch. After one a.m. Surely, she was home by now. Unless she wasn't coming home.

When the door suddenly opened, relief flooded him. Not that it lasted long. One look at her frown made sure of that.

"Stone?" Her voice hinted that the frown on her face wasn't a sign of confusion, but rather one of displeasure. "What are you doing here?"

He forced a smile. "I hear this is where one comes when they're looking for their very own fairytale ending."

When her brows creased, he pointed to the sign on her door.

"Oh. That." She opened the door wider and stepped aside. "Come in before you wake up Poppie and get his hopes firing in directions that won't pan out."

Did that mean Poppie was rooting for him? Stone's heart gave a hopeful leap. "I texted you," he said, following her into the familiar warmth of her apartment.

"I haven't looked at my phone since leaving for the ball," Sophie replied over her shoulder as she walked into the kitchen and flipped on the light. "What did you want that couldn't wait until tomorrow?"

He took a deep breath, preparing himself for the moment he had been dreading and anticipating in equal measure. "There's something I need to tell you, Sophie."

"Yes, I know. The secret. Considering how much I paid for it, I feel wine is in order," she said, sounding wary.

"It's not a bad secret," he assured her, hating that he'd made Sophie E. Clark—Professional Daydreamer—afraid to hope for a grand secret.

"Good to know." Sophie rummaged through several bottles before she grabbed a bottle of merlot out of the refrigerator, popped the cork, and poured two goblets. She handed him one. He resisted the urge to mention red wine was best served at slightly cooler than room temperature. Around sixty-six degrees. If she liked it cold, who was he to criticize.

Taking the glass, he cataloged the moment. The saying on her sleep shirt: *Daydream Enabler*. The heady fragrance of her skin after a shower: peaches and cream. The tightness in her lips right before she took her first sip of wine. Her lusty sigh of appreciation for the cheap, chilled vintage whose label read, *Fairytale Celebration*.

"Okay," she said, walking over to the window. "I'm listening." She turned and leaned against the frame.

"Maybe we should sit." He motioned to the couch. He'd had it delivered after they had split, with explicit instructions to the delivery team that if she tried to bully them into taking it back with them, they were to make excuses as to why that wasn't possible. It looked nice in her tiny apartment.

After a moment of hesitation, Sophie sat, and he sat next to her, their knees touching as they turned to look at one another. The lights flickered. Why had that happened? Was the spell Clarabelle had cast on him weakening?

"There's no easy way to say this without it coming as a shock," he began, reaching for her hands. Thunder boomed in the distance. "I'm about to tell you a secret I thought I'd take to my grave."

"To your grave?" Sophie yanked her hands out of his, clearly taken aback. "You said it wasn't a bad secret."

"Not bad." He reached for her hands again. "Sophie, I'm a bona fide Fairy Godfather."

Lightning was quickly followed by a loud clap of thunder, and then the lights went dark, preventing him from seeing her reaction.

"Damn." He quickly retrieved his phone, turned on its flashlight feature, and aimed it at her face.

Her eyes were wide, and her mouth open. "Define bona fide?" she squeaked.

"I have a wand." He waited for the shock to wear off. When it did, he breathed a little easier.

A look of pure enchantment filtered over Sophie's face. "Tell me everything."

The lights came back on.

He finished his wine and set the goblet down. "When individuals wish for a fairy godmother and one isn't available, the wish is passed to me and my brothers. They're also fairy godfathers."

A laugh burst from her, startling him.

"Ha," she exclaimed. "You had me for a moment. Tell me the real secret. Spit it out. Let's get this over with."

This reaction, he understood. He'd expected disbelief. Who in their right mind would accept his words at face value? "I know it sounds far-fetched, but I'm not lying."

She frowned. "Of course you're lying. You don't have an ounce of whimsy in your little finger. There's no way you're a Fairy Godfather."

He tensed. Was this the beginning of the end? Would she refuse to believe? Tell him to leave? "And yet, I am."

Emotions flashed across her face, the last one a mix of anger and hurt. "But you've done nothing but make fun of me for chasing my fairytale ending."

"In the beginning, I did. But then…" He trailed off. It wasn't time to admit she'd won him over and he'd fallen hard for every part of her. That there wasn't a thing about her he'd change.

"But then what?" she persisted, anger still evident in her voice.

Sweat broke out on his brow. She had every right to be mad. Hell, to send his sorry ass packing. It was time to be humble. "Can you ever forgive me?"

"I don't know." She scrubbed at a tear that had fallen on her cheek.

He held very still—afraid the wrong movement would make up her mind in a negative fashion—and forced himself to wait.

A lifetime later, she gave him a watery smile. "Tell me more about your being a Fairy Godfather."

He wiped the sweat from his brow and relaxed. "When we were little, we were bounced around from foster home to foster home. Then, one night, we overheard them talking about separating us because no one wanted to take on three boys. Unbeknownst to me, one of my brothers wished for a fairy godmother that evening."

"How old was he?" she asked.

"Five."

"That makes sense."

"Anyway, his wish was granted, and we were sent to a new foster home. To Clarabelle's home. A home we never had to leave because she adopted us…"

"And?" As if she were reliving history with him, another tear slipped down her cheek.

"Clarabelle was a fairy godmother." He left out the part about her new title including the word *ghost*. She was a fairy godmother ghost. Clarabelle now lived in the second veil in Harmony, Missouri.

Then again, why leave out that part? If fairy godfathers could be real, so could ghosts. And if he and Sophie were to have a chance at making their relationship work, he had to be transparent.

"Was?" Sophie asked, reaching out and taking his hands.

"She's dead now," Stone admitted.

"And?"

"When she died, she had unfinished business. And when that happens, Magicals have a system where they can ask for time to finish their business before crossing over."

"That's a nice perk," she said.

He nodded. "Her unfinished business was to tell her boys of her true identity. Once she did that, instead of crossing over, she somehow talked the powers-that-be in the second veil into letting her hang out there so she could run us through fairy godmother boot camp. A task we had to complete to earn our wands."

"There's a fairy godmother boot camp?" Sophie asked, jumping up and walking to the window again. "What does one do at this camp?" She turned to look at him.

"She trained us on how to help those in need." He resisted the urge to go to her, sensing she needed space. "And how to use our wands to conjure up the things our clients wished for."

"Let me get this straight. Your secret is to tell me you're a fairy godfather, you have a wand, you can conjure things, and your mom is a ghost?"

He swallowed hard. "That about sums it up."

"About?" Her eyes bulged. "What did you leave out?"

"Part of our becoming fairy godfathers was our promise that for every case we take to retrieve a kidnapped child, we would match it by completing a fairy godmother wish." In the beginning, the wishes had been simple. A pony. Long hair. Learning to ride a bike without training wheels. But lately, they'd become more convoluted.

"I once asked for a fairy godmother," Sophie said sadly. "I wanted to go to heaven and be with my parents. I never got one."

Fuck. "Yours wasn't a wish they could grant. They only respond to ones they can. And even then, not all wishes are granted."

"Why not?"

"Because fairy godmothers are in short supply. That's why Clarabelle was able to get it approved to start a fairy godfather branch. It was either that, or those children whose doable requests went unanswered would continue to be disappointed, and the more that happened, the fewer and fewer who would believe, and that would eventually cause the demise of fairy godmothers."

Sophie's eyes softened, and she looked at him with a mixture of understanding and lingering sadness. "So, it's not just about granting wishes. It's about keeping the magic alive?"

"Exactly," Stone said, relieved that she was starting to grasp the bigger picture. "We're doing our best to keep the belief in magic strong, to make sure that kids don't lose hope. It's a delicate balance."

She walked back to the couch and sat down, her expression contemplative. "Where's your wand? Can I see it?"

"Soon. This brings me to the next part of my reason for being here."

"Never in my thirty-two years," Sophie said with a bemused smile, "did I ever think a day would come when I heard myself say this, but here I go... This secret has been worth every penny of that million-dollar bid I made."

He laughed. Her enthusiasm was endearing. "Back to your question about my wand. You see, after the accident, my magic started glitching, which made me a danger in the field."

She frowned. "How was your wand damaged?"

"A bullet caught it and grazed my finger."

She went white. "A bullet. You take fairy godfather cases where bullets fly?"

He shook his head. "No. At least, we've never been given one where that was necessary. But we're allowed to use our wands in our retrieval of kidnapped children cases. By doing so, we practically eliminate the danger to the children. But on this particular night, right as I was casting a spell over the kidnapper, a child emerged we hadn't known was in the house. I was distracted, and my inattention gave the bad guy enough time to fire off a round before I could spell his gun."

"Was the child hurt?"

"No. Everything turned out okay, but my wand took a bullet, and my finger was grazed by the incident. As a result, my magic started glitching."

"What does glitchy magic look like? I mean, does your wand droop or something when you're spinning it?"

"I can say, 'turn those boots into stilettos,' and it turns the boots into a loaf of bread."

"Oh. I could see how that would be unimpressive to a child expecting big things out of you as their fairy godfather."

"Anyway, my wand hasn't been the same since."

She folded her arms across her chest. "I feel like there's more to the story than that. What aren't you saying?"

"It's been discovered that during the injury, magic from the wand leaked into me."

Sophie's eyes widened, her curiosity palpable. "What does that mean?"

"It means I now have some level of magic within me, independent of the wand. It's unpredictable and, at times, uncontrollable."

"Well, doesn't that just sound delightful?" She went back to pacing, her steps quick and purposeful.

Stone watched her in fascination. "I'm glad you feel that way because all the thunder, lightning, rain, freaky blinking lights... Those were all caused as a result of our interaction. It appears that every time you and I touched, my magic either seeped into you or you sucked it out of me. Or you are a sleeping Magical finally awakening."

She swirled around and came to him, eyes wide with realization. "Are you saying—" She stopped talking, twirled her pointer finger in the air, then pointed it at him and said, "Jazam."

He startled, taking a step back. "Whoa. Whoa. Let's not try casting spells without instruction. That's what boot camp is for. You do or say the wrong thing, and I'll be a toad."

She laughed, the sound musical and light, and tucked her finger into the waistband of her pajama shorts.

"I take it you're okay with everything I've told you tonight?" The question was rhetorical. It was obvious she was. He couldn't believe he'd ever been the dumb fuck who'd compared her to his last girlfriend and kept her at arm's length as a result. The two women were nothing alike. Of course Sophie would be thrilled to learn her boyfriend was a fairy godfather. She was Sophie E. fucking Clark. Believer in book boyfriends coming to life.

"Who wouldn't be?" Sophie enthused. "This is the best news ever. Like nothing you could say next would trump everything you've said so far."

Well, fuck. He should have started with "I love you." Saying it now would be the pure definition of anticlimactic. "Thank you for being so perfect for me."

She gave him a funny look. "Let's talk about that statement." Her voice was soft but firm. "Are you, or are you not, still a bachelor for life? And if not, what changed?"

"After you and I had our parting of ways, I was a mess."

"You're the one who kicked me to the curb. Why were you a mess?"

"Because I love you." Admitting it felt like a weight lifting off his chest and crashing down all at once. The vulnerability was terrifying, but it also felt undeniably right. He quickly continued, not giving her time to respond. "And I'd convinced myself that you were better off never knowing that. Not to mention, I'd made promises to my brothers I couldn't break. Loving you was inevitable, but acting on it would have been selfish." He stopped talking and waited for her to say *I love you, too.*

"Did you think I couldn't handle the fact you were a fairy godfather?"

He snorted. Yep. He should have led with *I love you.* Now, it didn't even garner a nod, a smirk, or a single flutter of her eyelashes. "By then, I knew you could. But as I told you before, I couldn't handle the idea of your life being in danger because of me."

"What's changed? You're here. You've told me you love me. You've told me your secret. Why? Are you getting out of security?" she asked in a no-nonsense tone.

There it was. The acknowledgement she'd heard his declaration. But still no sign of excitement. "Not that."

"Then you've decided to treat me like an adult and allow me to determine if I want to be in a relationship with a man who might get me killed? Or worse, break my heart by getting himself killed?"

His heart skipped a beat. Never that. Thank God that wasn't still an issue. "A way has been discovered where I am free to be in love with you, free to chase you and date you until I'm worthy of you falling in love with me, and keep you safe from danger in the process."

She grinned, and he breathed a little easier.

"You're going to chase me?" she asked.

"I am," he said solemnly. "And I expect you to play hard to get because you will be worth the chase."

"Damn straight I am, and I will not be easy to catch. Of that, you can be certain," she spouted without a second of hesitation. "But back to why you were finally able to tell me. What's this big plan?"

"How would you like to be our Fairytale Co-ordinator?" he blurted, knowing full well this would get a way bigger reaction than his telling her he loved her had. Of course, he deserved her less-than-ecstatic response. He had meant it when he said he'd be happy to chase her and prove worthy of her love.

As he had predicted, she squealed and threw herself into his arms. "Yes. Yes. Absolutely yes."

"But you don't even know what that means yet." He chuckled and pulled her into his embrace.

"It doesn't matter. The title is perfection. The only thing better than growing up to be a professional daydreamer would be to grow up to be a Fairytale Coordinator. Oh, my God. So many doubters are going to have to kiss my derriere for sure now! I am going to create a T-shirt saying as much. I'll wear it to my next class reunion."

He had no idea what she was talking about, so he let it slide...for now. "You would help us with our fairy godfather assignments. Help us create the perfect experience for every request. You would be in charge of making sure we get all the details right. And in return, you'll be under the protection of our magic. And, if you are Magical in your own right—which is a possibility—you will be taught how to use it."

"Holy Book Boyfriend Day. Tell me more about that?" Her grin took up her whole face.

"It is Clarabelle's strong belief that your mother was a Magical."

She gasped and slapped her hands over her mouth, shaking her head as if finding this the thing she couldn't accept as real. Slowly sliding her hands down and away from her lips, she whispered, "Like a fairy godmother?"

"Most likely...which would explain your mom's message on your nursery wall."

Sophie pivoted and headed toward the kitchen. "I'm going to need more wine," she said over her shoulder. "I feel like I've won the lottery, hit the jackpot at the casino, and discovered a magic spell to bring my favorite book boyfriend to life."

"The cinnamon roll one?" he asked, following her into the kitchen, acutely aware she hadn't yet said how she felt about him.

She shook her head as she reached for the bottle.

"Then which one?" he asked, his mind racing through all the other types. "Which one of them from tonight would you choose if you could make one of them your own?" He held out his glass for a refill.

"I'd choose...none."

"None?" he echoed. "Not even the one with a secret?"

"Nope."

He studied her. "I see."

"I don't think you do, you big idiot. I'd choose you. The real you. You're the perfect combination of all my favorite tropes. A little cinnamon, a little murky, a whole lot of delicious alpha yumminess."

"In other words, I'm book boyfriend-ish?"

"Yes."

"There's one problem. Your description of me left out one part." Stone inhaled deeply, prepared to give her his final secret.

"And that is?" she asked, taking a sip.

"Grumpy billionaire."

LISA WELLS

Chapter 36

"You're a billionaire?" Sophie repeated, as Stone wiped wine off his tux.

She didn't bother apologizing for spitting red wine all over him. He should know there are only so many surprises you can drop on a person at any one time before they are eventually going to explode wine out of their nose and mouth.

"A grumpy one." He removed his overcoat, slipped his bow tie off, and unbuttoned his top buttons.

"Then none of these revelations tonight are because you found out about my recent windfall, and you're not secretly hoping to get your hands on my fortune?" she teased.

He cocked his head. "You had a windfall, and you're now rich? Interesting."

"I believe so," she responded.

He tilted his head to the other side. "I look forward to hearing the story of your windfall on our first date. Say, tomorrow morning, for breakfast."

Sophie took a moment to steady herself, emotions swirling. "Are you really willing to chase me?" Now would be the right time to admit she loved him, but where was the fun in that? Not to mention, it deserved its own special night to be revealed.

"I am." He smiled, the tension between them easing. "I'm quite looking forward to dating the woman who turned my world upside down with her smiles."

"And this possibility of my being Magical?" *Oh, my God. I might be Magical.* "How will we research that?"

"That is something you'll have to take up with Clarabelle," Stone said. "She's the one who put my brothers and me through our paces at boot camp, but I'm not sure how it works if you have magic without a wand."

"I see. And if I am?" Sophie asked, internally pinching herself a thousand times a minute to make sure she was awake, and this was real. "Will my title change from Fairytale Coordinator to Fairy Godmother?"

Stone glanced at the liquid in his glass and thought. "I believe you could be a fairy godmother with the job title of Fairytale Coordinator."

"I do like the sound of that." Sophie giggled. "And this grumpy status of the guy who claims to love me? Is it negotiable?"

Stone sat both their wine goblets down, then moved into her space. "I think you'll find him less and less grumpy the more time he spends around you."

She placed her hands on his chest. "Poppie and I are a package. You get me, you get him."

He placed both hands on her face. "I like Poppie. That's not a problem. It's a bonus."

She licked her lip, anticipation building in her stomach. "And I'm not giving up my T-shirt business."

"I have every belief it will thrive." He stepped forward, and she stepped back until the counter dug into her hips.

"You have no idea," she said. "So much happened tonight I've not even shared with you."

He placed his hands on the counter on either side of her and placed his lips on her neck. "I'd love to hear all about it...later."

"I can't do breakfast or lunch. I have plans for both. The first with Ms. Birdie. The second with Poppie. I could pencil you in for dinner at a fancy restaurant?"

He nibbled the sensitive lobe of her ear, and she gasped.

"Nothing but the best for you." He pushed into her, and she felt his erection against her stomach.

"Just so you know," she said, tugging the tail of his shirt out of his pants and placing her hands on his back. "I most certainly do not have sex on the first date."

He chuckled. "Damn. How about the night before your first date?"

She reached for his belt. "This is all so incredible. It feels like a dream."

"I promise it's real," he said softly, his hands sliding under her T-shirt. "And it's just the beginning."

"Then let's make the most of it. Together."

"Together," he echoed, pulling back and sweeping her up in his arms.

As they gazed into each other's eyes, Sophie felt a sense of rightness, a feeling that this was where she was meant to be. With Stone, everything felt possible. Every challenge seemed surmountable. And every dream, no matter how fantastical, felt within reach.

Everyone who had ever told her she'd never be a professional daydreamer could kiss her ample derrière.

She'd done that and so much more.

Chapter 37

EPILOGUE

Eighteen months later, the wedding reception of the century—or at least that's how it was billed in Sophie's head—was in full swing, laughter and music filling the air.

Sophie and Stone, the newlyweds, sat at the head table, surrounded by friends and family. Overhead, twinkling lights mirrored the twinkle in their eyes as they basked in the glow of their big day.

Sophie's gown—a vision of lace and satin—had been designed by Clarabelle with love...and magic. The train and veil, which Sophie had designed herself, were adorned with delicate embroidery and tiny pearls that shimmered as she moved.

The sound of silverware clinking against glass quieted the room.

"Good evening. For those of you who don't know me, I'm Ryder, Stone's good-looking brother and co-best man. If you do know me, I apologize for any inappropriate jokes I've already made tonight."

Sophie laughed and glanced at Stone. His eyes were on her, the awe and adoration in his expression making her feel like the most beautiful woman in the world.

"Stone and Sophie, what a couple." Ryder said. "One is a strong, silent type with no charm, and the other is Sophie. I mean, have you seen her? Bro, you really outkicked your coverage here."

This elicited laughter from the audience and a nod of agreement from Stone.

"Now, let me tell you about my baby brother. He's always been the guy who wanted the world to see him as tough and broody. Broody—that's a new term I learned from Sophie, but I digress. Let's get back to Stone's aspirations to be Mr. Tough Guy. As it turns out, Stone is the only Navy SEAL in history who's afraid of needles. That's right, folks, the only SEAL without a single tattoo. Not one. While his comrades were getting inked with eagles and anchors, Stone was busy making sure he stayed a blank canvas. Tough, my ass." Ryder paused and smiled at his brother. "It's okay, little brother, I'm sure Sophie loves your tattoo-free, needle-phobic self just the way you are."

You're afraid of needles? Sophie mouthed to her new husband. How had she not known this already? When she'd asked him about his lack of tattoos, he'd made a joke about saving himself for marriage and then had distracted her with sex.

He leaned over and whispered, "Ryder's afraid of bubbles."

Sophie laughed and glanced around at those in attendance.

At a table nearby were eleven of the twelve book boyfriends. Her year-long column with *Naked Runway* had been a success. They'd offered her another column, but she'd declined. Her plate had gotten a little full, what with her T-shirt business booming and her side hustle as a Fairytale Coordinator.

And then there was the time now spent learning how to not only operate a wand but also cast spells.

Come to find out her mom had been a fairy godmother and her father a warlock. She'd discovered this when Poppie had given her two letters—one from each parent. Letters he'd received upon their deaths, with strict instructions to hold them until he knew she'd met the one she was meant to be with.

In the letters, they had explained she was a Magical and that she would come into her powers when she fell in love with the right man. They had also given her the names of two contacts she could go to for help in understanding her new identity. They lived in a haunted town in Missouri, and their names were Ruby Rae and Sara Ann. She and Stone had already visited the quirky little town of Harmony and its neighbor community, Mayhem, on several occasions. They loved the haunted towns so much that they were considering moving there once they had started a family.

Another tinkling of silverware against crystal pulled Sophie out of her thoughts. It was time for another speech.

"Good evening. I'm Donna, Sophie's maid of honor and the proud vice president of the Book Boyfriend Connoisseurs Club. That's right, I have the official job of critiquing fictional men for a living, and I must say, Sophie has set quite a high bar with her real-life choice."

The audience clapped, especially the two tables filled with members of the club. Considering Sophie's family consisted of just her and Poppie, she'd invited the book club and the book boyfriends to fill her side of the church. Stone had invited his Navy SEAL buddies and Clarabelle's family. His family via adoption. And, of course, all of *Naked Runway's* editors and their Glam Team were in attendance.

"Sophie and I met through our mutual love of romance novels," Donna said. "We bonded over swoon-worthy heroes, epic love stories, and of course, the occasional ridiculous plot twist."

Stone leaned over and whispered in her ear. "Like the bride is a witch and a fairy godmother? That kind of ridiculous plot twist?"

"Oh, hush up," Sophie said, playfully swatting his arm. *He wasn't wrong.*

Donna continued, "Sophie, with her endless optimism and boundless imagination, always dreamed of finding her very own book boyfriend in real life...thus her approaching *Naked Runway* to write a series of columns for them on the subject."

The book boyfriend table hooted and hollered.

"Little did she know," Donna continued when their antics died down, "her happily-ever-after was just around the corner, in the form of a grumpy Navy SEAL."

This caused deep, guttural hooyahs from their tables.

"The only thing making me grumpy right now," Stone whispered, "is wanting you out of that dress and knowing we're here for at least another three hours, during which those assholes are going to insist on dancing with you." He jerked his head toward his friends.

Sophie laughed. She'd told him in no uncertain terms they were staying for all of the reception. The details of both the wedding and the reception had been included in Sophie's letter from her mom. She'd written,

Sophie, if you're reading this, then I am not there to help you plan your special day. The thought breaks my heart, and I am so sorry I let you down by not living to see you in all your glory. It is a day I've dreamt about since you were born...

She'd gone on to write about how she had envisioned everything, right down to the glass slippers Sophie would wear.

Donna finished her speech and took a seat.

Poppie stood, looking handsome and happy in his tuxedo from the auction. He'd been thrilled when he'd learned he got to keep it. "I'm not much on speeches, but for Sophie, I'd do anything." He glanced her way. "Sophie, over the years, your spirit has kept me young, it's kept me alive, and it's kept me on my toes. Now, you have a new man in your life." He glanced at Stone. "And before it's too late to have this marriage annulled, I'd like to ask him a few questions. There will be a penalty for each one he gets wrong."

"Poppie," Sophie said. "In case you've forgotten, you're still on probation. If your plan is to shoot rocks at him with your slingshot for every answer he misses, you need to hop over to Plan B."

This caused some laughter.

"I'm willing to take my chances with the judge," Poppie said, pulling his slingshot out of one suit pocket and a fist full of rocks out of the other and placing them on the table.

More laughter.

"Son, it's time to see how much attention you've been paying to your courtship. Let's start with an easy one. Stone, can you tell all of us how it all began?"

Stone grinned, leaning back in his chair. "It all started in a coffee shop when the barista mixed up our coffee orders."

Sophie laughed, shaking her head. "According to the barista, she got them right. You chose to take mine so you'd have an excuse to talk to me."

"Umm," Stone said.

"I think the words you're looking for, Stone, are, 'yes dear,'" said Ms. Birdie.

As it turned out Ms. Birdie and Clarabelle had been in cahoots to matchmake Clarabelle's three sons for some time now. Sophie had discovered this while at brunch with Ms. Birdie the day after the auction.

Stone, dressed in a black tuxedo with a pink bowtie, turned to Sophie. "Yes, dear."

She smiled and patted him on his bald head.

Poppie cleared his throat. "Next question, who made the first move?"

Stone turned to Sophie. "Darling, would you like to field that question?"

She shrugged. "I may or may not have kissed him to make a point."

"And she made a fine point," Stone added, eliciting laughter.

"First date?" Poppie asked.

"I took her to a concert in the park. We had a picnic while listening to jazz," Stone said, looking quite pleased with his answer.

"It was a street fair, and we bought lemonade and hot dogs from a vendor," Sophie corrected.

"Hotdogs at a street fair? How in the hell did you get her to say yes to a second date let alone marriage?" Montgomery, Stone's oldest brother, chimed in.

"Asshole," Stone said, while flipping his brother the bird.

"Who said I *love you* first?" Poppie asked, looking quite bemused with all the comradery. Next to him sat his date. A woman he'd met at the auction. They'd been seeing quite a lot of each other, but Poppie clammed up anytime Sophie asked him his intentions toward her.

"This one I know," Stone said. "I said I love you before our first official date. And just so you all know, it took her three months to say it back."

"That's true enough." Sophie laid her hand on his arm, swooning at how his muscles tightened every time she touched him. "I did make him work for it. I mean, after such a dismal first date effort on his part, I was bound by sisterhood honor to put him through the wringer for everything he got past that point."

"Sophie E. Clark, you and I are cut from the same cloth," Isabella P. Chance said from her seat among the other bridesmaids."

"In my defense." Stone placed his hand over Sophie's. "It wasn't a planned first date. It was a spur-of-the-moment outing that ended up feeling like a date, so we gave it the official billing."

"Who is the most generous?" Poppie asked.

"Well, I did pay a million dollars to win him at auction," Sophie said.

"And I repaid you by telling you a secret that still makes you squeal with happiness over a year later," Stone replied.

"Tell us. Tell us. Tell us." The Navy SEALs chanted, pounding their fists on the table as they did, only to abruptly stop when Poppie picked up his slingshot and a rock and aimed it fully loaded in their direction.

"Worst date?" Poppie asked, putting his weapon of choice down unfired.

Stone frowned. "Darling, have we had a bad date?"

"Not unless you count the time you took me to the opera, and you fell asleep," Sophie replied sweetly.

He wiggled his eyebrows. "Only because you kept me up all night the night before."

"Worst habit?" Poppie asked.

"Easy. She makes me wear pink T-shirts with crazy ass sayings," Stone spouted off, winking at Sophie.

"Oh, come on, Stone," Frankie interjected. She was also part of the wedding party...reluctant, but Sophie had worn her down. "You look fabulous in pink. Almost as good as you did during that phase in your life where you wore a wig to impress your new wife." She held up her phone. "I have pictures if anyone wants to see them."

Stone groaned good-naturedly. He and Frankie had come to a shaky truce. He'd confronted her with his doubts about her, and she'd informed him to mind his own damn business. Other things were said, things Sophie had no knowledge of, but they had appeased Stone's worries.

Sophie patted him on the arm. "You made a wonderful-ish cinnamon roll. And I don't want to hear any complaints from you about my T-shirts. Not only do they now cost two hundred retail, but it's pretty much because of them that we met."

"True," he said. "Darling, have I mentioned yet today that saying yes to being your bodyguard was the best decision I ever made?"

Ziggy piped in. "And saying yes to hot dogs at a street fair. Don't forget that." He'd been their high-energy wedding planner. His date was Eddie, a guy who was a member of the Manhattan Knitters and an off-off-Broadway actor. He matched Ziggy flair for flair, inappropriate comment for inappropriate comment.

Sophie smiled at her husband. "I love you."

"Last question. What are you looking forward to the most in your future together?" Poppie asked.

Stone wrapped an arm around Sophie's shoulders. "Honestly, Poppie, just being with Sophie every day is what I look forward to. Whether it's an adventure or a quiet night in, as long as we're together, I'm happy."

Sophie's heart swelled. She thought about how much her life had changed.

As the reception continued, filled with laughter, love, and a hint of magic, Sophie knew that this was only the beginning. She squeezed Stone's hand, feeling his warmth and the promise of many more happy chapters to come.

The sound of a bell caught the attention of all those present who were in the fairy godperson business. It was the bell that indicated a child...or an adult...had just wished for their very own.

Stone leaned in, whispering in her ear. "Ready for our next adventure, Sophie Enchantment Clark...Blackthorn?"

Sophie smiled, her heart fluttering. He'd learned her middle name. "Always, Mr. Stone Cold-ish Godfather. Just not before the party is over. My dance card is quite full."

He raised an eyebrow. "You have a dance card? Why am I just now learning of this?"

With a grin, she pulled it out of the hidden pocket in her dress and laid it on the table. There were thirty spots on it, all claimed. "Don't worry, darling, I insisted you be initialed in for the first and last dance."

"And what if I don't want to share you?" he inquired, his eyes darkening with a possessive glint.

"I do believe that is something you'll have to take up with your brothers. You see, they created the card and then charged a thousand dollars a dance to all your SEAL buddies."

"Fucking assholes," he said before capturing her lips in a quick kiss. When the kiss ended, he pushed back from the table.

"Where are you going?" she asked.

"To bribe the band to play nothing but fast music except for the first and last dance."

She shook her head, amusement bubbling up inside of her.

As she watched him saunter away, her heart swelled with love and contentment. He was her new most favorite boyfriend trope. The alpha roll. The term referred to a hero who was all broody and macho on the outside but became warm and gooey on the inside...for the girl. One so gooey, she had no fear he'd balk at the T-shirts she'd created for them to wear on their honeymoon. Hers said 'Mine.' His said 'Hers.'

Her fairytale ending wasn't an ending after all. It was only the beginning. A beginning with no stop sign in sight.

A commotion on the dance floor caught her attention. The SEALs had joined Stone, and they appeared to be doing their own bribing of the musicians.

A sound of pure joy spilled out of her.

Sophie E. Clark had most definitely gotten the last laugh.

Dear Readers,

I hope you've enjoyed *Book Boyfriendish*. I had so much fun writing Sophie and Stone's story. If you fell in love with Sophie and her T-shirts, you'll want to check out her merchandise. It can be purchased from my website shop. On that site, find the category button *Book Boyfriendish*, and there you'll find all of Sophie's crazy fun creations. It's a great place to buy awesome gifts for the romance readers in your life, and for your single friends who are looking for a conversation starter in a crowd of potential dates. lisawellsauthor.com/shop/

If you'd like to be a member of Book Boyfriend Connoisseurs Club, join my Facebook group where conversations are held weekly about book boyfriends, and sign up for my newsletter, home of the original Book Boyfriend Connoisseurs Club.

About Author

Welcome to the whimsical world of Lisa Wells, a place where the paranormal waltzes with the everyday and contemporary romance sizzles with a humor that could lighten even the gloomiest of days. Nestled in the heart of Missouri, Lisa writes with a fervor that steams up the room—whether it be your eyeglasses or Kindle screen, nothing is safe from the heat radiating off her pages.

Lisa's own life is as full-flavored as her writing, with a taste for the finest dark chocolate, the richest red wine, and the most swoon-worthy book boyfriends—a trifecta of treats that inspire her storytelling. She's a maestro of indulgence, her writing days punctuated by the triumph of jeans that zip smoothly on miraculous mornings—a testament to life's simple pleasures (and the occasional indulgence that makes those jeans a bit snug).

In Lisa's tales, love is always in the air—whether it's tinged with the supernatural or wrapped in the warmth of real-world wonder. Donning her mom jeans with pride, she invites you to escape into stories where laughter blooms, passion ignites, and the possibility of a happy ending is just a page away. So settle in, pour yourself a glass of your best-loved beverage, and prepare to be delighted by the steamy romances of Lisa Wells—where every story is a love letter to those who believe in the magic of "What if?"

To stay up-to-date on book releases and news about this author:

Newsletter: https://bit.ly/LisaWellsRomanceAuthorNewsletter

Website: https://lisawellsauthor.com

www.ingramcontent.com/pod-product-compliance
Lightning Source LLC
Chambersburg PA
CBHW021232190726
48289CB00005B/1287